Encounter with ISIS

James Ward

COOL MILLENNIUM BOOKS

2

This is a work of fiction. All names, characters, and events are the product of the author's imagination, or used fictitiously. All resemblance to actual events, places, events or persons, living or dead, is entirely coincidental.

First published in KDP 2015.
This edition published 2021.

A CIP catalogue record for this book is available from the British Library.

ISBN: 978-1-913851-17-0

Cover picture shows Thames House, Millbank, London SW1.

This novel was produced in the UK and uses British-English language conventions ('authorise' instead of 'authorize', 'The government are' instead of 'the government is', etc.)

To my wife

Chapter 1: Everything You Never Wanted to Know About Alec

Alec stirred his tea twice, put the spoon on the saucer and leaned back. "You'll be coming to Turkey with us," he said.

"She'd just call us all together if it was that," Mordred replied. "She wouldn't tell us one by one. It'd be a waste of her time and ours."

"Not if we're all going over there to fulfil slightly different roles. Anyway, her office isn't big enough."

They sat in the first-floor staff canteen in Thames House. 10.40. Most people were busy downstairs this time in the morning, either examining intelligence files or filling in reports on real or virtual investigations, but Alec Cunningham and John Mordred's schedules had been cleared to make room for individual meetings. Without titles or agendas.

"She wouldn't need to announce it in her office," Mordred said. "There are plenty of seminar rooms."

Alec sighed, as if it was like talking to an idiot. "With something like this, you need to impress upon each individual member the importance of him or her fulfilling his or her role *exactly as specified*. Put it another way: Annabel's going to Turkey, she was interviewed alone; Gina's going to Turkey, she was interviewed alone; Phyllis is going to Turkey, she was interviewed alone; Ian's going - "

"Yes, yes, get the picture."

"I've been here longer than you, John. Much longer. I think I know what I'm talking about."

Mordred had the universally recognisable 'depressed by waiting' look: he was tall, blond, bulky, and wore a white shirt, and he was staring at the floor, slouching in his seat and had both arms extended uselessly on the table. By contrast, Alec, ten years older at thirty-nine, had the universally recognisable 'ready for action' appearance. He wore a short coat and a blue shirt; his features were sharp, his expression serious, and his hair jet black, where it wasn't retreating, but he sat up like he'd just been complimented, looked around himself frequently with a satisfied air, and had one hand flat on his chair, ready to spring up and walk to Istanbul, if necessary, at a moment's notice.

"There's no point in speculating," Mordred said. "I could even be about to be sacked."

"Who knows?"

"Not that it'd necessarily be a disaster if I was. Maybe I need a change of direction in life."

"Go and be a social worker, you mean."

"Why not?"

Alec took a deep 'superior wisdom' breath. "Shortly after I first came to work here, there was an agent in Red department, name of Jonathan Hartley-Brown. He wanted to be a social worker. He ended up getting killed by a foreign agent."

Mordred smiled. "So?"

"What do you mean, 'so'?"

"So ... what's the moral?"

"Prevarication, stupid. It's not good for your health."

"Silly me. Of course, yes."

They sat without speaking for several minutes. Alec finished his tea. Mordred's arrived. Two more agents – a man and a woman – came in and occupied opposite seats four tables away. Someone in the serving area shouted something about the lunch menu. A smell of frying onions filled the air. Rain assaulted the windows. Mordred wondered which of them – he or Alec – was the most boring.

"What's so bad about MI7?" Alec said.

He shrugged. "I can't put my finger on it. The meetings probably. Sometimes it seems like I'm always either in a meeting, or awaiting one."

Alec scoffed. "At least they're interesting, most of them. Take the one you're about to go into: you're going to Turkey. Probably. Most people's meetings aren't like that."

"No, I accept that."

"My brother, for example. He works in a primary school. The only meetings he ever has are prepare-for-OFSTED meetings. It's like that in most jobs, from what I've heard. All about inspectors and how to survive them."

"I guess so."

"It used to be that you were doing a good job if the organisation you worked for was making a profit. Nowadays, it's all individual. You've got to be minutely scrutinised to make sure you've got your nose to the grindstone."

"Big Brother's watching you."

"And he wants you to complete this self-appraisal form. It never used to exist. Not in my dad's day. I sometimes wonder how we got from there to here."

Mordred looked around him and shook his head. "If I do go to Turkey, it'll be just the same as here. An endless succession of different offices and computer screens."

"Bloody hell, what's wrong with you today? Why are you feeling so sorry for yourself?"

"Between-assignments syndrome, maybe."

"When's your appointment with Ruby Parker?"

"Noon."

"That's nearly an hour away. I'm not going to sit and keep you company for that long, not unless you make some sort of effort to cheer up."

"Sorry."

"Look, John, I'm the one that should be depressed. Let me tell you something. I really hope you *are* coming to Turkey with us. I'm going to need a very good reason to care a fig once we get out there."

"What do you mean?"

"Looking high and low for some teenage girl who's run away to join ISIS. She's fourteen. Old enough, you'd think, to understand the difference between right and wrong."

"Probably."

"I could just about get my head round someone making off to join the so-called Islamic State if, say, he or she didn't know it was fond of beheading aid-workers – *aid-workers*, for God's sake! – and genocide, and slavery, and mass rape, and burning POWs alive. But the fact is, you'd have to have lived on the moon for the last eighteen months not to know about those things!"

Mordred shrugged. "Granted."

"So here we've got a girl who not only knows about these things – she must do – but also thinks, 'Hey, I should really help these guys out. They might not triumph if someone doesn't support them'. Even at fourteen, you've got to think: that's pretty sick in the head. It's almost impossible to feel sorry for her. It's quite easy to go the other way. Imagine you're the parent of one of their victims!"

"She's been brainwashed. It happens all the time."

"There's no such thing as 'brainwashing'. It's been proved. The CIA invented it to explain why some POWs returned from the Korean war sympathising with Communism."

"There is for kids. We don't call it that, but it's what parents and teachers do with their children every day."

Alec grimaced. "Typical leftie bullshit."

"I'm not saying it's a bad thing."

"So what *are* you saying? It's good to brainwash kids?"

"You're a parent, for God's sake. You must teach them values. And you must teach them that your values are true. You don't teach them all the values in the world, then sit back and go, 'Hey, you make your own choice'. That'd be a disaster."

"I impose my values on them. So what?"

Mordred sat forward. "You don't give them a choice. *Because you're not supposed to, clot*. It's called, 'being a good parent'."

"What are you saying?"

"I'm saying, one day your kids will be teenagers. Then they'll visit the supermarket of new values. They all do. They might get in with a bad crowd. You're not going to go, 'That's fine. There's no such thing as brainwashing. Forensic psychologist Dick

Anthony disproved it in 1999. Let's just let her go with the bad crowd's values if she wants to.' It's your duty to intervene. That's not 'leftie bullshit'. It's the opposite. After all, no one loves your daughter more than you do."

Alec drew a breath and blew it out. "Yes, okay."

"And anyway, getting back to the actual kid in question, it's not just about her. It's about her parents. Do they really deserve what their daughter might be about to inflict on them? I admit, they don't sound like the world's greatest mum and dad, but hey."

They sat in silence for a while longer. It was obvious Alec was thinking. He had his I-need-to-say-something-sensitive-but-I'm-worried-you-might-not-see-me-as-James-Bond-any-more face on. He kept looking at different parts of the canteen, glazing into a hard stare and sighing.

"You and I make a good team," he said at last, "and after what you've just said, I want to get to the bottom of this one. I'm prepared to work twenty-four-seven if need be. You're right: probably Turkey will be a parade of desks and laptops, but we stand to do some good. We can get to the truth if we can stop that girl crossing the Syrian border."

"Which, given that no one's allowed to tell the media, seems unlikely."

"They're putting her photo out. Not over here, of course, but in Turkey, where it matters. No one on the ground there will make the connection."

"I'm sure her parents will be hugely relieved. Thanks to our discretion, their reputations will probably survive the family crisis unblemished."

"It's not chiefly about them. You're right, I can see that now. It's about her."

"So you won't be dragging me round the *meyhanes*?"

"Not after the conversation we've just had. It's funny you should mention her parents, too. I'm telling you, John, when Ruby Parker showed me that girl's photograph, I almost passed out. She looks just like my Sophie. A few years older, obviously. My eldest. I don't mind saying, I felt very equivocal. Deep paternal affection mixed with revulsion for ISIS. Weird. I don't recommend it."

"Sophie's mother's Kenyan, right?"

Alec nodded. "My second wife, yes. Cecily. The one I'm still in love with."

"The one you cheated on with that company director."

"The biggest mistake of my life. But she's praying for me, and I've started going to church." He laughed. "I'm literally begging God for a second chance, and I don't even believe in Him!"

"What does your third wife think?"

"Happy as pie. Rosaura was always far too young for me, and the culture leap was too big: from Kenyan to Guatemalan in under a decade: too much. Gastronomically, as much as anything. I've grown up. I'm almost as old and wise as you. Anyway, Rosie's moved in with a builder. Everyone wins, because it's Cecily I'm really in love with."

"And she's … five years older than you. Sorry, I have difficulty keeping up."

"I'm over obsessing about age and looks. They're meaningless. Anyway, I don't want to sound racist, but black people age better than white. Look at Ruby Parker. Has to be fifty-something, doesn't look more than forty. Cecily still looks like she's thirty. I don't care about that, though. It's what's inside that counts. Listen to me. I'm turning into you."

"And I'm becoming you, apparently."

Alec shrugged. "Call me selfish, but that's a price I'm willing to pay. Before you disappear completely into the abyss, though, thank you. I'm very grateful for how you've transformed me."

Mordred smiled. "Well, I'm quite looking forward to Turkey now I know we've a chance of doing something vaguely worthwhile."

"Attaboy." He held up his palm.

Mordred high-fived him. "Just out of interest, what does your first wife think of all this?"

"Jean? Oh, she passed away two years ago. Cancer of the spleen."

"Sorry to hear that. I didn't know."

"Marriage number one was a long time ago and a big mistake. Heady combination of infatuation and impulse. Credit to Jean, she realised that first. I was twenty, she was fifty-four. Too little in common once the sex stopped sizzling. The language-barrier didn't help. They played Mother's Little Helper as her coffin went through the curtains. It was surprisingly moving."

Mordred took a sip of his tea. "Complicated life you've got."

"If I could go back and change it, I would. Bits of it. But I can't. No one can."

Alec divulged more in thirty minutes than he had in three years. Vague outlines were filled in, stories aired and names revealed. Maybe it was just the mood Mordred was in, but that little jest about them swapping lives gave it a morbid twist. He didn't want Alec's life. His own wasn't brilliant, but it was relatively guilt-free. He drank his tea and went to tidy his desk and surf the net. Saturday was his youngest sister's birthday. He spent ten minutes designing an online card for her: 'Happy Birthday, Mabel' spelt out in bunches of flowers. Then he noticed it looked like a funeral wreath. Delete. 11.55. Time to do up his top button, tighten his tie and get moving.

He knocked on Ruby Parker's door and put his ear an inch closer so he could hear her reply. Once certain, he let himself in. She sat behind her desk, a small black woman in a suit, reading a document. "Apologies," she said. "Give me three seconds. Do sit down." The tropical fish tank on her right buzzed slightly. He liked that about her, her guppies. He wondered if they had names. Probably not, just codes.

She put the document to one side. "Has Alec told you about Aisha Sharif?"

"Not everything."

"Remind yourself out loud. We may save time."

"She ran away to Syria. Her father's one of four Parliamentary Under Secretaries of State in the Department for Communities and Local Government. He doesn't want anyone knowing until they absolutely have to."

"Anyone in the media," she corrected him.

"In practice, that means virtually everyone," he replied, "since, once they find out who she is, most people are likely to tweet it, or know someone who will."

She passed a photograph across. A head and shoulders of a young girl in school uniform. Long hair, wide smile, light make up, intelligent-looking.

"No hijab," he remarked.

"She's a recent convert," Ruby Parker replied.

"To Islam?"

"To Islam*ism*. 'Islamofascism', as some of my older colleagues would call it."

"Do we know that for certain, or is it just speculation consistent with her behaviour?"

"She posted an update on her Facebook page two days ago. By 'recent', I mean extremely sudden. Up till Tuesday evening, she hated what she called 'brain-dead fundamentalism'. She seems to have had a Road to Damascus experience."

"Unfortunate turn of phrase."

She ignored him. "Take a good look at her face. I want you to remember it. There's a very small possibility you may see her on your travels."

"I very much hope so."

"In Southwark."

It took a second for this to sink in. "So I'm not going to Turkey."

"Not yet. And I don't want you to take that the wrong way. The fact is, I've another job needs doing, and it requires someone with good interpersonal skills. No one else here fits the bill as well as you do. In any case, we've no reason to think it's going to take more than a day or two, so I'd advise you to pack your bags for Istanbul anyway."

"I was recruited to MI7 for my language skills, as I remember. And I don't think my interpersonal skills are a patch on Gina's. Wouldn't I be better employed in Turkey? I'm not trying to get out of what you're proposing, by the way. It's just, I can capture precise nuances of local accents. I can pass myself off as a local. I might be able to get something - "

"Everyone knows you're MI7's greatest linguist, but Gina's already out there, and it so happens you have a multiplicity of skills, of which approachability isn't the least."

"What's going on in Southwark?"

"Another disappeared teenager."

He tried to conceal a groan. "Another Islamist?"

"The son of the founder and director of Chewton Black, the private security company."

"*The* Chewton Black? One of MI7's biggest rivals?"

She laughed. "Yes, that Chewton Black. 'Chewblacca' as I believe Phyllis calls it. One of our insignificant imitators."

"Sir Ronald Chewton's son's an *Islamist?*"

"No, I didn't say that. Perhaps let me explain your assignment, John, then you can ask questions? That's how it usually works."

"Apologies. Yes, go ahead."

She leaned back. "We don't know precisely why Chewton Junior disappeared, but we do know that, until a few days ago, he was engaged in sixth-form work experience with his father's outfit. CB was contracted to launch a mock cyber-attack on the private equity company, JM Cranenburgh Bradley, with a view to testing its digital defences. Sebastian's viruses penetrated the system, then he removed them. Now he's vanished."

"He didn't leave a note or anything?"

"No."

"I assume they've called the police."

"Of course, but they're not taking it terribly seriously just yet. The point is, however, it does have a national security connection, however tenuous. I've assigned you because Sir Ronald's an old friend of mine, and his son's disappearance falls within the letter of our remit. My guess is he's gone off to some pop festival or other, or he's staying at a friend's, and it's nothing to worry about. Finding him's hardly going to be any skin off our noses, and one day, we may need the favour returned. It pays to stay in credit."

"What could Chewton Black conceivably do for us?"

"I don't know yet, but it's unwise to be arrogant. I'm not going to tell you any more, because I don't know an awful lot, and since you're in charge of the investigation, you need to get as much as you can from the horse's mouth. Pick up the address from Amber on the way out. Grab a sandwich on your way over. I told Mr and Mrs Chewton you'd be there no later than two o'clock. With luck, he might even have returned home by the time you arrive."

He bumped into Alec on the way out. The entranceway was full of secretaries, guests and civil servants coming or going during lunch hour. The high ceilings and the glass doors gave everything a cold look. Colin Bale stood behind the reception desk looking dour.

"Well?" Alec said.

"I'm not going to Turkey," Mordred replied.

"You really know how to play an April fool's trick, has anyone ever told you that? Except: well, it needs to be before twelve o'clock, and on the first day of the month, and in April. Otherwise, John, it's just not funny. Now, shall we start again? What time does your plane leave?"

"I've just said: I'm not going. At least not yet."

He frowned slightly. "You're *not* joking, are you? You're actually not joking. Well, where the hell *are* you going? I was looking forward to us working together."

"I've been promoted."

"What?"

"That's right. Station controller, Budapest."

The bottom seemed to drop out of Alec's world for a moment, then he grabbed hold of it and rammed it back into place. "Wait a minute. This is your standard witticism, isn't it? We've been here before. I - "

"I'm going to Southwark to look for a missing teenager. Not an Islamist, just a wayward white boy who's probably a bit footloose. Satisfied?"

They were walking at speed now, exiting the building. "Is this the truth, John? Because no one can ever tell with you."

"Cross my heart and hope to die. Anyway, I told you the truth first time round, and you refused to believe me. You accused me of playing a prank."

"But that's the point with J. Mordred esquire. Sometimes, it's impossible to tell what's true and what isn't. I don't think you even know yourself, most days."

"That's why I'm such a bloody good spy."

"Really? Is that the reason you've been assigned to look after a rebellious teenager? Is that what spies do? Listen, John, it sounds to me rather as if Ruby Parker may have overheard you angling for a job in Social Services. I think she's decided to give you a taste of your own medicine."

"You really think so?"

Alec slapped him on the shoulder. "Best of luck, dunce. I've a plane to catch."

Chapter 2: At Home With the Chewtons

The Chewtons lived in a small Edwardian detached house, surrounded by other similar buildings, just west of One Tree Hill. It abutted onto a narrow pavement and sat behind railings with a black bin discreetly tucked to one side. The upstairs room had a well-stocked window box. A faded 'Vote UKIP' sign clung to the inside front window of the house opposite. He knocked.

Mrs Chewton – he assumed it was her: she looked distressed enough – admitted him after he showed his card. As far as the police were concerned, he was a private detective hired by the family. The Chewtons knew the truth. The case wasn't expected to last long enough for complications to occur.

Mrs Chewton looked to be in her mid-forties. She had long dark hair, brown eyes, a small nose and big lips made even more prominent with scarlet gloss. She wore a navy blue skirt and blouse. She led him through into the living room - essentially a sofa and TV space with antiques for the edification of guests - and asked him gloomily to sit down. On one of the two armchairs, a young WPC in full uniform sat with a notebook. She stood up when Mordred entered, smiled and offered a handshake.

"I'm WPC Goodchild. I was just taking the details of Sebastian's disappearance."

"John Mordred, private detective."

Mrs Chewton flopped down on the sofa and looked at her knees, as if she'd forgotten either of her visitors existed.

"There, there," Goodchild said loudly, as if she was addressing a geriatric, "I'm sure he'll be home soon. He's probably just gone off for a bit of an adventure. Teenagers do these things. We're keeping a beady eye out, though. We'll find him, don't you worry."

"Do you mind if I listen in to your questions?" Mordred asked.

"I'm just about done, actually," Goodchild replied.

"What have you got?"

"Sorry, data protection. You need to ask Mrs Chewton yourself. I've got to go."

"Yes, go," Mrs Chewton said softly and firmly, the first words Mordred had heard her utter since she came in.

Had he been alone with Goodchild, he'd probably have offered some advice along the lines of 'don't make promises' – *We'll find him, don't you worry* was surely tempting fate - but it didn't seem appropriate with Mrs Chewton present. "Nice to have met you," he said.

"I'll let myself out," Goodchild said.

"May I sit down?" Mordred asked, when he heard her close the front door.

"Please do," Mrs Chewton replied mordantly. "I'm forgetting my manners. Even in my state of mind, there's no excuse for that. Can I get you anything? Tea? Coffee?"

"I'm fine."

"My husband tells me you're a 'spook'."

"I've been called worse. What can you tell me about Sebastian? If you could repeat what you just told WPC Goodchild, it should save time, then I can ask any further questions of my own. Will I … have a chance to speak to Mr Chewton?"

"I would imagine Ronald's banging his secretary. It's how he copes when events run beyond his control."

"I see." He swallowed. "Maybe I'll speak to him later."

"Or maybe I'm just imagining it. Ronald and Sheila, Sheila and Ronald, ever one body in the beast with two backs."

The door opened and a man of about sixty strode in with a tumblerful of whisky. He wore a grey suit and tie. His face was ruddy, his hair thin and ginger, and he had a well-trimmed moustache. His feet were bare. "Has she gone?" he asked. He spotted Mordred. "You – are you the man from MI5? It's gone two. You must be."

Mordred stood up. "Sir Ronald?" Obviously. "I'm agent John Mordred. Pleased to meet you."

"I told him you were off with Sheila," Mrs Chewton said. "In bed."

Sir Ronald scowled and closed his eyes. "I told you thirty minutes ago before I went," he said, "I was *going upstairs to get out of the way while the WPC was here!*"

"Upstairs, to give Sheila a good seeing-to," Mrs Chewton said.

He seemed torn between mortification and rage. "Excuse me," he said under his breath.

He strode out of the room in the same determined way he'd entered it, and left the door open.

"In flagrante," Mrs Chewton whispered, apparently to herself.

They heard cupboard doors banging. Mrs Chewton sat immobile and looked at her thighs. Finally, they heard a tap roar, and Sir Ronald returned with a glass of water and a wet hand and sleeve, and some tablets. "Here, Elaine, my sweet," he said, kneeling down before her, "take these."

She took the pills on her palm, but hesitated to take the glass. "Do you still love me, Ronald?" she asked.

"Only you, darling. I've never loved anyone else."

She shook her head like a little girl. "And not Sheila?"

"Never. You know that. You do. Really, you do."

She put the tablets in her mouth and washed them down. She cried. He looked at her for a few moments, stroking her hair, then he began to cry too.

"Where's Sebastian?" she asked.

"We'll find him, darling. He'll come back. You've had a hard day today. I didn't know you'd forgotten to take your tablets. If I had, I'd never have left you with that wretched woman." He turned to Mordred. "Young man, would you do me the favour of picking my wife up, and depositing her in the bedroom? And don't get any ideas."

Mordred put one arm under her back and another beneath her knees. She was almost asleep now. He carried her upstairs and laid her gently on their four-poster, then retired and went back to the lounge. He sat down and waited nearly three-quarters of an hour. Eventually, Sir Ronald reappeared.

"Sorry about that," he said. "I, er, had to console her. She takes on the persona of this 'Sheila' from time to time, usually before she falls unconscious. The irony is, I've never even known a woman called Sheila, and I've never had a secretary." He sighed bitterly. "Anyway, you may be able to speak to her tomorrow. With the tablets, she has days, sometimes weeks, of perfect lucidity. Without them … well, I'm afraid you saw."

"I'll keep it entirely to myself, obviously."

"I'm very grateful you arrived when you did. If WPC Whatshername had seen what you just did, there's no telling where it would have ended. Data protection, my arse. It'd have been all over the Met."

"Could I ask you about Sebastian?"

"How about I tell you what I know, and you can ask any questions to fill in the gaps?"

"Sounds like a good idea."

"Whisky?" Sir Ronald asked. "I'm having one."

"Not for me."

"You're driving?"

"No, I came by taxi. I'll be returning that way."

"Then you'll have a whisky, young man, and like it. Don't worry, your secret's safe with me. I won't tell Priggy Parker."

"I - "

"Put it this way. If we share two tumblerfuls of scotch, I'll know I've something on you. Something you don't want people to know. Just as you've now got something on me, regarding Elaine. We'll be quits, and more than that, we'll be partners in crime. Friends, almost. Now, surely I'm much more likely to open up to a friend than some Johnny-come-lately from the City? It's your duty, John."

Mordred laughed. "You do realise that if I'm found out, I can just use that argument to prove it was all in the line of work?

Which means you'd have nothing 'on me'." But he already had a tumbler in his hand and his host was already filling it.

"Say when," Sir Ronald said.

"That's enough."

"What? I'm deaf."

No point in protesting. Mordred waited till it was full to the brim and resigned himself to drinking it. This was worse than a bar crawl with Alec.

"That's a good fellow," Sir Ronald said. "Put hairs on your chest."

It seemed odd he wasn't more concerned about getting his son back. As if the real problem was Elaine and people finding out about her; as if he thought he was doing Mordred a favour by helping his investigation forward. Didn't he care about Sebastian? Or did he believe, like nearly everyone else, that his son would be home in a jiffy? Maybe Sebastian had done it before. Maybe he did it to get away from the Ronald-Elaine-Sheila love triangle. Teenagers absconded daily for lesser reasons.

"Sebastian's at sixth form, as you probably know," Sir Ronald said. "Rheeming Hall, one of the most expensive and prestigious institutions in the south east. Anyway, they have a 'work experience' week. All schools do it, nowadays, apparently. Sebastian's never been a very outgoing child, so he couldn't bring himself to ring round the local employers and arrange a placement – well, that's not true: he could, but only to idiotic places: corner shops, delivery companies, *Lidl*. The other students were doing theirs in Threadneedle Street or New York or bloody Washington or Toronto. I didn't want my son driving a sodding milk float for a week. I decided I had to save him from himself, so I offered him a placement with us. He wasn't keen, but I insisted. You've got to be cruel to be kind as a parent, sometimes. Everyone knows that.

"In any case, I genuinely thought Sebastian could be useful to us. He's something of a computer whizz-kid, you see. Exactly what Chewton Black's looking for. And of course, he's the company heir. There is no 'Black', you see. I just added that because it sounded good. It just so happened he started at a very good time. We'd just been contracted to launch a pretend cyber-assault on the private equity firm, JM Cranenburgh Bradley, see if we could get past their security firewalls. Sebastian devised something of his own. Melted their defences like butter. In and out before they knew what had hit them.

"We gave them enough information back to prove we'd done the job, and destroyed everything else. That's normal, of course, but when I looked in the contract, it didn't require such a thing. I still can't see why not. After all, as a cautious company, you only need to know whether your system's been penetrated and how deeply. You shouldn't need a copy of all the accessed files. If we've got them – if we've unzipped them, let's say – who's to say we're not going to keep them on our computers, even accidentally? No, it's standard practice to require a blanket destruction.

"Anyway, we had a little disagreement over price. They'd paid half upfront, and it seemed obvious we'd struggle to get the rest – rare, but it happens - but they may have worried about us leaking their precious information, because it arrived Sunday evening, just as Sebastian was due back at school."

"When did you last see him?" Mordred asked.

"Sunday afternoon. Elaine took him to the station that evening. Rheeming's in Kent, near Margate. He caught the 19.15 from Victoria – she watched as he got on – and that was the last anyone we know saw of him."

"When did you first realise he was missing?"

"Monday morning, when the school contacted us."

"It's a boarding school?"

"Yes. Does that make a difference?"

"I'm assuming they've done their own internal investigation: questioned his friends, that sort of thing?"

"So they say. I've no idea how thorough they were, but the police have been in touch with them, so I'm sure they're treating it pretty seriously."

"I'd like to go over there at some point. If you could let them know I'm coming, that would smooth my path."

"Of course."

"How did he seem when he was doing work experience?"

"Do you mean, 'did he seem resentful'?"

"You said parents sometimes have to be cruel to be kind. I'm sure you're right, but I'm equally certain the thoughtfulness isn't always perceived as such."

"I appreciate that, yes. No. he seemed okay with it. Mind you, he's never been very communicative."

"How does he feel about Mrs Chewton's illness? Generally?"

"He doesn't really have to cope with it most of the time. That's one of the reasons we sent him off to boarding school. During the holidays, he spends a good bit of time at my sister's, for the same reason. We've been in touch with her, before you ask. She knows nothing. Mind you, Elaine's all right when she's taking her tablets. That's most of the time."

"Where do you think he is? You must have a theory."

"I believe he ran away because he thought he'd let me down. Bloody Cranenburgh Bradley quibbling over money. Came as a bit of a shock to all of us. Maybe he misinterpreted it, assumed it was his fault. If so, my guess is he's begging on the streets somewhere."

"Why call MI5 in then?"

"Because the other possibility's that he's been nobbled. Someone thinks he's got secrets to sell, and they want them. One of JMCB's rivals."

"Does he?"

"It's possible. He dipped his line deep in the well of that company and I imagine he came up with some pretty strange fish. Like I say, I didn't ask, because the company policy is destruction of anything that might compromise our clients. In all the wrangling over payments due, I lost sight of what Sebastian might have discovered."

"Did his behaviour seem different in any way, after he'd been into JMCB's secure areas?"

"I don't know. Yes, maybe. The truth is, we see him so seldom, it's difficult to judge. But perhaps, yes."

"In what way?"

Sir Ronald laughed humourlessly. "You've just heard how hesitant I am about the fact that he even *was* different, and now you want me to tell you precisely *how*?"

"Just try, please."

"Very well. Quieter. Elaine might not agree, though. She knows him better than me. She might not have noticed a thing."

"Different people latch onto different things. How soon before I can speak to your wife?"

"If you come back tomorrow morning, I'll make sure she's fully dosed up and lucid."

"I'm sure the police are onto this as we speak, but what about Sebastian's Facebook page? What about Twitter, Instagram, Pinterest, etcetera?"

"I don't know the passwords, but I run a private security firm, so I'm familiar with the territory. There have been no updates."

"Send the links to my phone. What about his friends' Facebook accounts?"

"I hadn't thought of that. Should have done. Mind you, I don't actually know he's got any. Must have, though. Everyone's got friends. A problem shared is a problem halved."

"What do you mean?"

"I think he's perceived over there – at school - as a bit of a loser." He blushed and looked at the floor. "Pardon my French, but you might as well have the full picture."

Mordred let it pass. "Final question: is there a picture of him I could have? Obviously, I'll bring it back once we've taken a copy."

"We don't take that many photos in our family, but I'm sure I can find something."

"I'd like to look at a *few*, if you don't mind. You see a person from three or four different angles, you get more of a sense of how they probably look in the flesh. I don't suppose you've any videos?"

"Of Sebastian?" He laughed. "Not likely. He didn't even like having his photo taken. Perhaps when you see him, you'll appreciate why."

He left the room again. Mordred looked at the whisky he'd been given. He hadn't touched it yet, and Sir Ronald hadn't insisted. If this had been a sitcom, he'd have looked round for a potted plant and poured it away. But there weren't any plants in here. Could he pour it out of the window? Not in the time he probably had. His fate seemed sealed.

"Here we are, here we are," Sir Ronald said from somewhere outside. He came in shuffling three or four photos, apparently examining them to judge their suitability. He sat down opposite Mordred and handed them all over at once.

Sebastian Chewton was very tall and thin with a stoop. His hands and feet were large, his hair unruly and he had buck teeth and his mother's big lips. In each photo, he was alone, and looked as if he expected to be hit by an iron girder.

"Ugly, I'm afraid," Sir Ronald said. "Which matters a lot when you're his age. When he gets older, he'll come into money, and his personality will count for a lot more, as of course, it always does in the adult world. We tried taking him to the orthodontist."

It seemed an odd point with which to conclude, but it was clear Sir Ronald was embarrassed by his son now in a way he hadn't been previously.

"Which photo would you like me to take?"

"Take your pick. Have all of them if you like."

Even odder. But then, he had been drinking. His tumbler was empty and he was eyeing Mordred's greedily. Nothing to worry about then.

"I'll follow up the leads you've given me," he told Sir Ronald, "and I'll get back to you. If – when - I need to speak to your wife, as I'm sure I will unless we hear from Sebastian pretty soon, I'll ring ahead to let you know. That'll be two days at the outside."

"You've been very helpful, young man. Allow me to show you out. Are you sure you won't finish your whisky?"

"It's a lovely gesture, but no, thank you."

Sir Ronald shrugged as if the ways of the young were truly unfathomable. "As you wish then."

Chapter 3: I Spy Iblis's Stooges

When Mordred got back to Thames House, he found a request from Ruby Parker waiting for him at reception. Another meeting. It couldn't be that urgent or she'd have rung him, but it wasn't good to go home with that hanging over your head. *Either in a meeting or awaiting one.* 5pm. Clocking-out time in thirty minutes … in the usual course of things. But you could never tell in this job. He had a sinking feeling this was going to be one of those 8, 9, 10pm days.

He took the lift to the first floor underground and knocked on her door. She looked exactly the same as she had at noon. Nothing of the this-has-been-a-long-day about her. There never was. She was feeding her fish. He knew from what others had told him that this probably meant she was about to go home.

They sat down on opposite sides of the desk. "Two things," she said. "Firstly, I'm not sending you to Turkey after all. Not even if – or when – Sebastian Chewton turns up. There's been a sinister development in the Aisha Sharif case. It appears she's been making regular guest-appearances on the dark web."

"Never good news."

"My initial reaction exactly. But it turns out I was wrong." She picked up a document. "I quote: 'where do you get off being such a fat-headed loser, SuperBeliever01? Just because a girl does a bit of modelling doesn't make her a "whore". Newsflash: you ain't even a real Muslim.' That was on the second of April. Then, twelve days later, 'Yet another brilliant triumph for internationally-famous cavemen with guns outfit, Incredibly Stupid in Iraq and Syria: brackets: ISIS. I really hope one day you saddos meet a real army. You won't last five minutes.' April the seventeenth: 'Do you want to know what ISIS stands for, dumbass? I Spy Iblis's Stooges. Go figure.'"

"That puts a very different slant on matters."

"Forum comments, almost instantly deleted by the moderator, but we used her computer to retrieve them and also to penetrate that little bit of the darkness. We've got the site administrator coming in shortly for interview. Not here, of course: at the police station on the embankment by Waterloo Bridge. I'd like you to be present. You've a talent for spotting micro-expressions. You might see something we don't."

"What are we trying to find out?"

"You'll recall I said this was a 'sinister' development. Given the strength of her aversion to ISIS, it seems unlikely she's gone to Syria willingly. Even if she'd had a blinding conversion, one that persuaded her to reverse her previous beliefs, she'd have to know she'd passed the point of no return with that lot. Public repentance doesn't usually cut the mustard,"

"Did she specifically say she was going to join ISIS?"

"No. but that's irrelevant. Most of the opposition groups out there are Islamist now."

"So we think she's a kidnap victim? And that's how we'd account for the final message on her Facebook page? What did it actually say?"

Ruby Parker picked up another document and read: "'Allah Akbar, I've seen the error of my ways. Forgive my sins, O believers, and may I atone for my *shirk* with a martyr's blood' – 'martyr' spelt M-A-R-T-E-R."

"Martyr. Has she ever used that word before in writing?"

"Not that we know of. We've trawled her school notepads, web pages, e-mails, everything. But of course she sounds far too articulate, and much too well-informed, to make such an egregious error. One of the reasons I read you some excerpts."

"If she has been kidnapped, that would make our job much more difficult."

"Which is why time's of the essence. I don't know if you've plans for tonight, because I'd like you to cancel them, please."

They sat in silence for a split second longer than was normal.

"What's the matter, John?" she asked tetchily.

"I'm just trying to get my head round the course of events. Aisha Sharif leaves a number of hostile messages on Islamist forums. The moderators delete them, but they also want to know the identity of the culprit. After some time – this was April, right? – they locate her. Then there must have been a moment of shock. Astonishment that she's the daughter of a prominent politician. Only that would explain why they went to all the trouble of dragging her across the continent rather than killing her on the spot. Her publicity value to ISIS."

"Sorry, I can't see where you're going with this."

"Something here doesn't add up. Firstly, why delete the messages if you want to discover their source? That would probably make your job more difficult. Secondly, why did it take them so long? Thirdly, I just called her father a 'prominent politician', but he's not. He's one of four Parliamentary Under Secretaries of State in the Department for Communities and Local Government. That's not going to mean anything to your average Islamist. It doesn't even mean much to *me*. And how do they even *find out* who he is? He doesn't live in an unusual house in a strange location, he's probably not followed about by the media; he probably gets on the tube every morning just like any other commuter. And finally, if you're going to take the risk of kidnapping her, why leave a message on her Facebook page *that very day* saying she's gone to Syria? Why take the risk? Why not wait till you've got her there and *then* update it? Not that you *would* update it. You wouldn't want people thinking you were beheading a sincere convert. No, you'd want them thinking you were executing a *Kufrul-Istihzaha*, a disbelieving mocker."

Ruby Parker was kneading her chin. "This is why I always ask for a face-to-face meeting with you, John. You're good at making connections … and spotting disconnections." She sighed. "The question is, where does it leave us?"

"Perhaps we should go back a bit."

"I'm still listening."

"That 'moment of shock' that she's the daughter of a prominent politician. Let's assume, for the sake of argument, that's what happened. At that point, whoever was out to get her must have changed his assassination-plot into a kidnap-plot. Which would require a lot of networking."

"Okay."

"The other possibility is that she genuinely has had a religious conversion, and she's gone with them willingly. But that requires the independent, highly unlikely conjunction of two major events: them finding her and her having a blinding religious experience."

"Remind me: why can't she just have gone on her own? That way, you've only got one event: the conversion."

"She'd have needed to prepare. Even if she was going with friends. Just leaving a farewell note on Facebook and setting off into the sunset wouldn't get her very far."

"Her passport's gone, her bank account's been cleared, and she's taken several changes of clothes."

"How much money did she take altogether?"

"Including the money she removed from her father's account, about five thousand pounds. We've CCTV footage of her at the local cashpoint."

"And no one's with her?"

"Not in shot."

"Do we have any *bureau de change* report of a fourteen year-old girl swapping pounds sterling for Turkish lira? Or footage of her at the airport? Or of *any* lone fourteen year-old girl?"

"No, but ..."

"Either she had accomplices, or she's still in this country. Once I've met this forum moderator, I should know which of those alternatives is true."

"Optimistic. I'll let it ride for now. He's due to arrive in about thirty minutes. That's not all, John."

He successfully suppressed a deafening groan. "Fire away."

"We've had a notification from the National Fraud Intelligence Bureau about JM Cranenburgh Bradley. They believe their systems may have been compromised from abroad. I had a word with a Detective Inspector Collingdale this afternoon. It turns out JMCB *didn't* request a mock cyber-attack from Chewton Black. They knew nothing about it. Obviously, we haven't told them yet. They still think Chewton Black's little incursion came from overseas somewhere. I'd like you to go and see them, disabuse them as gently as you can."

He grinned. "In all honesty, I'm not sure I can cope with Sebastian Chewton *and* Aisha Sharif *and* this. Know your limits: the first rule of good spycraft. Isn't there someone else we can assign to one or the other?"

"I only want you to go and see this moderator, then you're back with the Chewton boy. We've got too many agents in Turkey, John. Prime Minister's insistence, unfortunately: he and Yousaf Sharif are good friends as well as work colleagues. You might as well cancel tomorrow night's plans too. I know I have. We're seriously overstretched."

"Am I seeing the moderator and JMCB-whoever tonight?"

"You might as well. If that's okay. Amber will set up the introductions. Read the file on Terence Dimbleton, JMCB's chairman, before you leave the building. I've told her to have it ready and waiting for you. On no account are you to divulge its contents anywhere at any time, even to Amber herself. Understood?"

"What's in it?"

She looked at him expressionlessly. "Dirt," she said.

Chapter 4: Two Baddies in One Chapter

Thirty minutes just wasn't long enough to read a file as fat as the one on Terence Dimbleton and get over to Waterloo police station in time to meet the man he was already beginning to think of as 'The Moderator', as if that was his handle in a team for a heist. However, he got the gist. Dimbleton was a man given to sexual violence, some of it against children. Owing, the report strongly implied, to his wealth and connections, it was never possible to prove anything significant against him, but he was on a to-watch list in twelve different countries, half of them in Southeast Asia.

Mordred entered the police station at six-thirty and was shown to an interview room on the first floor. Outside, four uniformed officers awaited him, three men and a woman. They shook hands. Mordred was tactfully reminded he was only there to observe. He asked for a seat facing the suspect.

Inside, an Asian man in his early thirties sat at a table beside an elderly white man in a suit, obviously his lawyer. Two empty seats faced him and a cassette recorder lay to one side. Mordred took his chair, and the woman and one of her colleagues sat down facing the suspect and his lawyer. The two other officers stood at sufficient proximity to prevent an outbreak of violence if necessary. She switched the tape on.

"Sergeant Aadila Aziz and Constable Ben Sykes," she said. "Interview with Mohammad Ali Abdullah, twentieth September, 6.50pm. Now, Mr Abdullah, you do know why you're here, don't you?"

"What do you want me to say?" Abdullah asked. "It wasn't me! I don't know who put up that website! I swear on my mother's grave!"

"We've got your hard drive," the male policeman said. "We've looked in your folders. We've got a list of texts that were copied and pasted into the forum, with matching dates."

"I don't know who that was! Who the hell it *could* have been! All I know is, it wasn't me!"

"Your mother says you boasted to one of your cousins about it, and gave him a password."

"No, no, that's not true! I've never done that!"

"We've actually spoken to the cousin. He says you did."

"I absolutely never! I didn't! It wasn't me!"

"We've also got webcam footage of you uploading *London Loves ISIS* banners onto your jihadist forum."

"No, no, that can't be!" Something seemed to snap in him. For a full minute he looked around the room, then shrugged. He turned to his lawyer. They had a whispered conversation and finally he said, "Okay, yeah, it was me. So what?"

The lawyer threw up his hands.

"So I'll ask you again," Sergeant Aziz said. "You do know why you're here, don't you?"

"Yeah."

"Do you admit administering the website 'Death to All Kafirs' between June 2013 and September 2015?"

"Suppose."

"Yes or no?"

"*Yes*. Bloody hell."

"We found one forum-post that was particularly interesting. It reads: 'Listen, SupremeMuslim' – that's you, Mr Abdullah, isn't it? – 'hate to break it to you, but sooner or later, the scales are gonna fall from your eyes and you're going to look anew at your precious little kill-'em-all website and realise what an infantile little plonker you've been. By then, innocent people may have been killed, because not everyone can see what a 100% loser you are. Good luck then with the living-with-yourself thing'."

"I don't remember that one."

"Must have stung a bit, though, surely?"

"People are always putting the soldiers of Allah down. It only makes us stronger."

"Ever heard the phrase 'Infernal Stink in Iraq and Syria'?"

He shrugged and shook his head.

"A contributor going by the name of 'Sufi Seven'?"

"Never."

"It didn't occur to you to try and track down individuals who made argumentative comments on your website?"

"No."

"Not even if they tried to personally humiliate you in front of your followers?"

"No. All right, yes. But I never did it."

"Never tried? Or never succeeded?"

"Neither. I never did neither."

"Did you have any idea who the mockers might be?"

"Americans, probably."

"Why do you say that?"

"Just a guess. I don't know who they were. That's the point about the web. You don't know who anyone is. That's why Death to All Kafirs is supposed to be off the radar."

"So you've got someone out there making hostile comments about you and your website. Obviously, they don't approve of you or what you're trying to achieve."

"Yeah, shit happens."

"But you don't seem to have considered that they might go straight to the police. All you do instead is delete their comments. That doesn't sound very plausible to me, Mr Abdullah. If it was me, I'd probably make an effort to locate them and silence them."

"How can I, if they're in America?"

"You don't have any followers in the USA? Because that's not what we discovered."

"What do you want me to say? If anyone tried to kill anyone, it wasn't me! I don't know anything about it! I swear on my mother's grave!"

"But there are several incitements to murder on your website."

"I didn't do those."

"Oh, come on."

He sighed. "Okay. But they weren't serious. I was just messing about."

"I think a judge might see the matter differently."

"It's not like I'm going to get a fair trial anyway, so who cares?"

"*You* must, otherwise you wouldn't be denying it."

The lawyer leaned forward. "You're attempting to lead my client, Sergeant Aziz," he said. "I'm having none of it."

It was a pretty ineffectual interruption. Sergeant Aziz acted like it hadn't happened. "It must take a lot of skill to set up a website," she said, "and keep it out of sight of network surveillance."

"Not really. You just use Tor. I guess that's what she must have done."

"'She'?"

Abdullah looked thunderstruck. He swivelled his head as if he might discover his words floating about and swallow them before anyone noticed. "I only thought because it sounded like a woman!"

"Really? How did it 'sound like a woman'?"

"I don't know! I deleted all the messages! Leave me alone! I'm not saying any more!"

"Did the messenger *say* she was a woman?"

His lawyer leaned over and whispered in his ear. He sat there like a dead man. Eventually, Sergeant Aziz leaned over the cassette player. "Suspect declines to answer any more questions," she said. "Time: 7.15pm. Interview terminated."

Mordred found a car waiting for him outside the police station as soon as the interview was over. The driver handed him a secure phone and set off for Canary Wharf at speed. He called Ruby Parker.

"I'm pretty sure he knows nothing," he told her. "The interviewer asked him twice if he ever tried to locate people who posted negatively. He said no. I don't believe he was lying."

"What did the interviewer think?"

"She thought he was. She was bloody good at her job."

"Could you be mistaken?"

"No one's infallible, but kidnapping a fourteen year-old girl's pretty serious stuff. I didn't get any sense that Abdullah thought there might be an invisible elephant in the room. He seemed entirely focussed on his website."

"I've spoken to Tony in IT. He thinks it's unlikely the moderator of a website like that could have traced an individual. Mostly, users are advised to anonymise themselves as a condition of service."

"There was a moment of high drama at the end. Abdullah said he thought the person posting on his website was a 'she'."

"Interesting."

"Sounds so, but I'm not even sure he knew why he said it. I think he was confusing the website taunter with Sergeant Aziz, and he's probably a bit of a misogynist."

"Complicated theory, John. You're saying he thought they were both taunting him?"

"Maybe a lot of women taunt him."

"I sincerely hope so."

"I think there's a real possibility Aisha Sharif's still in this country. I'm not saying it's one hundred per cent, by any means, but I'd suggest it's more likely than not."

"Why did she run away then?"

"My guess is someone told her they were on their way to get her. They were probably bluffing, but she believed them and she panicked."

"I'll call a couple of agents back from Ankara and we'll launch a new search. Are you on your way to Dimbleton now?"

"I believe that's where your car's taking me, yes."

"You read his file, I hope."

"I skimmed it. There wasn't time for any more. But I got the general idea. Nasty piece of work."

"You're DI John Mordred from the National Fraud Intelligence Bureau. Don't tell him anything about Chewton Black, it'll only complicate matters. We need to find who hired them first."

"Have you told Sir Ronald?"

"Better than that. I've sent a police artist round to make drawings of the men he dealt with. Somebody must recognise them."

"Send the pictures to my phone as soon as they're complete."

"Consider it done. Have you eaten yet?"

"Not yet."

"Ask Geoffrey to pull in somewhere. I don't want you working on an empty stomach. It's been a long enough day already."

He considered 'yes mum'-ing her, but thought better of it. It was the sort of thing you only did when you were hungry and tired, or drunk. On balance, he preferred to keep his job.

He checked into One Canada Square and took the lift to the top floor, where JMCB's office suite was. The doors opened onto a carpeted reception area with a massive curved desk and a young woman behind it in a red jacket. He gave his name and sat alone in one of the five armchairs set out for guests. The spotlights gave a warm feel. A vague smell of herbs and lemon, as of a very expensive air-freshener, pervaded the air. He waited for the 'Mr Dimbleton will see you now, sir' that he could see coming with hard precision. Despite his wealth and connections, Dimbleton had never appeared in any honours list. He was still plain 'mister', and given what everyone seemed to know about him, he looked set to stay that way.

"Mr Dimbleton will see you now, sir," the receptionist said, as if it was a fairly cheery bit of good news, but not too wonderful, because that would be vulgar. "Go straight ahead, along the corridor, and it's the room at the end."

"Thank you." He put down his copy of *The Financial Times* and followed instructions. Dimbleton wasn't waiting for him with the door open, or anything hospitable like that. He knocked. Silence. He tried again.

"Come in!" came a voice, as of, I've already said it once, moron.

He entered. The light was much less intense in here. Dimbleton sat behind a large desk. He looked to be about forty, lean and floppy-haired like a dandy. He wore a blue suit and a cravat. His eyes were small and close together, his nose was cosmetically too-perfect and he had thin lips and the weak, receding chin of a safe-seat MP. He was playing Peg Solitaire on a wooden board.

"You're DI John Mordred," he said without standing up, or taking his eyes from his game. "Odd name, that. Are you Scottish?"

"Northumbrian."

"Same thing."

Mordred had had this discussion before, and knew it led nowhere. "I understand someone's breached your computer security, Mr Dimbleton," he said.

He suddenly had a sense of someone else in the room with them. He turned instinctively. A thin, black man of about forty with a goatee sat on a hard chair in the corner, just looking at Mordred. His expression remained the same even after they made eye contact.

"Musa Farole, my bodyguard," Dimbleton said. "He's Somalian."

"Pleased to meet you," Mordred said, although he was pretty sure the feeling wasn't reciprocated.

"To business, Detective Inspector," Dimbleton said. "You're quite right: someone's breached our computer security. The question is, what are you doing about it?"

"I need to ask you about your rivals."

"Business rivals."

"I'm from the National Fraud Intelligence Bureau, Mr Dimbleton. If it's some other variety of data you've lost, you need to contact another department."

Dimbleton smiled. "Just checking. Yes, I can tell you all about JMCB's rivals. You think they might be responsible?"

"It's the obvious first hypothesis."

"Isn't it. I'll tell you what, Detective Inspector. This isn't the sort of thing I can just cook up at a moment's notice. How about you call back tomorrow morning, and I'll give you a list?"

Mordred must have hesitated a moment too long, because the next moment, Dimbleton said: "What's the problem, flatfoot? Shoo, go on."

"You don't seem very concerned, sir. If it was me, I'd probably have anticipated that question. I'd have a list ready and waiting."

Dimbleton looked at if someone had egged him. "How *dare* you? How bloody *dare* you? How bloody *dare* you come here and start lecturing me about how to look after my own company?"

"I just thought I'd better say," Mordred replied calmly, trying not to look agitated.

"Get out. *Get out!*"

"Well, I'll see you tomorrow morning then. Try to have that list waiting, sir. That is, if you want our help at all."

"Get him *out*, Musa! Throw him out of the *window* if necessary!"

The bodyguard was on his way over. He made a move to grab Mordred, but Mordred feinted and picked him up by his own torque and tossed him over the desk. Normally, that would have been merely the beginning, and with someone trained as a professional bodyguard, Mordred would probably have been on the receiving end of the rest of it, but he got the distinct impression the Somalian didn't want a fight; more, that he actually let himself be thrown. Maybe he was an illegal, and didn't want to go home. Dimbleton wouldn't care about that. Bodyguards were probably ten a penny when you had your own office on the top floor of One Canada Square.

"Well, good bye," he said. He opened the door and was out. He wasn't behaving very much like a policeman, but it was too late to go back and get all blustery and start ranting about the full force of the law, etc. He went past reception and pressed the lift button. The light came on above the door. Bloody hell. 27, twenty-three floors away. That could be ten minutes. Farole and his master would probably be along any second.

"Where are the stairs?" he asked the receptionist.

"Just go through that door" – the opposite direction to Dimbleton's office, thank God – "and carry on to the end. Last door on your left. It's marked 'fire exit'. But we're fifty floors up so I definitely wouldn't recommend - "

He heard Dimbleton's door swing open hard as he entered the corridor. He'd be alone on the stairs, but it was a risk he'd have to take. Maybe Farole and he could work something out.

He bounded down the steps two at a time. Not very James-Bondlike, but at least he was being true to himself. Maybe it'd be quicker to slide down the stair rail - like a *Beano* character? He started laughing with the adrenalin, and the breathlessness, and the mental picture of himself and Farole zooming down the bannisters in hot flight and pursuit, a kind of 20mph car-chase equivalent in one of the City's most prestigious piles. Bet the architect never envisaged that. Be great in a film. Suddenly, he was in the zone. Laughing at your enemies, yes, that *was* JamesBondlike.

Two-thirds of the way down, he stopped running and started walking. He wasn't being chased, not unless they'd taken their shoes off and were immune to breathlessness. If they'd decided to come after him at all, they'd have taken the lift, and they'd be waiting for him either at the bottom or somewhere a few floors before in an ambush. He needed a strategy. Probably best to toss Farole out of the way, then start running again.

But that probably wouldn't work. Dimbleton had seen his bodyguard fail once; he wasn't going to tolerate two let-downs. Go for Dimbleton himself then. Knock him out, maybe. Have a pow-wow with Farole. Concoct a plausible story, save both their faces.

What the hell was he thinking? He was supposed to be a policeman. Dimbleton was the one who should be having kittens, not him. For all Dimbleton knew, he might have called for assistance. The whole bloody Met might be on its way over right now. He wouldn't dare push his already over-extended luck any further. That word: 'dare'. How dare you, get out of here, how utterly dare you. Talk about strange. Bit like the *Beano* again. Chasing Mordred with a cane, alternating how dare you and Grrr! He laughed again.

He reached Ground and pushed through into the restaurant. It was full, even at this time of night, so no chance he'd be attacked here, even if that was still on the cards, which it wasn't. Unless Dimbleton *knew* somehow that he was from MI7? He had 'connections', so it wasn't impossible. Did that make it more or less likely he'd be attacked? He couldn't think.

Suddenly, he sensed two figures approaching fast on his left. He turned. Dimbleton and Farole. Farole stopped deferentially, allowing his employer to close the space between himself and Mordred.

"I'm really sorry for what happened upstairs," he said. "I'm on medication. I'm not supposed to drink with it. But sometimes, I do. Thank God for my bodyguard. He could have killed you up there, but he chose to go through the motions of defeat, just to save my skin. Please. Dine with me."

"I've already had a veggie burger with all the trimmings."

Dimbleton smiled. The stuff about medication and drink was almost certainly a lie. "What are the 'trimmings' for a veggie burger?" he asked. "Just out of interest?"

Not the question he expected. His mind went blank. "Ketchup," he said, "and, er, a bit of lettuce. Fried onions. That's it. Sometimes a sliced gherkin."

"*Tomato* ketchup?"

"Is there any other kind?"

"Absolutely. There's mushroom ketchup, oyster ketchup and walnut ketchup, to name but a few. Please sit down with me.

Allow me to make amends. Yes, you may be full of vegetable burger, Detective Inspector, but I'm sure you've still room to experience the various types of ketchup. You may never get the opportunity again. Please."

He sighed. "Yes, fine."

They went to an empty table – God knows where it had materialised from, but Dimbleton probably had massive influence here - and sat down. "I'd like to order off-menu," Dimbleton said, when the waiter – a man of about thirty with thick black hair and a chiselled jaw - arrived.

"I'll have to see if the chef has the ingredients. What would you like?"

"Three authentic ketchups. Walnut, mushroom, oyster. Tell the chef it's for Mr Dimbleton of JMCB."

"Just one moment, sir."

"You must be quite tired after your walk down fifty flights of stairs," Dimbleton said. "Why didn't you take the lift?"

"It's easier for two men to beat up a third in a lift."

Dimbleton scowled. "Well, you've nothing to worry about on that score. Not any more. I've got tablets, you see, that counteract the effect on alcohol on the first set of tablets."

Another waiter brought some bread and three napkins.

"I don't understand," Mordred said. "You've got tablets that you're not supposed to take with alcohol, but the doctor gave you some more tablets, so that if you do drink, say, a glass of vodka, you can just take them, and it's as if nothing happened?"

"That's right."

"Why don't they just combine the two? Make one tablet that it's safe to drink alcohol with?"

"I don't know," Dimbleton said irritably. "I didn't get the second set from the doctor."

"Where did you get them?"

He seemed to realise he was talking to a policeman. "A chemist."

"What? Like *Boots?*"

"For God's sake!"

The waiter arrived. "The three kinds of ketchup should be about thirty minutes, sir," he said. "Would you like anything while you're waiting? Drinks, perhaps?"

"Water for me, please," Mordred said.

"Just water," Dimbleton said sulkily. He wiped his forehead with a napkin. "He'll have water too," he added, gesturing at the Somalian.

"You can have alcohol if you want," Mordred said.

"No!"

" ... Okay."

"Let's get down to business. You're here about the cyber-attack on JMCB. Can I ask who it was that reported we'd been attacked?"

"I assumed it was you."

"It wasn't anyone in JMCB. Certainly not me."

"Are you saying you haven't been attacked?"

"No, I'm saying: yes, we have been attacked. But it happens all the time. Our rivals strike us, we retaliate. It's like a computer-game, but with real money stakes. Not everyone sees it like that, of course. But it makes the whole business of being super-rich a little more bearable, and when it happens, we tend not involve the police. It's bad form. So even if you find out who attacked us, we won't be pressing charges. *Under no circumstances,* do you understand, Detective Inspector?"

"Got you, yes."

"I just want to make it crystal clear, that's all. Forgive me if my tone appears a little aggressive, but these are my good friends we're probably talking about, and I don't want them embarrassed by PC Plod. They'd do the same for me."

"Right."

"What I would like to know, though, is, who told on us? Who reported the attack to the NFIB?"

"As I said earlier," Mordred replied, "I assumed it was you."

"How much would it take ... for you to find out for me?"

"You're offering me money?"

"I realise there is such a thing as Data Protection, and that circumventing it comes with a price-tag. How much?"

"What are you going to do to whoever's responsible?"

Dimbleton frowned. "That's none of your business."

"I don't like to see people get hurt, that's all. A million pounds?"

"Oh, for God's sake! That's just plucking a figure out of thin air! *A million pounds?"* He laughed. "Who the hell do you think you *are?"*

"Okay, eight hundred and fifty thousand."

"How *dare* you? I'll give you twenty! – a two with four noughts on the end, which is ten times more than I anticipated – and not a penny more!"

"Sorry, seven hundred and fifty's my final offer. Plus VAT."

Dimbleton pulled his chin back. "I see. VAT." He laughed artificially. "I thought ...? You were joking. Of course. We both were."

"Trying to bribe a police officer. That's a pretty serious offence."

"Okay, *okay!* Seven hundred and fifty! Bloody *hell!"*

"Plus VAT."

"But ... but – *what?"*

"Twenty per cent?"

"But – but – er, that's *nine hundred thousand!"*

"I did offer to do it for eight-fifty, but you said no."

Dimbleton put his elbows on the table and lowered his head into his hands. "I don't get it. Are we still joking here?"

Mordred laughed. "Well, *I* was. I thought you were."

Silence. Dimbleton and Farole exchanged sombre expressions. Dimbleton leaned across the table. "You'd better enjoy your three kinds of ketchup, Detective Inspector," he hissed. "You're not going to make it back to base alive."

"Why, what's wrong with them?"

"Carry on being funny, that's good, yes. Being droll. Make the most of it."

"You do realise I'm wearing a wire, right?"

He blanched. "What? … Oh, God." He filled with rage. "I might have *known!"* He lunged across the table with a half-grasp, half-punch, but Mordred jerked out of the way. "You're *dead!"* He stood up and threw the table over. *"You're DEAD! You slimy little piece of dirt! How dare you! How DARE you!* You're *DEAD!*

The whole restaurant was focussed on them now. The waiters made robotic gestures as if nothing had prepared them for this sort of thing so they were forced to go on standby. One by one, they stopped operating. A woman shrieked. A man said 'Whoa! whoa!' as if that was all that was needed to restore normality. Suddenly, there was silence.

"Take it easy, Terence," Mordred said. "I was only joking."

No one laughed. The silence disappeared as quickly as it had arrived in a roar of astonishment and anxiety and one or two people asking for their coats, please.

Mordred looked around himself. One more second and Farole would leap. "Well, bye," he said. "Thanks for a lovely evening."

"Er, where are you going?" someone shouted – a man, three or four tables away. "I've called the police!"

But Mordred was through the double doors and out of the building. Behind him, a man stood in Farole's way in a misguided attempt to be heroic, but the African brushed him aside as if he was a mannequin.

Mordred was running now. Towards the tube station, that's a good idea, lead him down there. Get your card out, through the barriers, nice and easy. Crouch down behind the turnstile, peek out. There he was.

From this side, a uniformed attendant was approaching. *Hiding behind the barrier's not allowed, sir: move on quietly or I'm going to have to call the police.* Probably has me down as a drunk. He's not in a hurry. Sensible chap. Possibility of violence.

Farole wouldn't have a ticket, that was the beauty. And – yes – he clocked the attendant coming. He'd have to rush if he was going to make that train and kill Mr Three Ketchups. No time to lose.

He broke into a hard sprint and leapt over the turnstile as if he was an Olympic hurdler. Too late for him to stop, Mordred stood up, slammed him in the chest while he was still in mid-air and grabbed his calf. His vault turned into a grotesque tailspin and Mordred brought the side of his knee down hard on the blockade-bar. Something inside crunched, and he toppled backwards like a Guy Fawkes doll and screamed and writhed and hammered the floor with his fist.

Mordred leapt after him, then over him, and ran up the stairs and out of the station. He walked calmly into *Charles Tyrwhitt*, bought himself a complete set of new clothes, and took a taxi from Upper Bank Street.

Chapter 5: Great News From Great Yarmouth

Ruby Parker leaned across her desk and glowered. Mordred sat up a little bit more rigidly than he was used to. Remember, don't argue with her. You want to keep your job, and she's your boss. The clock on her desk said 9.05am. He'd been sitting here in silence for ten minutes while she silently re-read his report in front of him. Keep cool. Don't quibble.

"I'll be honest with you, John," she said at last, "Sir Ranulph Farquarson warned me something like this might happen when I oversaw your transfer from Grey. You're very talented, but you've a huge Achilles Heel. Let me ask you a question: where do you think things went wrong last night?"

"I shouldn't have goaded him. But in my defence, he did try to bribe me."

"Which could have been a useful lead. Instead of following it up, though, you squandered it in a half-baked game of point-scoring. The only thing that's stopping me disciplining you now is the fact that he was apparently just as immature as you. It appears you met your match on this occasion."

"I'm sorry."

"What makes you behave like that?"

"I don't know. Boredom, maybe."

"Boredom?" She laughed, obviously despite herself. "How childish. You could have been killed!"

"He thought 'three varieties of ketchup' was interesting."

"And you didn't. I wouldn't call that boredom."

He waited to hear what she'd call it. Then it dawned on him that maybe she expected him to continue the discussion. "I don't know then," he said. "He threatens me and, instead of exchanging thinly-veiled escalatory remarks, I try to defuse the situation with a bit of light humour. Except he hasn't got a sense of humour. If it was Alec, he'd just go with it, as would any normal person. I mean, it's not like I'm not making fun of myself as well."

"Give me an example, please."

"He asked me how much it'd cost for me to be bribed, and I gave him a quote, then I added VAT. I mean, it's a bloody bribe. It's not like I'm going to have to account for it to HMRC, come the end of the financial year. But I was playing the part of someone who thought he would."

"I see."

"A joke's never funny when it has to be explained."

"I see that, as well."

"I didn't throw the table over. He did. Not that I'm trying to defend myself."

"You deliberately provoked him."

"I've already admitted that. I'm sorry."

"Do you know what I think your problem is, John? You're a moralist, that's what. I think it was a big mistake for me to show you Terence Dimbleton's file before sending you over there, because it upset you. It was the exact opposite of what I should have done. I should have buried it in a deep hole and sent you in the other direction. I'm not the only person in MI7 who thinks that about you, either. You've a lot of strengths, but one day, your high moral scruples are going to let you down. You just can't *do* the sorts of things we sometimes have to do and maintain a rigid conscience."

"I thought Red department was supposed to be different."

"We are. But we're still spies. It's a morally dubious activity in itself. Even before it's been used to achieve any goal."

"That's probably true, but it's irrelevant."

"I don't know what you mean. Irrelevant to what?"

"Living your life. People go through the world thinking they're always confronted with the choice of good or evil. But that's wrong. Mostly, you've only got greater and lesser evils, and your job is to stick to the lesser. In that context, the fact that spying's 'a morally dubious activity in itself' is irrelevant. The only relevant consideration is: what end does it serve?"

"And 'how can I avoid the glaringly immoral ends'?"

"If someone asked me to do something blatantly unjust, I'd refuse. There, I've said it. Even for Queen and Country."

"You're probably never going to be promoted, you realise that."

"With respect: think about that for a moment. What does it say about you?" He realised as soon as the words were out of his mouth how stupid, even infantile, they were.

She smiled. "*Touché*. Luckily, I'm not as sensitive as Terence Dimbleton, and I rather like my desk the way it is."

"I apologise. I shouldn't have said that. It was unjustifiably personal and completely uncalled for." He realised he was probably blushing. He could feel it.

"You're too valuable to lose, John. And you're very popular with your colleagues. Contrary to what you're thinking, I haven't really brought you in here to change your personality. Immature though it may sometimes be. A person's weaknesses and their strengths are the same character qualities exhibited in different contexts. Just be careful, that's all."

"I'd like to retract my last remark. Last but one. The really rude one."

"I can see you're mortified. Stop mentioning it now. It's hardly the worst thing anyone's ever said to me, and certainly not as bad as some of the things I sometimes think about myself. The fact is, however, I haven't really done anything seriously wrong in my life. Maybe you and I are more alike than I imagine. Perhaps there is hope for you yet. Promotion-wise," she added. "I don't mean: that you should turn out like me."

"I wouldn't mind turning out like you," he said. "Except that I don't know anything about you, of course."

"No one does," she replied. "And I intend to keep it that way. Let's move on."

"So what are we going to do about Dimbleton now?"

"Nothing at all. I doubt even the police can do much. He can't be charged for attempting to bribe a bogus police officer, and without that, it's entirely a matter for the restaurant to resolve.

Unless they press charges, that'll be that. I imagine he'll compensate them for the inconvenience - at worst he might be barred - and they'll agree to forget all about it. No one was hurt, after all."

"So that's the last I'll see of him."

"Until his face turns up in the papers, yes. In my experience, luck only accompanies those sorts of people so far."

"Have we anyone coming over to take charge of the British end of the Aisha Sharif case yet?"

"Phyllis and Annabel should be on their way from Heathrow as we speak."

"Which leaves me to concentrate on Seb Chewton. I said I'd go and see his mother this morning, if I could."

"Well, you can. Get moving. And don't call him Seb."

He took the tube over there and walked from the station to their house. He'd speak to Mrs Chewton first, then he'd spend the afternoon with Sir Ronald. He still hadn't seen the pictures of the men who'd ordered the cyber-attack. Ruby Parker had probably been too annoyed to send them, which was fair. But that didn't alter the fact that they might be his biggest lead. Once that was done, he'd take a taxi to Rheeming Hall, have a word with Seb's – Sebastian's – friends. At that point, he should have a fairly complete outline. He could begin filling it in.

Might there be a connection between Sebastian Chewton and Terence Dimbleton? It couldn't be ruled out, though best not to pursue it till the dust of last night's fracas had settled in Thames House. *It's like a computer-game, but with real money stakes*. Maybe that's the sort of thing you would say if you were trying to cover your tracks. He seemed pretty eager to get his hands on the person who'd reported him to the NFIB, which seemed at odds with his all-chums-together claims. Maybe he knew much more than he was letting on.

He was being stupid, when he thought about it. Much more likely the teenager's disappearance had something to do with school. He was being bullied, or exam revision was getting on top of him, or he thought the teachers didn't like him. He'd disappeared on his way back there, after all. The good thing was, his body hadn't washed up anywhere yet. If he was suicidal, he probably hadn't taken action. No one had found a note. Which meant there was hope. It was just a question of finding out where he'd gone.

"Brilliant news!" Mrs Chewton said, when she opened the door to him. She wore a summer dress and beamed. "We've only just heard. We were about to contact you!"

"Sebastian's back?" Mordred said.

Sir Ronald appeared behind his wife and took her hand. "Come in, young man, come in. No, he's not back. But someone's used my credit card to draw two thousand pounds out of a cash machine in Great Yarmouth. It must be him. No one else knows the number. And I haven't taken it out of the house since he left. He must have stolen it! Hooray!"

"Have you let the police know?"

"First thing we did after we put the phone down on the bank!" Mrs Chewton said. "Oh, this is wonderful!" They went into the living room together. She sat down on the armchair and wept.

"Would you like a whisky, John?" Sir Ronald asked. "Just a normal one this time?"

"Mr and Mrs Chewton," Mordred said, "I don't want to seem negative, but it may not be a good idea to build your hopes up. Not just yet. There are other possibilities. Someone may have taken the card and forced Sebastian to divulge the number. Do you have family in Great Yarmouth?"

"No," Mrs Chewton said. "But he wouldn't go to his relatives. He'd go to his friends, or friends of his friends."

"John's right," Sir Ronald said. "One swallow doesn't make a summer."

"I'd like to take a look at his room, if I may," Mordred said. "There may be some hint of where he's gone in there."

The couple exchanged unhappy glances, as if they knew this was coming and dreaded it. "We've checked already," Sir Ronald said, "but … if it makes you happy."

"I won't speak for myself," Mordred said, "but I will speak for the police. I think they may have expected him to return by now. Pretty soon, they'll raise the investigation to another level, but the sooner we – you and I - act, the better."

"Of course," Mrs Chewton said. "I'll come with you."

They went upstairs. She seemed entirely normal today, nothing of the split personality about her at all. It was a small room. A lattice window looked out onto the street. Plain lamp-shade and curtains. She sat on the bed while Mordred went through his belongings. He had a desk piled with copies of *BBC History* and *New Scientist* magazines either side of a PC. A single bed stood against the wall. There were two posters on the wall, one from Lord of the Rings, the other, Game of Thrones. Under the bed, old childhood toys.

"Ronald buys him the magazines," she said. "He seems to like them, though. He reads them."

"Do you mind if I switch his computer on?"

She shuddered. Somewhere along the line, she'd completely lost the exultation with which she'd greeted him at the front door.

"Yes, fine," she said tersely.

He got the impression it was something to do with him, something he was doing to her. Something she didn't want him to find out. It suddenly hit him: this room hadn't just been cleaned: it had been cleared. And recently. There was too little of the teen-ager about it. Even the atypical sort.

Sir Ronald arrived. "What's going on?" he asked. "You can't just go through a person's computer."

"It may be a question of finding him or not," Mordred said.

"No, absolutely not," he repeated. "Your tea's downstairs. It's getting cold."

"What are you afraid of finding?" Mordred asked.

"Come on … he might have pictures of *girls* on there."

"Well, he's a teenager, so let's just assume he has."

"But – no. No, I draw the line at looking into his personal information."

Mordred was becoming irritated. "And yet you didn't draw the line at me searching his bedroom. I'm going to speak to his friends at Rheeming later today, but you don't object to that. Sometimes, if you want to find a missing person, you've got to do a bit of digging. You may not like what you find, but it's got to be done. You must know that. You're in the security business yourself. Put it another way: if he later turns up dead, and something on his computer could have saved him, you're going to find it very difficult to live with yourselves."

"No," Sir Ronald said. "Absolutely not."

"Maybe we should," his wife said.

"*No!* Look, young man, I'm going to ask you to go now. I can see it was a mistake to call MI5 in. I might have known you'd make a meal of it. Let's just leave it in the hands of the police, eh? Now we know he's in Great Yarmouth, I'm sure it's only going to be a matter of hours. No need to further humiliate him by having a look at his pictures."

"He needn't know." But it was obviously pointless arguing. "Very well, I'll leave."

"Have some tea on the way out. I don't mean to be rude. I'm really sorry if I came across that way. It's just … certain lines shouldn't be crossed. That's all I'm saying."

"I think it depends on the stakes," Mordred replied.

He went downstairs, sat on the sofa and drank his tea. Unfortunately, it was scalding, so there was no hurrying it. The three of them sat in a surreal silence without making eye contact. The clock ticked.

"Would you like an Oreo biscuit?" Mrs Chewton asked weakly.

"I'm fine."

Another truck of silence arrived and emptied its load. The clock ticked a bit more.

"I think we should tell him," she said.

"No!" Sir Ronald barked for the second time, making everyone jump, even himself.

Suddenly, it all fell into place. It wasn't pictures of girls Sir Ronald was frightened of him finding. It was pictures of boys. Of course. He'd only just found out, and he hadn't come to terms with it. He assumed it was cause for shame. Bless.

Mrs Chewton saw him to the front door. As she closed it, he saw her glance fleetingly at the wheelie-bin behind the railings. Whether she knew what she'd done or not, he couldn't tell. Either way, it was too late. He knew.

The secret was in there.

Chapter 6: The So-Called 'Hidden Curriculum'

The wheelie-bin would have to wait till tonight. In the meantime, he had a school to get to. He wasn't going to give up on Seb – Sebastian – just because his dad was homophobic. He'd come too far, and he had the sense of being on the verge of a breakthrough. Besides, he was always up for a trip to Margate. He rang Thames House and told them to formalise the arrangements. They'd already been agreed provisionally.

He took the train from London Victoria and arrived two hours later. From the station, it was a short taxi ride to Rheeming Hall, an exemplary specimen of Victorian gothic with twenty-eight rooms – now all classrooms or offices - that had been home to the family whose surname it still bore until World War One, when both heirs had died on the western front. Set in four acres of playing fields dotted with trees deemed too ancient to chop down, it had been converted to a school in 1974, and the current headmaster – Derek Bolam, BSc. – was part-owner. It was boys-only.

Mordred gave his name and card in at reception, and was taken in to the Head's office, a wainscoted former drawing room with a view of the sea in the distance. Mr Bolam was a bald, red-faced man of about sixty. He wore a moustache and spoke with a loud voice. He shook Mordred's hand.

"I assume you've talked to your staff about Sebastian," Mordred said, as they sat down. "Did he seem withdrawn at all?"

"I've already spoken about this. To a different officer. But I suppose it can't hurt to go over the same ground again. Sebastian was Sebastian. He was a loner. Not that he didn't have friends, but they were ... well, I suppose quiet, sensitive sorts. More like poets and painters, I suppose, than sportsmen."

"Looking back, could you have foreseen his disappearance? I mean, with the wisdom of hindsight?"

"*I* couldn't. His friends have a different story to tell."

"You've interviewed them, I imagine. I thought speaking to you first might save me some time."

"They believe he had a girlfriend. And that she ditched him, and then he became suicidal."

"Is that just a theory, or do they have evidence?"

"Personally, I think it's codswallop. They never met her. It's the sort of thing you tend to claim when you're gay and in denial. Don't get me wrong: it's the statutory duty of every school nowadays to prevent all forms of prejudice-based bullying. We take that very seriously. We have a zero tolerance policy on homophobic - and transphobic - behaviour here."

"What makes you say he was 'gay and in denial'?"

"I'm just saying it's a possibility. I'm certainly not saying there's anything wrong with it. Adolescence is one of the most difficult, confusing times of your life. We try to help them through it. It helps sometimes to try and anticipate things."

"Not all parents feel as you do, of course. Do you think Sebastian's may have found it difficult?"

"We don't know he was gay."

"Hypothetically."

"You never know how parents will react to something like that until it happens. I don't know Mr and Mrs Chewton well enough to be any more specific."

"Did any of the boys think he might be gay?"

Bolam scoffed. "They *all* accuse each other of being gay at one time or another. You're 'gay' if you don't like rugby or football or cricket; you're gay if your interests overlap at any point with those of a stereotypical girl; you're gay if you like poetry; you're gay if you don't like misogynistic rap; you're gay if you want to be alone; you're gay if you're too expressive; you're gay if you have a certain kind of voice, or walk, or run. Let me tell you something, Mr Mordred. This is a boys' school, so I speak from experience. People talk about the Taliban, or ISIS, or the Nazi party, or the Khmer Rouge, or the Ku Klux Klan, as if they're what's wrong – beliefs, in other words - and if we just got rid of those ideas, etc.

But ask yourself, what do all those movements have in common? They're led by men. Where do you ever hear of an organised group of women spontaneously terrorising males? Ever in the world? It just doesn't happen. That doesn't mean that all males are pathological, of course. Far from it. But a significant minority probably are. The rest risk getting their necks broken in the flight to the lowest common denominator."

"You think Sebastian may have felt victimised?"

"I'm sure of it. He saw the school counsellor, Sue Pierce, on three occasions. She said he claimed he was 'in love' with this 'girl'. But she couldn't get him to be any more specific. Sue's non-judgemental: she won't say she thinks it was a fantasy, but she will admit she got nowhere near discovering the identity of said female. Look, we did try to ease the pressure on him a bit, but we didn't think he was in any way close to running away from home. As it is, I'm confident he'll turn up. That's how it nearly always pans out."

"Sorry, in what way did you try to 'ease the pressure' on him?"

"He went to do work experience with his parents. Normally, we don't permit that. It defeats the object a little bit, because parents tend to be a little too indulgent. But we made an exception with Sebastian. Sue advised him to speak to them. Whether he got round to doing so, I don't know."

"Thank you, Mr Bolam, you've been very helpful. I wonder if it would be possible for me to speak to his friends now?"

He wasn't allowed to conduct the interview except in the presence of another adult who'd been CRB-checked. The headmaster took him along a corridor, up a flight of stairs and knocked at an office door. A sign below the fire-glass said, 'Mrs Pierce is in Da House'. He introduced Mordred to her and sent a passing sixth former to summon 'Dale and Graham'. Mrs Pierce was tall, thin, very friendly and about forty with thick blonde hair and a suntanned face. She wore a track-suit. On her wall, there were timetables, different coloured bulletins and a big notice saying, "'When you do what you fear most, then you can do anything' – Stephen Richards." Her desk had an in and out tray, and the obligatory PC with the school homepage on. Four chairs had been laid out. The Head made his excuses, shook hands with Mordred again and left.

"I won't say anything unless I absolutely need to," she said. "It's a tough time of your life, school. I wouldn't go back there. Not for the world."

"I was educated at home," Mordred said. "My parents thought school was too much like being in the army."

"The so-called hidden curriculum," she replied. "You used to hear a lot about that years ago. No one talks about it nowadays. Mind you, no one thinks any more. They just follow diktats." She laughed gently.

"It may be necessary for me to use your PC at some point," he said.

"It's the only one in the school that isn't filtered," she said. "I quite often need to access social networking sites to monitor cyber-bullying."

Dale and Graham knocked at the door and came in. Mordred had forgotten they were sixth-formers. All the talk about 'school' had temporarily misled him into thinking they'd be younger. They had to lower their heads to get under the doorframe. They wore uniforms. They were thin-faced and spotty. Dale wore heavy-rimmed glasses. Mrs Pierce introduced them. They shook hands with Mordred and sat down.

"Of course, you both know I'm here to talk about Sebastian," Mordred said.

Dale sighed. "He's just gone for a bit of a bunk-off. He'll be back by the end of the week. Just leave him alone. With respect."

"I admit, you may be right," Mordred said, "but we can't afford to be complacent. If we took that approach with every young man of your age who went missing, we'd have left some people in grave danger."

"I guess so," Dale said. "What do you want to know? He hasn't tried to contact either of us, if that's what you're going to ask. And he hasn't updated his Facebook page or any of that stuff."

"I'm particularly interested in a girl he may have been seeing."

Graham leaned forward slightly. "Do you know who she is?"

"No."

"But you know she exists, right?"

"Again, no."

Dale gave another sigh. "So what you're asking is: does she exist?" He laughed. "I don't know. I don't think so."

"Why would he make something like that up?" Mordred asked.

"Why would anyone make anything up? This is a school. People are always making things up. How rich they are, where they go on holiday, how their dad owns this yacht in the Caribbean, how they've got a really tough older brother – everything. Especially about girls."

"But you're his friends. I can understand someone making up a story to impress a person they don't know very well, in order to win them round, but why would you do that to someone who's already been won round? What did he have to gain?"

"I guess he must have thought *we* thought he was gay," Dale said. "Some guys are paranoid about that."

"People change as they get older," Graham added. "He may not have wanted to impress us once; maybe lately he did. I don't know why. It happens, I've seen it."

"Don't take this the wrong way," Dale said, "I'd never say this to his – or anyone's – face, but Sebastian's ugly. He looks like Plug from The Bash Street Kids. Women don't want that. They want someone who looks like One Direction or Zac Efron. Especially at our age. They want someone who'll look good in a selfie with them."

Graham turned to his friend. "Yeah, but he was quite good with computers. That can be quite cool. Nowadays, you can be quite a hard man if you're good at infecting other peoples' systems. Like their phones or their homepages. Everyone's scared of that."

"Yeah, I accept that might get you a certain kind of girl," Dale said. "You being ugly might actually help in that case. Make you more of an outsider. Providing you didn't smell. No girl likes that. But Sebastian never smelt."

"Maybe he *did* have a girlfriend," Graham said. "She'd be like an online girlfriend he never saw. Or rather, she never saw him."

"That's rather implausible, isn't it?" Mordred asked.

"In the age of Skype, I suppose," Graham said.

"Maybe he went off because she saw him," Dale said, "and she dumped him. Maybe that was it."

"Have you examined his hard drive?" Graham asked.

"Not yet," Mordred replied.

"Maybe you should," he said.

"When did you last have contact?"

"Before work experience."

"Did you notice any ways in which he was behaving uncharacteristically?"

Something seemed to hit Graham. "No," he said. "… No, he *did* contact me during work experience week. I'd completely forgotten … I was supposed to be in a meeting at the time. It was a text message. He said he'd been to a mosque and it was, er, 'wonderful'. Something like that. I thought he was joking because he was always watching news clips about ISIS."

"Oh, come on," Dale said. "He wasn't 'always watching news clips about ISIS'. That's rubbish. He watched them when they came on."

"Yeah, but he always made a point of it."

"But he didn't watch them over and over again like a mad obsessive. That's what you just implied."

"Did I? Yeah, I guess I did."

Dale laughed. "You've got to be careful. You'll end up making everyone think Sebastian's gone off to join ISIS."

"Sorry. That's weird. They'd burn him to death as soon as they set eyes on him. He's not that mad."

"He's not mad at all. He's a great guy, deep down. He's just having a tough time with his 'girlfriend'." They laughed. Dale shrugged pleasantly. "Seriously, though, he's a great guy."

"Did you keep the message?" Mordred asked.

"Hey, it was just a joke," Graham said. "He was making fun of himself, that's all. You don't need to see my phone, do you?"

"Absolutely not. You've both been very helpful. Thank you."

"Any time," Graham said. "Thanks for getting us out of lessons. And hey, don't worry. He'll be back before you know it."

They shook hands again and Mrs Pierce escorted Mordred out of the school building, where a taxi awaited him. On the way to the station, he rang Ruby Parker.

"Have someone collect Sir Ronald Chewton's domestic waste for examination," he said, "as a matter of urgency. And see if there's any way of remotely accessing his son's computer and his digital profile."

"Any particular reason?" she asked.

"If I tell you now, you'll laugh," he replied. "And I'd like a hold on disposal at his local amenity tip. Please. I suspect he may have anticipated me."

"When I said, 'any particular reason'," she replied, "I meant: I need an actual reason. I don't do Christmas and birthday surprises. Tell me what's going on."

He smiled. "All right then. But remember. It's only a few hours since you said I tend to see connections. That gives me credit in the bank, right? Well, I'm about to cash it in."

Chapter 7: A Trip to the Tip

The waste-disposal lorry came on Friday, but it was Thursday, and Sir Ronald's bin was still completely empty. Either no one in the household was eating and drinking, or something was up. After a request from MI5, the police closed the local amenity tip, and Mordred and three other agents crawled into two household waste skips and began untying refuse bags. Ian interviewed the recycling operatives, one of whom recalled having seen Sir Ronald, or someone very like him, about eight hours ago – roughly half an hour after Mordred had left his house. It all seemed to fit. It was dark now, and they had to work under the floodlights. The sky threatened rain and the wind roared in the surrounding trees.

"I think I may have found it!" Sylvia called, after thirty minutes. "This one's got bits of his address in."

She brought it down and the other agents huddled round. This was Mordred's baby, so they didn't try to pre-empt him. He reached inside and began removing the contents, item by item. Halfway down, he found what he was looking for. What had once been a bundle of leaflets, but was now shreds. Someone had covered them in cooking-oil, possibly as a reconsidered prelude to burning them, or perhaps simply to make them less retrievable. However, once you knew what you were after, they were easy to reassemble. Mordred put four pieces together. *How to Become a Muslim by Dr Nawaz Raza, BA (Hons).*

Thames House. 10.45pm. Seminar room C11. Mordred and Ruby Parker, and Annabel and Phyllis sat opposite each other. On the table, twenty-five leaflets, recreated from their pieces, about Islam and conversion.

"I must admit, I thought you were barking," Ruby Parker said.

"So you think Aisha Sharif and Sebastian Chewton are together," Annabel said, as if she still couldn't get her head round the idea. "But why?"

"They disappeared on exactly the same day, at more or less the same time," Mordred said. "What we need now is information about her academic side. What subjects does she do in school? She doesn't live anywhere near Sebastian Chewton, not really, although they are sufficiently close to make the occasional meeting possible."

"He lives in Southwark, she lives in Richmond-upon-Thames," Ruby Parker said. "That's about twelve miles. They'd probably meet in the City if they met at all."

"Why do you need to know about her school life?" Annabel asked. "I assume you mean over and above talking to her friends about her social connections and atypical patterns of behaviour?"

"They must have met somewhere," he said. "He doesn't sound like the kind of boy who's very confident with the opposite sex, and from what I've heard, if a girl was to make a policy of looking for boyfriends, Sebastian Chewton wouldn't be an obvious choice. So it can't have been opportunism. No, they must have been thrown together somewhere. And long enough for her to discover he's got hidden depths, and for him to realise he may have a chance with her."

"So where does that get us?" Phyllis asked.

"If they're doing the same subjects at school," he continued, "and they both went on a conference somewhere … I'm thinking residential, though it wouldn't have to be."

"I don't like banging on people's doors in the middle of the night," Ruby Parker said. "It's not good for our image. But if you're right, we're going to have to get our hands on Sebastian Chewton's computer soon. The only thing that's stopping me going over to Southwark now is it's all so speculative. What have we got? Twenty-five torn up leaflets and a timing coincidence. That's not enough."

"I asked Ian to look at the CCTV from Great Yarmouth," Mordred said. "I know the ATM footage is no good – apparently, he's wearing a mask and a hood? – but now we've got a theory it might yield something."

"I think everyone needs to sleep now," Ruby Parker said. "We're running on empty. Phyllis, Annabel: I'll get the night shift to trawl the police interview documents with Aisha Sharif's nearest and dearest, and see if they can match anything to Sebastian Chewton. I'll explain what you're looking for. John: I want you to go round to Sir Ronald's house first thing tomorrow morning. Tell him you've been to the school, and you've reason to believe his son's converted to Islam. Don't be any more specific than that. Once he realises his terrible secret is out, my guess is he'll give in over the computer. You may even be able to bring it back here with you. Don't go home, it'll take too long. Use the sleeping pods in Western Basement One. I've already asked Amber to take your spare clothes out of mothballs."

None of them had ever used the sleeping pods before. They picked up their passes to WB1 at reception and descended by lift to First Underground. They took the shuttle to the ladies' and gents' cloakrooms – directly beneath St John's Gardens, so he'd been told – where they parted company. He changed into a pair of pyjamas and went through into a bare metallic room with about ten large drawers. He was alone. He pressed the button on the nearest. Out came his bed. He climbed on, lay down and felt it return to its original position. The lights went off. He slept. At eight o'clock, he reversed the process. His new clothes – socks, underwear, white shirt and a dark suit - were in the cloakroom. He showered and put them on. He ate two slices of toast and Marmite in the canteen with Annabel and Phyllis. When he left the building, his ride to Southwark – in a company Vauxhall, driven by a man who never spoke – awaited him, with that morning's *Independent* on the back seat.

"I must say, some days, you do feel you're well looked after here," Mordred said.

The man who never spoke looked at him in the rear-view mirror. He didn't smile.

"They've quite a decent canteen upstairs," Mordred said. "Name me a breakfast cereal. I bet they've got it."

The man who never spoke remained silent. He stopped looking at Mordred.

"You look like a bacon and eggs man to me," Mordred continued. "Could that be right? I bet it is, eh?"

The man who never spoke put a pair of sunglasses on.

"What do you think of the situation in the middle east?"

They carried on in this vein all the way to Southwark. Mordred knew he *could* talk, because he'd seen him with his friends in a bar on Horseferry Road. And he knew he didn't have orders not to talk, because he'd enquired. So why he wouldn't was a mystery. Halfway along, it occurred to him that this was precisely the kind of behaviour Ruby Parker considered immature: firing endless, trivial questions at a man who never spoke. But it passed the time. Anyway, he wasn't being unreasonable. T.M.W.N.S. was.

"Penny for your thoughts," he said, as the car slowed at their destination.

The man who never spoke apparently didn't want a penny. He let Mordred out and zoomed away with a screech of rubber like a New York City cop drama.

Mordred mounted the steps and knocked at the front door. Mrs Chewton answered. She wore black trousers and a buttoned-up pink cardigan and looked at him without surprise. "Ronald," she called indoors. "Your friend's back!"

Sir Ronald appeared from the background, doing up his cufflinks. "Ah, John boy," he said, as if it was a nice surprise. "Come in. Sorry about the misunderstanding yesterday. The fact is … well, Elaine and I have decided to come clean. We think Sebastian may be gay. We found a huge folder of homosexual pornography on his hard drive, and we've – I've – been finding it difficult to process the thought that our son may, well, never marry and have children."

"Unless he adopts, of course," Mrs Chewton said, "but it's not the same."

"Yes, of course, you can adopt. Like Elton John and that Furnish chap. But still. It's not your seed. Bloody disappointing."

"Still, we love him, so we'll get over it," Mrs Chewton said.

"I just wanted to save you having to see the pictures," Sir Ronald said. "For your sake as much as ours. Some of them are *horrible*. Imagine someone shows you a picture of two men really – well, you know – and then they say, 'By the way, your nearest and dearest downloaded this from the internet, and a lot more besides!' You'll get a sense of our mortification."

"Sebastian's been silly," she said, "but it's not a crime, and we forgive him."

"Unreservedly," Sir Ronald agreed.

"We're not proud of him," she said. "But life doesn't always go according to plan."

Mordred didn't know quite how to pierce their bubble. He felt sorry for them. They'd obviously spent a long time rehearsing. "So could I see his hard drive now?" he asked.

"I really don't think that's necessary," Sir Ronald said. "You'll only be ill. It's absolutely hideous, some of it."

"Utterly *ghastly*," Mrs Chewton agreed. "I had nightmares."

"We won't keep you, John. There's no need for any more MI5. We'll let the police take it from here."

"Would you like a toasted sandwich?" she asked.

"Or a whisky?" Sir Ronald asked.

"I went to Rheeming Hall yesterday," Mordred announced. "I was told Sebastian converted to Islam recently. We've also come into possession of some of the leaflets he owned. It appears we may still need to examine his hard drive."

It was as if they were hot air balloons ready for lift-off and he'd pierced them with a hole just big enough to ensure slow but complete deflation. There'd be no lifting off in this house now. No one was going anywhere. Their eyes filled with defeat and terror.

"Is – is that right?" Mrs Chewton said. She put her fingers to her mouth and trembled and looked to her husband for support.

"Why are you so afraid?" Mordred asked. "It's only Islam."

Sir Ronald sat down on the sofa and buried his head in his hands. His wife left the room. He heard her go upstairs – to hang herself, for all he knew, but there was nothing he could do about it. It was fully five minutes before Sir Ronald spoke.

"You found our rubbish, didn't you? Of course you did. It's what you lot do. I don't resent you for it. We asked you in – Elaine and I - and you're only doing what you do best. I bloody knew I should have burned it."

"Had you better check on Mrs Chewton?"

"Yes, probably." He left the room. Another ten minutes passed, and he re-entered, holding her hand. He led her to the sofa and they sat down side-by-side. She'd obviously been crying hard. She was still sniffing

"You can have the hard drive," Sir Ronald said. "We might as well tell you the truth. You'll find out anyway now. You already know half of it."

"We only want to help you find him," Mordred said.

"I've already been through his computer," Sir Ronald said. "I'm the head of a private security firm, and I taught my son a lot of what he knows about information technology, so it's not as if I'm a dilettante."

"When did you do that?"

"After you called the first time. It didn't occur to me at first. Like everyone, I thought he'd just come back here – or turn up at school – the next day. Bit of a walkabout, few drinks at a pal's house, hangover, regret, face the music. But then it just went … on."

"When did you find out about the Islam?"

"I've known he was interested in it for some time. I mean, I didn't know he'd converted. It's not that. Regular Islam, that's all right. It's just another world view, like Buddhism or Hinduism. I wouldn't give a bugger if became a conventional Muslim. But now I've looked at his web history, I know he's been dipping his soul in the so-called 'dark web': I'm talking Islamism here. There: it's out in the open. Islamism. Terrorism, or would-be. People who want to blow this country up. Traitors. Scum. He's one of those."

"But we still love him," Mrs Chewton said.

"Until he blows someone up," Sir Ronald said. "Then he can go to hell. Come that day, he's nothing to do with me. Or you."

"That's why we were so happy to think he might be in Great Yarmouth," Mrs Chewton said weakly. She sat up. "Because, obviously, it's in the opposite direction to Syria."

"You thought – think - he may have gone to Syria?" Mordred said. "But he's Caucasian. And I wouldn't imagine he can speak much Arabic."

"I don't suppose for a minute he's gone over there alone," Sir Ronald said. "Yes, once he crosses the border, they'll probably just put him in a cage, soak him in paraffin and set fire to him, but he's too young to see that. You can't see the evil side of people when you're that age. Although you've got to be pretty blind not to be able to see the evil side of that bunch."

"You think everybody's your friend!" Mrs Chewton wailed. The bit about Sebastian being burned alive had renewed her grief, as, of course, it was bound to.

"Naturally, the Great Yarmouth thing was a red herring," Sir Ronald said. "Some bloody thieving hoodie most likely, just like you suggested. Either that, or Sebastian's hoping to cross to the continent from there. It's on the coast, after all."

"We should tell Mr Mordred something," his wife whispered.

Sir Ronald looked at her and seemed to understand. "Sebastian's not gay," he said. "There is no folder full of pictures of men doing things."

"I'd already guessed that," Mordred said.

"Though it would be preferable," Sir Ronald said. "Vastly preferable."

Mordred stood up. "I'm going to call for a car to come and pick me up," he said. "I'd like you to help me get his computer ready to transport. Any data storage devices, anything you think might be remotely relevant, I'd like you to submit that too. We'll keep this out of sight of the media for as long as we possibly can, and we'll do everything in our power to locate him before anything happens. We've got agents on the ground in Turkey. We'll add him to our list. Being Caucasian and sixteen, he should be fairly recognisable."

Sir Ronald sighed. "At least we won't have to keep pretending to you all. And he's not alone. I read the other day that over five hundred people in this country have gone to Syria to join ISIS. *Five hundred!* I mean, I'm not saying I'll *ever* feel pity for them or anything – I don't believe any sane person will - but just out of interest: how the hell will they live with themselves when they finally wake up?"

The car arrived half an hour later. Mr and Mrs Chewton stood at the front door and waved him off like he was an old friend. The man who never spoke took him back to Thames House – he was too depressed to bombard him with one-sided banter now – and left him on the pavement. He took the computer straight down to IT and sent a 'mark urgent' request up to Ruby Parker. It arrived completed five minutes later and he attached it to the machine. He noticed she'd ticked the highest priority box, meaning probably within the hour.

When he got back to his desk, Phyllis was waiting for him, sitting in his chair, using his PC. She logged out when she caught sight of him, but not like she thought she was doing anything wrong. "Good news," she said, without standing up. "You were right."

"About what?"

"They share a school subject. Obviously, she's doing GCSEs and he's doing A Levels, so it's different stages, but they're both doing Religious Studies. That makes it doubly interesting because she's in a school where you have to opt for it. It's not like you're just made to do it."

"I see what you're saying."

"It would be another matter if they were both doing Maths. She'd be doing Maths anyway at GCSE, because it's compulsory. So it wouldn't indicate that she was interested in it."

"Whereas, of course, RS indicates that they're both interested in religion."

"Bit like you, John," she said. "And Gina."

"Gina?"

"Oh, yes."

"Right. Do we have any idea where they might have met?"

"We certainly do."

He grinned. "Are you going to tell me, or would you like me to guess? Because you're dealing with the wrong man here."

"Go on then, Smartypants."

"I originally thought: conference. Some sort of London lectures put on by Heythrop College, say, but I gave up on that idea. Unless it was residential, it wouldn't have allowed them enough time. And it'd be too expensive to run a residential course in London over several days, and so there wouldn't be enough of a take-up. And of course, there'd be the problem of pitching your lectures. Something useful for GCSE would be too simple for A Level students, and something for A Level students might go way over the heads of GCSE candidates."

She looked impressed. "True. So what's the alternative?"

"A summer school. Somewhere in the heart of the countryside, far from the capital, specifically designed to get bright students top grades. You'd actually encourage the different levels to meet and mingle. The A Level candidates would benefit by having to explain their ideas to younger students, and the GCSE contingent would pick the older students' brains. Everyone benefits."

"Bloody hell. You're good. I'm not just saying that, John. If this was a film, I'd probably offer to sleep with you, you're so clever. But it isn't, so keep your distance. I've got a boyfriend."

"Where is it then, this summer school?"

"Bamford, in the beautiful Peak District. One whole week, the middle of last summer. Outstanding weather too. I checked the reports."

"The perfect place to fall in love, I'd say. Not you and me, of course. Him and her."

"Ho, ho."

"Yes."

"Be careful, John, it's all still circumstantial. Don't get carried away."

"I've just deposited Sebastian's Chewton's hard drive downstairs for analysis."

"Is this you trying to chat me up?"

He blushed a bit. "No. Of course not."

"Just asking. You're perfect, incidentally."

"Thanks. Has anyone spoken to the owners of the summer school yet?"

"For sure. They remember them well. Couldn't say definitely that they became an 'item' – their words – but they think it's possible. They were definitely on their to-watch list."

He laughed. "They operate a to-watch list?"

"They have to, don't they?"

"What do you mean?"

She laughed. "Come on, John, use your nous. Let's say that, thanks to summer school, my daughter gets a lovely A-star. That's not going to be much compensation if, thanks to same institution, she's now having a baby."

"I've never heard of that happening, but I suppose it must do."

"They'd hardly advertise it. Their job's to be aware and to take all necessary precautions. Sounds like a good place to send my own children, actually. You know: Jocasta and Liam?"

"No, I ... sorry, I wasn't aware - "

She sighed. "An Alec joke. I thought you'd be in on it. I haven't given birth to them yet. Apparently, I'm still saving for their school fees."

"So we know they definitely met. It was 'possible' they became an 'item', he's interested in Islam and accessed Islamist websites - "

"I didn't know that. I thought you'd only just taken the computer down to IT?"

"Mr Chewton did some searching of his own. But it's kind of irrelevant, in a way. She accessed Islamist websites too. It wasn't because she was one. It was the flat opposite."

"How are the Chewtons?"

"Pretty demolished. I thought Mrs Chewton might kill herself this morning. I still do. It's weird. I feel a kind of *human duty* to be there for her somehow. But I also know that officially – socially, conventionally – it's 'none of my business'. I can't get involved because I'm already not."

She shook her head. "You should see the Sharifs. He wanders round the house like he's only just learned to walk. You try talking to him and he keeps breaking off to go to the letterbox or check his e-mail. She just sits by her phone with the charger permanently plugged in, looking into space. If you look closely, you can actually see them both ageing. They're in their forties now. In six months' time, they'll be in their eighties. I feel so sorry for them."

"I've just had an idea. I need to see Ruby Parker."

She stood up. "Is this one of your eureka moments, John? Because I really want to be in on it if it is."

"What's it worth?"

"What do you mean? I've just told you I've got a boyfriend. Although I am free for dinner next Thursday. Strictly food and conversation. Nothing more."

"Are you paying?"

"What the bloody - "

"When I said 'what's it worth', I meant: will you come with me to Ruby Parker and say you're 100% behind me?"

She narrowed her eyes. "What if it turns out to be a stupid idea?"

"It won't."

"Okay," she said. "Go on."

Chapter 8: The Drunkard's Search?

They were striding along a corridor on their way to Ruby Parker's office when Phyllis had a thought. "We really ought to include Annabel," she said. "If she thinks we're doing major work-y things behind her back, she'll go ape."

"Only if she's prepared to say she's 100% behind me," he said. "Otherwise, she'll just have to seethe."

"Come on, she'll always be 100% behind you. She loves you, remember?"

"What, because she cooked me a quiche when we were carrying out a burglary?"

"That's how the mating ritual begins, numbskull."

"Give her a ring. If you must. But I'm not sure three of us will fit in front of Ruby Parker's desk."

But Phyllis already had her phone out. "Hi, listen, John's just had one of his brilliant ideas. We're on our way to see *la patronne* now. Are you coming? There isn't time to explain. Meet us by the lift on Basement One." She took her phone from her ear. "She's on her way."

"You didn't say anything about her getting fully behind me."

"For God's sake, John, she cooked you a bloody quiche during a burglary!"

He sighed. He should have kept his 'brilliant idea' to himself. On reflection, it wasn't even that wonderful. Not for the first time, he wondered if Phyllis was making fun of him.

Phyllis knocked and put her head round the door. "Could we just have a quick word?"

They squeezed in and stood roughly to attention in front of Ruby Parker to indicate they weren't trying to intimidate her. She sat with an expressionless face.

"John's had an idea," Annabel said.

"And you're both here to support it?" Ruby Parker asked.

"Yes," Phyllis replied.

"Well, it's either a good idea or a poor one. Either way, its chances aren't going to be affected by the presence of a committee. This isn't a secondary school. Nominate one of you. The others can return to their desks."

Mordred was stymied. He couldn't propose Annabel because she didn't know anything about it. He couldn't put Phyllis forward because that would upset Annabel.

"We'll let John do it," both women muttered together. They shuffled past him and left.

"You do realise," Ruby Parker said, when they'd closed the door and were safely out of earshot, "that they're probably both slightly in love with you?"

"I hadn't noticed, no."

"What did you want to see me about?"

"I think we've now enough evidence to make it a working hypothesis that Aisha Sharif and Sebastian Chewton ran away together. The summer school evidence makes it more than idle speculation because we now know they actually met. If we're going to get any further, we need to start asking why. What provoked them into running away."

"Granted. What's your theory?"

"The obvious one, although it's quite a complacent option till we've got hard evidence, so I've got others in reserve."

"You think she may be pregnant," Ruby Parker said, "and they ran away together as an alternative to facing the music."

"It makes perfect sense. If you scare your parents into thinking you're dead or on your way to join ISIS, they're much less likely to explode when you tell them the truth."

"Unfortunately, I'm ahead of you. Aisha Sharif has been suffering serious period pain recently. Three days before she disappeared, she accompanied her mother to the doctor's for a full check-up. I've accessed the results. She's not pregnant."

Mordred nodded. One hypothesis down. But he wasn't finished. "In that case, I need the faces of the people you got Sir

Ronald to recall the other night. You said you'd send me them. You didn't."

"Matters changed when Terence Dimbleton said he wouldn't press charges. I assumed you'd realised that. It looks as if one of JMCB's rivals wanted to steal a commercial march on them and duped Chewton Black into providing the necessary intel. But JMCB doesn't want to prosecute, and the head of Chewton Black's got other things to worry about. It's therefore out of our hands. I implied as much the other day when you asked whether you'd see Dimbleton again. The police have the pictures. I'm not sure what they intend to do with them, but that's their concern."

"I'm only thinking: Dimbleton was desperate to know who'd reported the security breach. Nine hundred thousand pounds desperate. There must be something he really doesn't want people knowing."

"If that was the case, he'd go through the motions of prosecuting Chewton Black and reach an out-of-court settlement with them in which certain confidential bits of information were surrendered as part of the deal."

"Except that obviously, Chewton Black wouldn't know who'd squealed on Chewton Black."

"Nor do we."

"What if it was Sebastian?"

"Why would he do that?"

"To trigger an investigation by the proper authorities."

"If so, Dimbleton obviously doesn't know it's Sebastian, otherwise he'd hardly have offered you all that money. So why would Sebastian be running away?"

"Because Dimbleton *does* know. But he wants to know if we know. That would explain why he was okay with nine hundred thousand. He actually thinks we *don't* know. And if we don't, he doesn't have to pay up. If we do, maybe he does, but - "

She rubbed her forehead. "Slow down."

"He wants to know … if we know … that it was Sebastian. So much so that he was willing to pay through the nose and risk imprisonment for bribing a police officer."

"Okay. And you think the pictures of the men who hired Chewton Black might help – how?"

"If he's after Sebastian, he may well be after them too. And one of them may have had dealings with Sebastian, personally. They may know what he found out."

"Why doesn't Sebastian just go to the police?" she asked. "And how's Aisha Sharif connected to all this?"

"That's what we need to find out. It's an investigation bursting with possibilities."

She shook her head. "It sounds more like the principle of the drunkard's search."

"You've lost me."

"The drunkard looking for the keys he lost beneath the lamp post, only because that's where the light is. When questioned, he admits he actually lost his keys in the park."

"I think it's more than that."

"Here's another hypothesis," she said. "Aisha Sharif and Sebastian Chewton fall in love. Their interests centre on religion and they develop a taste for comment-bombing Islamist websites. It's fun, after all, and it's risky. They get to see themselves as a kind of anti-Islamist Bonnie and Clyde. But one day, something goes wrong. One of them carelessly neglects to cover their tracks, and someone manages to trace them. By this point, they've upset an awful lot of very nasty people, and there's a rush to Southwark and Richmond to behead them. And that's why they run off. They go north, and to create a false trail – either for her, to hinder her parents, or for both of them, to stall their pursuers - she leaves a message saying she's had a blinding enlightenment and she's on her way to another continent two thousand miles away in more or less the opposite direction."

He frowned. "Okay. I agree her conversion message was likely posted for those reasons, but why didn't Mohammad Ali Abdullah know anything about any of this?"

"We don't know he didn't. He might just be very good at managing his body-language."

"We've got a number of Islamist websites under surveillance," he carried on. "Where is there any indication that any of them know anything about Aisha Sharif and Sebastian Chewton?"

"Most of them suspect they may be being watched. They're not going to broadcast an explicit incitement to murder. That would be playing into our hands."

"What about a *coded* incitement?"

"There may or may not have been several of those. Until we've broken the code, it's difficult to tell."

"What about incitements from abroad? Syria say?"

"Here's another hypothesis. They're actually on their way to Syria as we speak."

"Have you ever watched *The Million Pound Drop?*"

"The TV programme? I've heard of it. Why?"

"The contestants are given forty bundles of fifty pound notes, adding up to a million pounds, then they're asked a series of multiple choice questions. If they don't know the answer, their best strategy is to spread the money evenly."

"Right. A long-winded way of asking whether I think it'd be wise for us to hedge our bets."

"With an added bonus of a TV recommendation."

She rubbed her chin and sighed. "Sit down."

"What's the matter?"

"You've made a good case. My concern is that it puts you back in the way of Terence Dimbleton again, and we both know what happened last time. I'm not sure I can rely on you not to wind him up again, and there's a fair chance he'll attempt to even the score. I don't like macho men, and I like the games they play even less. You're best kept out of his way. For everyone's sake. But especially your own."

He shrugged. "It's a good job Phyllis and Annabel left the office. If they were to hear you call me a macho man, they'd wet themselves laughing."

"I'm sure just about everyone in this organisation would. And I intend that as a compliment. But all men have their moments. I don't want yours turning into a full-blown set of aspirations."

"I'm only thinking of the investigation. I've no axe to grind. I won the Mordred-Dimbleton Clash of the Titans last time, and my policy in these sorts of cases is usually to quit when I'm ahead. Give it to Annabel and Phyllis. The chief priority is that we don't leave some major stone unturned. Not for my sake."

"If that's how you feel, then hooray. Send them in and I'll brief them. Better still, why don't you brief them? In the meantime, I'm deploying you to track the Islamist connection. Which is highly fortuitous, because I understand Tariq, in IT, is downstairs waiting to speak to you about the Chewton boy's computer. I'll tell him to expect you in forty minutes. That will give you time to speak to your colleagues."

"Where will they get the pictures Sir Ronald devised?"

"There are copies in the archives. Tell them to see Amber."

Chapter 9: Tariq's Underground Kingdom

He found Phyllis and Annabel on two chairs at his desk, waiting for him. They didn't smile when he came over.

"We made ourselves look stupid there," Phyllis said. "Ms Parker was right. We behaved like a bunch of schoolkids piling into the head teacher's office to complain about too much homework."

"Good news," Mordred said. "You're following up the JMCB aspect."

They both looked at the floor, obviously still mortified by the too-much-homework thing. Maybe it was going to take more than being upbeat.

"How fruitful is it likely to be?" Annabel asked eventually. "Phyllis has been trying to explain your bright idea, but I'd rather hear it direct from source."

"My 'bright idea'," he replied irritably, "is that Sebastian Chewton found something while he was burrowing into JMCB's records. And Terence Dimbleton's after him. And that's why he ran away. I didn't ask for you to be assigned to it. Ruby Parker insisted."

"No need to snap," Annabel said.

"I didn't ask you to follow me into her office. Don't blame me."

"Okay, okay, John," Phyllis said. "Sorry. You're right, we brought it on ourselves. Your stock probably went down too. Anyway, we're still all best friends, that's the main thing."

"Oh, yes," Annabel said opaquely.

"I actually think it's the side of the investigation most likely to lead somewhere," Mordred said. "You need to find the men who came to Sir Ronald pretending to be JMCB. If you succeed in that, you might even crack the case."

"Let's not get carried away, sweetie," Phyllis said. "But it's a nice sentiment."

"I can see where John's coming from, though," Annabel said. "One thing leads to another. Who knows?"

Phyllis shrugged. "Come on, let's get started. Where do we get those pictures?"

After he'd left them, he went downstairs to IT. Tariq al-Banna was a thirty-five year old male with hair gelled flat and flawlessly side-parted. He wore a white shirt, very pointy brogues and a pair of wire-framed spectacles. Mordred had never met him before, but he'd once heard Gina talk admiringly about his 'Indonesian jacket' – whatever that was. More generally, he had a reputation in MI7 as the god of elegant attire. To cap it all, he also 'smelt good', which is to say: of men's fragrance.

The computer forensics room, which al-Banna ruled, was about the size of a garage forecourt. Twenty men and women sat staring at laptops and tapping keyboards. There were no windows, but the light was supposedly engineered to resemble sunshine. Occasionally someone leaned over to his or her next door neighbour and said something. A whispered conversation took place, and a few discreet chuckles were had. In that respect, it was just like any office. Mostly, these were confiscated machines under investigation. Data analysis and retrieval happened ninety-five miles away in Cheltenham.

They shook hands. "Interesting piece of equipment you've brought in," al-Banna said. "Very thought provoking."

"I wasn't sure there would be anything on it," Mordred replied. "I got the impression his father tried to wipe it clean."

"The owner of this computer's on the side of the angels, I would say. Sufi Six, he calls himself. Sebastian Chewton."

"I'm assuming there's a connection to Sufi Seven?"

"Aisha Sharif. You're quite correct. They seem to have been … I don't know what the term is, nowadays. Boy and girl friend? Anyway, they had a thing about entering Islamist websites, posting put-downs, then leaving before the hosts knew what had hit them."

"I was present at the police interview with Mohammad Ali Abdullah so I got a taste of their sense of humour."

"Abdullah? How did he come across?"

"Limited intelligence."

"An out and out geek? Most of them are. That's why the ISIS thing attracts them."

"Maybe."

"Beheading people or using them as sex slaves is the opposite of geeky, you see. That's all they want. The highest good: becoming their own opposite. The paradox is that, when you think about it, that's about as geeky as you can get."

"I get the impression that Aisha Sharif and Sebastian Chewton were both a bit that way."

"I've glanced through your reports on them. And you'd be correct. That's why, when they met by chance in the Peak District last year, she was apparently on the verge of departing for Syria. She planned to leave the UK as soon as she got back. There were fighters lined up to meet her in Turkey and everything. She kept a diary of sorts on her computer. We've only just gained access to it. Hidden in a corner, inside three password-protected folders, bless."

"And Sebastian Chewton dissuaded her?"

"From what I've read, he confused her. According to the radicalist script, anyone opposed to ISIS has to be part of the western *kafir* culture of secular materialism, and entirely comfortable with it. But it was obvious as soon as they met that he was as much of an outsider as she was. They fell in love because she tried to persuade him to come with her. To Syria. And she didn't do that because she *liked* him. She did it because she felt sorry for him. And she probably recognised a fellow loner."

"What was his reaction?"

"He didn't laugh at her, I know that. For all I know, he may even have considered it for a while. But not for the whole week. When she came back from the Peak District, the first thing she did was unpack her bags, so to speak, and cut off her Syrian contacts."

"And after that, she turned against them."

"There's none so bitter as those who know they've been duped."

Mordred smiled. "I think 'groomed' is a better word. Is there any clue on there as to why they're running away, or where they may have gone?"

"I don't think they disappeared because they were found out. There are over forty-five thousand different web accounts linked to ISIS, so obviously we can't check them all, but I don't get any sense that they were unmasked by their enemies. No one on the net's talking about Sufis six and seven. They were just slightly irritating, that's all. Mostly, the site hosts simply deleted their comments and forgot about them. That's my impression."

"What about Sufis one to five? Or eight, nine, ten, etcetera?"

"If they existed, there'd be evidence on one or both computers. In any case, they actually discuss it at one point. She took seven because it's sacred in Islam, and he took six because it's beneath seven. A symbolic reversal of gender roles as ISIS prescribes them."

"Pretty sophisticated for teenagers."

"They're geeks. They're not stupid."

"They definitely couldn't have changed their minds, done a *volte-face* and gone to Syria together? Her final Facebook post talks about having a conversion."

"Not a chance. There's no communication with anyone over there."

"But you wouldn't expect that, would you? Conversions don't happen to order."

"True, But they'd have to discuss it, and after discussing it, they'd probably bide their time. Unless you're suggesting they both had simultaneous conversions?"

"You're right. It doesn't make sense. But why put your parents through something like that? Unless …"

"Unless you're so scared, you'll do anything to put your pursuers off the scent. Even to the point of devastating your nearest and dearest. I'm not an expert on this case, John, but as I said, I glanced through your report. Now, I don't want to sound as if I'm teaching my grandmother to suck eggs, but if it was me, I'd be concentrating my energies on the possibility that one or both of them may simply have failed to take proper precautions, and she's on the road to single motherhood. I honestly think the Syria connection's a dead end."

"It can't be that. We know for a fact she wasn't pregnant when she left."

Al-Banna frowned and drew his eyebrows together as if it was a technical problem. "Not pregnant and not in Syria. A real conundrum."

Afterwards, Mordred went up to the canteen for a cup of tea and half a jam scone. So that was the end of that particular lead. At least now there was no doubt they were together. He needed to let Ruby Parker know. He e-mailed her on his phone, put it to one side and settled down to think. There was a real possibility Phyllis and Annabel had got the better half of the investigation. Not that he could have done anything about that, even if he'd foreseen it.

He was them. They had money, lots of it. He'd got some out in Great Yarmouth – if it was him; let's assume it was – and she'd cleared her bank account. Where do you go? Relatives? No, because they'd just get back to your parents. They might pretend not to, but they would. And your parents wouldn't sit there crying, assuming they decided to play along with the charade. No, not relatives. Friends, then? But all your friends at that age had parents, and it was term time. No, friends was impossible.

So what do you do? You've got to stay somewhere. You can't live on the streets, especially not if you've got money. Well, you go and stay in a guest-house or a caravan. How do you do that, if you're only fourteen and sixteen going on seventeen? Well, you'd have to look older than you are. So you need to buy new clothes, probably some make up; do yourself up like a twenty-something. You could probably pull that off.

Normally, all that would be necessary now would be for information to be fed to the nation via the media: *the public are requested to be on the lookout for a pair of teenagers, 14 and 16, Asian and white, police believe they may* … But both sets of parents had ticked the 'no publicity' box, so that was a non-starter.

But hang on. Obviously, they'd change their minds once they realised they were in Britain. Wouldn't they?

What were the risks with that? It would depend on who they were being chased by, if anyone.

This was ridiculous. He had to go and see Ruby Parker. He needed in on the Dimbleton side of the investigation. That was where the truth and the sole hope of progress lay.

His phone jingled. He looked at the screen. Ruby Parker. *I'm calling everyone back from Turkey now, John. Well done.*

Couldn't have come at a better time. Yes, he'd brought a crowd into her office; yes, he'd been a macho man; yes, he was MI7's own 'Mr Immature'. But right now, she felt grateful to him.

Time to go and take advantage of her largesse.

Chapter 10: At Home With the Sharifs

"John," she said, when he went in. "What a surprise. Before you say anything, I know exactly why you're here. You think the Islamist side of the investigation's a cul-de-sac, and you want to join Annabel and Phyllis. In fact, you're willing to beg me on both knees."

He shrugged. "How did you know?"

"Because I'd be feeling exactly the same in your position. However, I'm going to say no, and when you hear my reasons, I think you'll be pleased. Have you heard of Fatima Wilson, Mariam Khan and Bidisha Mubarak?"

"Not yet."

"They're Aisha Sharif's school friends."

He put both hands on his hair. "Bloody hell."

"What?"

"I finish talking to Tariq, then I go up to the canteen for an extended think, and I have one, and *never once* does it occur to me to think of her friends! What the hell's the matter with me?"

"It would have occurred to you sooner rather than later. We're all human. Reading, John: that's what helps us progress. Studying each other's reports. I know it sounds boring, and maybe it is, but it's what drives us in the right direction."

"We need to tell both sets of parents. Before I forget."

"Explain."

"Now we're certain they're not on their way to Syria."

"We'll only be 'certain', when we discover where they are. Until then, we don't rule anything out. However, I concede your more general point. As a probability, Syria's slipped right down the table. If I was a football fan, I might even say it's in the relegation zone."

"I still say we should let them know. Firstly because if those kids do turn up, say, in Norfolk, and we haven't said anything, it'll make it look as if we didn't know. We'll appear incompetent.

Secondly because they might have useful ideas about where they could be."

"I agree. We need to be careful, though. There are no final facts at this stage, just greater and lesser probabilities."

"Of course."

"In that case, I'd like you to go and see Mr and Mrs Sharif first. You haven't met them yet, and bringing them good news would be a good way of introducing yourself and getting them on your side. Now, to the three girls I spoke to you about a moment ago."

"Maybe I should read their reports first."

"They're on the Met staff intranet. You'll need a 24-hour password, so see Amber. You'll probably be able to download them and read them on your way over to Richmond. Obviously, take a briefcase to keep them in and don't on any account leave it behind. I'll let Kevin know to remind you."

"Kevin?"

"Your driver."

"What, the man who never speaks?"

"The one who drove you to the Chewtons this morning. What do you mean, he never speaks? He's perfectly civil to me."

"I can't seem to get him to talk to me."

"He was talking to Phyllis and Annabel when he took them into the City. I saw them all laughing. I've seen him speaking to Alec too. You must have done something to upset him. Anyway, let's concentrate on business, shall we?"

"The three friends."

"Whose parents all contacted the police independently yesterday. All three girls have drawn money from the bank and they've all been packing bags. One of them – Fatima - has been in contact with an ISIS recruiter inside Syria called Umm Ibrahim."

"Wow."

"That's why I'm almost certain Aisha Sharif isn't in the middle-east, and wasn't ever on her way there. The first time Fatima asked about her, Umm Ibrahim had no idea what she was talking about. Since then, she's adjusted. It's all been, *your sister's here and expecting you; your sister Aisha says what are you waiting for*, etcetera, and of course, a series of direct messages from someone pretending to be her."

"But curiously, no photos."

"And of course, she never seems to be around when Fatima has something specific to ask her."

"It would help, of course, if the real Aisha Sharif would just stand up."

"I'd like you to go to the Sharifs now. Speak to the parents, see if you can get any leads. I'm sending Tariq and another technician over to the girls' houses. They're at school for the next few hours, so we may have time to get something set up."

"Such as what? We know they're on their way to Syria, don't we? Why don't we just stop them?"

"That's the plan. But it's flexible. If we bide our time a little, we may be able to discover the identities of other at-risk teenagers. And of course, we may be able to use the girls to discover the whereabouts of Aisha Sharif. Now that we know what they're planning, we've got all exits covered. They're in no real danger any more."

"If I've got time after speaking to her parents, is it okay if I ring Tariq and join him?"

"I was just about to suggest it."

On the way over, Mordred read the files on the three girls. Each insisted she had no idea where she'd gone. Syria loomed large throughout. *Has she changed recently, seemed withdrawn?* No, not at all. *You've seen her Facebook page, right?* Yes, but I never saw that coming. *Have you ever been contacted by anyone suspicious on the internet?* No. *What's your opinion of ISIS?* I think they're, like, Nazis. *Do you know anyone who supports them?* No. *Do you think she could be lying?* And so on. Not terribly useful.

When they reached the Sharifs' house, Mordred made a show of packing the briefcase so the driver wouldn't have to relinquish his principles. He got out and the car screeched away unnecessarily.

The Sharifs house was a mini-mansion in an area of mini-mansions. Detached, made of red brick, with a mansard roof, it had eight Georgian front windows with white frames and an ornate front door. The gravel forecourt was big enough for five or six cars. Perfect for when your fellow Under Secretaries came round to watch an England match.

He knocked on the front door. Mr Sharif – he assumed it was him – answered quickly. He wore a grey cardigan, a polo shirt, trousers and socks and was about half a head shorter than Mordred and fifteen years older. His black hair was just turning grey.

"Hello?" he said, as if it was a question.

"I'm from the police. DI John Mordred. I'd like to talk to you about Aisha."

He took the card and examined it. "I haven't heard of you. Are you new to the case? You're not a reporter, are you?"

"I was given to understand you might want to call base, confirm my credentials."

"Your card looks in order. I don't suppose it matters much anyway. It's bound to come out eventually. Come in, come in."

They went through into the living room. Large, three piece suite, mostly white and cream, except for the family photos, the TV and a large brass dolphin on a low table.

"It's not – bad news?" Mr Sharif said weakly. The thought seemed only just to have occurred to him.

"No. I only came to tell you - "

"Excuse me, I'll just get my wife. She thinks I'm keeping things from her. I'm not."

But Mrs Sharif had already appeared in the opposite doorway. About the same age as her husband with big hair and a puffy face. She shuffled across the room, without looking at either man, as if she was ill, and sat down on the sofa.

"I won't beat about the bush," Mordred said. "I think it's highly unlikely your daughter's in Syria. The message on her Facebook page was deliberately designed to mislead us. I think she's still in this country."

It took a while for either of the Sharifs to digest this. They looked as if they were being stabilised in a decompression chamber, then Mr Sarif said, "Is this your private theory, or is it the consensus?"

"It's more or less the consensus now."

"And yet, they send someone over who we've never met before to divulge it. Wait here."

He left the room. Mordred heard him talking on the phone somewhere else in the house.

"Would you like a cup of tea?" Mrs Sharif said, "even if you are a reporter?"

"I'm not a reporter," Mordred said. "And I'll have one if you're having one, thank you. Milk, no sugar."

Mr Sharif returned as if he couldn't believe his luck. "He's not a reporter!" he told his wife. "He's an actual, genuine police officer! Where the bloody hell is she, then, Detective Inspector? Sorry, sorry, that wasn't me swearing at you, you understand, that's just - "

"We think she may have met a boy. They're on the run together. I can't divulge his name, but he's a boarding sixth former, and he disappeared at exactly the same time as your daughter."

"Is that all you've got?" Mr Sharif said.

"Let him finish!" his wife snapped.

"Yes, yes, sorry. Yes."

"We know that the two were in almost constant communication by text and e-mail before their disappearance. And that goes back for about a year."

"Is he Asian?" Mr Sharif said. "Is his name Ayaaz or Gafoor or Mudassar or Obaid or Faisal - "

"Let him answer!" his wife yelled. *"Just let him answer, will you?"*

"He's not Asian," Mordred said. "He's white."

"What's his last name begin with? What letter?" He put both hands on his forehead and took a deep breath. "Sorry, I'm not thinking straight. Of course you can't tell me that, obviously you can't. Sorry, I'll stop asking. Sorry." He giggled slightly. "So she's all right? She's probably okay?"

"It's not quite as simple as that," Mordred said. "We're working on the hypothesis that one, or both of them, might be on the run in response to a perceived danger of some sort. We've yet to find out what that danger was, or is."

"This isn't to do with her taunting Islamists, is it?" he said. "Because we didn't know anything about that. If we had known, we'd have put a stop to it. We didn't find out till the police told us, after she'd gone." He sighed. "The trouble is, you never know what your son or daughter's doing online. You think you do sometimes, but really you've no idea. You can't look over their shoulders to see whose website they're downloading, and most of them are more technology-savvy than we are, so you can't even scrutinise the history folder afterwards. They've got ways of encrypting things and they're careful to delete things they don't want you to see. That's why we gave her computer to MI5."

Mordred took a deep breath. "Are you suggesting you suspected she may have been up to something?"

"No," he said. "Well, yes. But no more than any caring parents. If your child spends a lot more time on the internet than she does with you, obviously you get jealous, and you want to know who or what's giving her the satisfaction. Some of it's revision, of course. You try to tell yourself most or even all of it is, sometimes. You don't *want* to know. Because you can't."

"How sure are you that it's a boy that's made her leave?" Mrs Sharif asked.

"They haven't actually been seen together. But we've got their computers, we know they think they're in love, and we know they disappeared at almost exactly the same time. The best way of finding them would be to get the public involved. That would mean telling the media, perhaps holding a press conference. If you're happy with that, I'll talk to the parents of the boy and we'll get moving."

"Will we meet the boy's parents?" Mr Sharif asked.

"That would seem sensible. If you both give me permission to release your identities, it should be even quicker."

"Is it a good family?" Mrs Sharif asked. "I mean, just out of interest?"

"That's for you to judge," Mordred replied.

An hour later, he had a similar conversation with the Chewtons. Then he handed the matter over to the police: MI7 didn't do press conferences. It was nearly five. No possibility of meeting Tariq *in situ*. The IT man was almost certainly back at Thames House by now, maybe even on his way home for the evening. The man with no voice drove through the traffic jams, twice almost hitting a cyclist, and dropped him outside Thames House before rocketing off.

Mordred suddenly realised he'd left the briefcase on the back seat. At exactly the same moment, as if by a psychic link, the car screeched to a halt and reversed until its back door was level with him. One way, among others, of issuing a non-verbal reminder. 'Kevin' must have put a lot of thought into it - which was almost flattering.

He went straight to his desk. Fifteen minutes to begin writing a report. Mind you, this one was probably too important to leave half-finished. Still, 6pm should do it if he bought a coffee and wrote quickly. Two coffees.

"Tariq's waiting for you downstairs," Colin Bale said when he handed his card in at reception.

Mordred got in the lift and went down to IT.

Al-Banna was waiting outside the computer interrogation room, looking anxiously at his watch. "Thank God," he said when he saw Mordred. "I've a date tonight, early. I've got to get home and get spruced up. I was beginning to think you were never going to show."

"Anyone I know?" Mordred said.

"Annabel Gould?"

Ouch. "I know Annabel, yes."

"Well, her."

They went into the room where they met this morning. However, now only one person was at work. Al-Banna led Mordred to an oversize PC at the far end of the room and switched it on. It resolved into four equal squares, each an independent screen. The top left showed Wikipedia, its next door neighbour, GCSE Bitesize Maths. The bottom left was blank. The one beside that was open in what looked like a Word document. Letters were appearing at speed: ' … and so in 1933, Hitler …"

"What am I looking at?" Mordred asked,

"The PC activity of your three leads: Fatima Wilson, Mariam Khan and Bidisha Mubarak. It's all being recorded. If you see anything suspicious, all you've got to do is note the time and the screen." He pointed. "We've numbered each one so you don't forget. Conveniently, the bottom one's vacant. Ruby Parker wants you to use it to type your report. You're to ring over to the canteen when you get hungry. The phone's just through there. You've been granted permission to spend the night in one of the pods, so no need to go home if it's too late. But it should be all over by eleven at the latest. They're schoolkids. They can't stay up all night."

"What about their phones?"

"That's why Annabel and I are going out so early. I'm going over to the girls' houses at around 2am. The parents should have sneaked upstairs to get the mobiles from their daughters' bedsides, and be ready and waiting with them. It should only take a few seconds to put something in, then we'll have six screens on two PCs."

"So am I going to be sitting here all tomorrow as well?"

"Don't be silly. Even we have to do this sort of thing in shifts. Your job, tonight, is to get a feel for the territory. You are in charge of this side of the investigation, so I've been told. Then we'll keep monitoring and let you know if anything significant occurs. If you sit here too long, you go blind."

"The parents are probably going to be holding a press conference tomorrow. I think Aisha Sharif may well turn up in the next few days. Once Fatima Wilson realises she's been taken for a ride by Umm Ibrahim, I imagine Syria will be right off the menu."

"Let's hope so. Coffee's at the far end if you want to make yourself some, but I'd ring up to the canteen if it was me. They've orders to bring you down whatever you want, *gratis*. Goodnight, John."

"Have a good date."

Al-Banna smiled. "You can rely on it."

Chapter 11: Jairmany Calling!

Al-Banna left, followed by the sole other technician, and Mordred found himself alone in front of four screens, one of which he was supposed to write his report on. He should have been going home now. Did Ruby Parker ever go home, or did she just sleep in a pod every night? Sheesh.

The door opened and Alec Cunningham came in. He wore a black coat and had one hand in his pocket. He was slightly tanned. "Greeting and salutations, John," he said. "I was told you'd be down here. Gina and I just got in from Istanbul." He pulled up a seat. "What are you looking at?"

"These are the screens of Aisha Sharif's best friends. They might be on the verge of setting off for Syria. Well, at least one of them, anyway."

"Not abloodygain. I don't believe it. What is it with these kids? Are they completely brain dead or something?"

"I don't know."

"I mean, can *you* see the attraction?"

"In a way."

Alec did a double-take. "Er …?"

He didn't really want this discussion, but it was bound to happen sooner or later. "I've been thinking about it a lot, as it happens."

"Let's hear your nuggets of wisdom then."

"They think they're supporting a cause that must win. Because it's got divine sanction. If it's got that, it *can't* be wrong, no matter how appalling it might seem. It ties an enclave in the middle-east to the whole human race, the past to the future, the eternal to the temporal, the majesty of providence to your little life here on earth. If I was a teenager, that might make me feel giddy. And yes, maybe I *would* go and live in Raqqa, even though I know in my rational self that it's full of ruin and disease, and ISIS doesn't stand a cat in hell's chance, and all my friends and I are all going to die. In fact, that might make it even more attractive."

"Whoa. Don't let anyone else in this building hear you."

"I don't *believe* it, obviously. I can just see it."

"Keep your voice down then."

"Go back to where I said it made me feel giddy. At that point, I want it to be true so badly that I blind myself to the public crucifixions, the immolations, the beheadings, the genocide, the rape, the slavery. I watch the videos and read Umm Layth's blog and look at the web pictures of cute kittens in Raqqa. I adopt an Arabic-of-the-Qur'an lingo, and I lap up the tweets about how wonderful it all is, and how much the western media's lying, and I start to feel superior, because I can see the truth, and I can articulate it in the argot, and hardly anyone else can. Next thing you know, I'm packing my bags."

Alec shrugged. "Teenagers are always nutters, that's the bottom line."

"Another excellent way of putting it."

"I wanted to kill myself quite a lot of the time when I was fourteen. Spent most of my time listening to The Smiths. But what if had been Germany in 1933, and you had kids blogging saying, I don't know: 'come and join us in Berlin'?"

"It'd be just the same, I suppose. More than anything else, teenagers want to be with like-minded people the same age as them."

"Maybe."

"Come on, it's true. If you twist their world-view so drastically that it alienates them from all their school friends, then you offer them other kids halfway across the globe with the same outlook, they'll do whatever it takes to close the gap. These are just children. They're being abused. It's just like any other form of child abuse."

Alec scoffed. "As bad as paedophilia? I don't think so."

"Not all child abuse is sexual."

"True, but we're all victims of our childhood in a way. There comes a point when that's no longer a valid excuse. Age sixteen, I'd say."

"But we can't give up the fight before then. That's why we're sitting here, by the way. Because these are just three confused children."

"I really hope you do become station controller in Budapest someday. You're a good guy. How about I bring some whisky down, and we take turns watching your screens?"

"I don't think it's allowed."

"Bloody hell. It's way past five-thirty. I'm not saying let's get drunk, but I think you're entitled to one or two glasses. There's only so much the Big Parker can reasonably forbid."

"I'm not much of a one for spirits, but okay then."

"Good, because I brought this." He reached into his pocket and brought out a half-bottle of *Teacher's*. He went to get two cups from where the coffee stuff was. "God, I keep thinking about my Sophie," he said. "This could happen to her. She's mixed-race and a big churchgoer, and I know it happens to black Christian kids. Grace Dare, ever heard of her? They target them. They target all the ethnic minorities. Listen, John, if it ever happens to either of my girls, I'll go to Syria and bring her back myself in person. I should never have left Cecily. Well, I didn't leave her, but in a manner of speaking, yes I did. Kids are more vulnerable when they come from broken homes. Speaking to you makes me feel better, by the way."

"Don't you think you should go home to actually be with Cecily?"

He put two mugs in front of them and poured the whisky, "She's going out tonight with a man. A lawyer. I hope she's just doing it to make me jealous, but I can't assume that. She hasn't asked me to babysit."

"I think if she's a Christian, sometimes they see marriage as sacrosanct. What God has joined together, let not man put asunder, that sort of thing. But not always. She might be a Christian feminist. A bit more savvy."

"You know the Bible quite well, don't you?"

"I've read it."

"Drink up. There's all this to go yet."

One by one the computer screens in front of them went off. Mordred frowned. "That shouldn't happen," he said. "I don't understand. They've done their homework and ... what? They've logged off and shut down? No social networking?"

"You must have heard of 'phones', John. They're the new big thing."

"I can understand you reverting to your phone when there's no alternative. But the text's small. Bad for your eyes. Why would you go to your mobile when you've got a keyboard and a monitor to hand?"

"Maybe it's dinnertime."

"All simultaneously?"

"It's possible. What's the alternative? I'm assuming you've got some sort of theory to hand here."

"Unless there's a problem with the wiring, our end?"

"There probably isn't any wiring."

"Come on, Alec. There's no such thing as 'wireless'. It's just an advertising gimmick."

"Now you've said that, I can see it makes sense; you're right."

They drank their whisky. There didn't seem much else for it. Mordred checked the wires, then Alec checked his checking. Nothing. After an hour, none of the three friends had logged on again. Ditto after two hours. At nine o'clock, something seemed definitely wrong. By this time, they were nearly at the end of the bottle. The funny thing about whisky was, the first half-mugful was always the hardest. After that, your taste buds became anaesthetised.

"Have you had anything to eat?" Alec asked.

"I'm allowed to order anything I like from the canteen."

"How about a bottle of Jack Daniels? You allowed to order that?"

"I don't think that's strictly canteen-fare. What sort of pizza do you like? I could order a twelve inch."

"Pepperoni?"

"Afraid not. They know I'm a vegetarian."

"Well, you could have a turnip pizza or something, and I could have a pepperoni. I'd pay for my own. They'd only have to bring it down. But since they're already coming down with yours, that wouldn't be too much of an inconvenience, would it? I just don't want to leave the excitement."

Mordred raised his mug. "Here's to brutal sarcasm."

Alec chinked. They drank. There was a knock at the door. "Enter!" called Alec, as if this was his office.

Annabel came in. She wore a black evening dress and heels and make-up.

"Bloody hell," Alec said. "You look good."

"I – I'm here to see John," she said.

"Would you like a *Jack Daniels?"* Mordred asked her.

"It's not JD," Alec said. "It's bloody *Teacher's*."

"What difference does it make?"

"Women like JD. *Teacher's* just doesn't sound that sexy by comparison. 'A *Teacher's* and coke, please, barman' – a phrase you never hear. God knows, Annabel may be different."

"Alec, would you mind leaving the room a minute?" she said.

"I'll be back," he reassured Mordred, as he got laboriously to his feet. "Call me if you need anything."

He left and closed the door gently behind him.

"We were just about to order a pizza in," Mordred said. "Would you like one?"

"I've eaten. I only wanted to tell you, Tariq and I aren't exclusive. Just because we went out tonight, doesn't mean you can't ask me out on a date. There, I've said it. You can call Alec back in now if you like."

"Sit down. Alec was right. You look very beautiful. I mean, more than usual."

"I've just been out to an expensive restaurant."

"I know. Tariq said."

"He told me you were down here and what you were doing. I felt sorry for you. I thought I'd come and keep you company. I didn't realise Alec would be here. I didn't realise you'd have been drinking either. Sorry, that sounded judgemental. I didn't mean it like that."

"Go on, have a cup."

"A 'cup'?"

"A glass in a coffee mug equals a cup. That's what we call it."

"Who's 'we'?"

"Me. That's all."

"How many have you had?"

"There's the bottle. Most of it's air. I've had half the air-bit."

She smiled. "Okay, which is your cup? I don't want to drink out of Alec's."

"You don't have to stay if you don't want to," he said. "It's pretty grim down here."

"Would you like me to stay?"

"Obviously, yes."

"Why?"

"Because we're really good friends."

She drew a sharp breath. "I like you too. It's cold down here. Is there a heating switch?"

"Probably. I don't know where. Here, put my jacket on."

"Put your arm around me."

"Okay, but what if Alec comes back?"

"I'm sure he will. What of it?"

"He might tell Tariq."

"Let him. It's only an arm. I'll just tell him I was cold. If he doesn't like it, hard luck."

The door burst open. "Surprise!" Alec said. He was holding a bottle of *Teacher's*. "I had the option of JD," he explained, "but I thought: what the hell, Annabel's here, we might as well start a new fashion while we're in the company of high glamour. I see you've got your arms round each other. You realise Tariq's probably watching you on his webcam?"

"They're only arms," Mordred said.

"John and I are sharing a cup," Annabel said.

Alec's eyebrows flickered. "A 'cup'?"

"It would thousands of years to explain," Mordred said.

The three computer screens stayed off, which, if you thought about it, must mean the machinery had malfunctioned. They ordered two pizzas: pepperoni and vegetarian. Alec went to one of the other PCs and found BBC iPlayer and watched a week-old episode of University Challenge. Annabel drank the *Teacher's* and grimaced. Occasionally, she shouted at Alec's screen. "Epideictic pheromones!", "mammalian lordosis!", "Androstadienone, idiots!" At eleven, Mordred rang Tariq.

"None of the screens seem to be working," he said. "Apart from the report one, sadly."

"Is Annabel there?"

"Yes, why?"

"Must be very cosy down there, just the two of you."

"Three." He passed the phone to Alec. "Tariq wants to say hello."

"Hi, Tariq," Alec said. "I've been here since seven. Thought I'd keep John company. Then along comes She. Don't worry, I'm keeping an eye on them. We're watching University Challenge right now. Why don't you come and join us, if you're worried? Everyone's welcome … Don't deny it. You're worried. I would be, with Manly Mordred in the house."

"Shut up, Alec," Annabel said. "Changes in skin conductance," she told Jeremy Paxman.

"No sorry, you lose five points. It was changes in skin conductance," the TV said.

"I love you, John," she said. She burped slightly. "Sorry, I shouldn't have admitted – said - that. I'm drunk."

"Tariq says 'put him back on'," Alec said, passing the phone back. He pressed the speaker button so everyone could listen in.

"None of the three screens connected to the girls' computers is working," Mordred said. "They all went off together at about half six and they haven't come back on."

"All went off *together*, you say?"

"More or less."

"You're right. It must be a malfunction of some kind." There was still bitterness in his voice. "Sorry I put you through the inconvenience. I'll check it tomorrow morning. On the plus side, you did get to spend several hours with a fabulously attractive woman, and the night's still young."

Annabel grabbed the phone. "What are you implying, Tariq?" she said.

"Nothing!" There was a tremor in his voice which, since he'd only spoken one word, was quite impressive. "Sorry, I didn't know - "

"I'm not going to *sleep* with John, if that's what you're insinuating."

Alec looked as if he was keeping a tight rein on a crippling desire to laugh. He stared fixedly at the screen.

"I didn't think you were!" Tariq protested.

"What do you mean then: 'the night's still young'? It's eleven o' bloody clock! What *else* do you think we're going to be doing this evening?"

"I meant to tell you tonight, that's all: I love you!"

"What?"

Suddenly, Alec wasn't laughing any more. He blinked slowly like he was watching a car crash live, somewhere so remote he couldn't do anything about it.

"I love you!"

"No, you don't," Annabel said. "You've insulted me, so you think you'll change the subject with flattery and that'll kill two birds with one stone. Deflect my annoyance and make me go weak at the knees. Well, it hasn't worked. We'll talk about this tomorrow. Good night."

She hung up, poured herself a large whisky and downed it in one gulp. She gurned, then blinked three times, hard. "Men," she said.

"Sorry about men," Mordred said.

"Yeah, sorry about us," Alec added. "To be fair to Tariq, though, I also thought you might sleep with John."

Annabel shook her head. "So did I." She regarded them both looking at her with slightly open mouths. *"What?"* she demanded. "I'm *drunk!"*

"Come on, let's scoot," Alec said. "Annabel, we'll walk you home. No buts. Incidentally, let that be a lesson to you, John. Never play the 'I love you' card in the heat of an argument. It's the weakest card in the pack and once you've put it down, what's left?"

Mordred reflected on this for a moment. "If it's the weakest card, and you play it," he said, "you must have stronger cards left. Unless it's a game with just one card."

"Yes," Alec replied. "But there's a rule that once you've played this particular card, you're not allowed to play any others."

"Why would you bother then?" Annabel said. "Sorry, you've got this *one card* that you know is the weakest in the pack, and you also know that playing it'll prevent you playing any more. Why not just throw it away?"

They left the computer room and went to the lift. Alec pressed 'Ground'. "I'm not making myself clear probably," he said. "It's like a Joker. All or nothing."

"But you just said it was the weakest in the pack," Mordred said.

"And that's an actual quote," Annabel added. She linked arms with Mordred.

"It's a really good card in *some card games,* that's the thing," Alec said. "In others, it's terrible."

"So in some games, it's the strongest in the pack," Mordred said.

"I didn't say that exactly - "

"You did call it 'a very good card'," Mordred persisted.

Alec stopped. He put his hands on his head. "Sorry, I've forgotten what card we're talking about again. Remind me. What is it?"

"The 'I love you' card," Mordred and Annabel said together.

They walked into the foyer, signed out at reception and left the building. A cold wind blew from the Thames and the street was filled with the first leaf-falls of autumn. Cars raced across Lambeth Bridge and down into Millbank.

Alec took a deep breath. "Let's say I'm having an argument with ... I don't know: Phyllis, and I've got a pack of cards, and each has a response on, some reply I could credibly make to what she's accusing me of. Now, I've got this one card with, 'I love you' on. Now, if I'm an amateur, I might assume that's my best card. So I play it. Disaster. Because it's the weakest card in the pack."

"We've been through this," Annabel said. "If you've got other, stronger cards, you just play them."

"Yes, but you can't."

"Why not?"

"Because the 'I love you' card has a certain embarrassment value. It's like putting a card down and discovering it's from a different pack. Which it is."

"How do you know it is?" Annabel asked.

"Slightly different design probably," Alec replied.

"So it's not actually from that pack at all," Mordred said. "That's a bit like saying an apple's the weakest of all the vegetables, or a lion's the weakest rodent."

"No," Alec persisted, "because a lion couldn't take its place amongst rodents. But if you've got a full pack of cards and you lose, say, the ten of spades, you can perfectly well take the ten of spades from another pack. It'll work just as well."

"Yes, but the ten of spades must have had a role in the original pack," Mordred replied. "If it works as a replacement, it must fulfil exactly the same function. To all intents and purposes, it's the same card."

"You've taken the 'I love you' card from its original pack," Annabel said, "and put it in a new pack?"

"I think so," Alec said.

"So what was it in the original pack?" she asked.

"It was the 'I love you' card," he replied.

"Should we get a taxi?" Mordred asked. "Where do you live, Annabel?"

"You shouldn't have linked arms with John," Alec told her. "Tariq might be watching. You're already wearing John's jacket."

"Oh, leave me *alone!"* she said, startling him. She swung round in front of Mordred and forced both men to a juddering halt, facing her. "I love you, John. There, I've said it. I know this is completely sudden and out of the blue, and I don't expect anything to happen, because I know you're probably still in love with the Chinese girl from Black department, and I'm actually clinically frigid – if there is such a thing - but I might as well tell you while I'm drunk, because everything will be back to normal tomorrow morning, and I'll be trapped once again in the prison of being Annabel Delores Gould. I was only going to sleep with you to get you to love me back. I didn't expect to enjoy it. And before you ask, Alec, no, I'm not a lesbian. Maybe I would enjoy it with you, John, I don't know. I haven't tried it for such a long time. The fact is … I was very badly abused as a child. I'll spare you the details, but I've got 'baggage'. Tons and tons of it. And that's why" – she laughed and cried at the same time – "I need to be … left … alone, Alec."

She turned and strode to the pavement's edge. She'd obviously seen a taxi coming from the direction they had their backs to, and, somehow she'd flagged it down. She threw open the back door. "Thanks for a lovely evening," she told them. She was back in control now. "I mean it, I'm not being ironic. We had the best time ever. Brixton, please, driver."

The two men came forward, but the car pulled away. They had no option but to watch it disappear.

"Bloody hell," Alec said. "That was … Whoa, that was *intense.*"

"I always thought she was out of my league."

Alec laughed. "I wouldn't get involved, if I were you. Poor old Annabel. Everyone knows she's strange, but I never expected that was behind it."

"What do you mean, 'I wouldn't get involved'?"

"You can't take the problems of the world on your shoulders. Ah, no, sorry: I'm forgetting. You already have. You're John Sisyphus Mordred."

"I wonder where I could take her on a date."

"Aren't you forgetting about Tariq? Her current beau?"

"Oh, sod Tariq. You just heard her say she loves me."

"Well, that's the thing about damaged goods. What they say and what they mean aren't always the same thing. Trust me, I've got experience with women. And crackpots, male and female."

"Somewhere we could talk? She seemed to enjoy that. Hampton Court maze, maybe."

"Tomorrow morning, it'll be as if you've never met. That's how she is. You think you've really hit it off with her, then twenty-four hours on, it's as if someone's pressed the reset button. *Er, and you are …?*"

"According to Phyllis, her father's doing twenty years in HM Prison Manchester for aggravated burglary."

"I knew that. I didn't know you did. He's an evil piece of work."

"Phyllis seemed to think she had the use of his property in Devon."

"Not bloody likely. That's not his, it's hers. She's very good at saving money. Do you know why? Because she's got no family and no friends. No one to spend it on except herself. I'm not saying people don't want to get close to her. Lots do … well, mostly men, if I'm honest. But she shows no interest."

"Don't you see? Everything seems to have been against her, and yet she's not only survived but flourished!"

"You don't know that," Alec said. "My guess is that each day's a renewed struggle just to keep it from falling apart at the seams. See how her mood changed just then? We were all just having a laugh, then she turned on us and started pouring her heart out."

"That's no evidence at all. Everyone does that."

"Even on the most optimistic interpretation, now's probably as good as it gets. You marry her and you'll have one or two kids she can never relate to, and she'll become more and more estranged and odd. Even to you. You'll rue the day you met."

"What's the hell's the matter with you?"

"It's my duty to warn you, that's all. As a friend."

"Look at how far she's come. Why should she stop here? Why can't she go on to become the greatest woman the world's ever seen? That's her trajectory. All I've got to do is not hinder her."

Alec laughed. "I think that's the whisky talking. And the fact that she played the 'I love you' card. I take it back. It may not be the weakest card in the pack, after all."

They hadn't moved since Annabel's departure. Alec sauntered to the railings that ran alongside the pavement and leaned over to look across the little strip of Victoria Tower Gardens at the Thames. He signalled for Mordred to join him.

"Don't turn round," he said when they were looking at the black nothing that was the river at midnight, "but we're being watched. Two Asian men, leaning on the workhouse. They followed us when we came out of the building. They haven't moved since."

Mordred put his phone up, pretending to access it, and looked at the dim reflection in the glass. Bloody hell, yes.

Chapter 12: Two Shadows

"Don't forget," Alec said. "They're only the two we can see. If they're making that little effort to conceal themselves, they must have reinforcements."

He and Mordred stood leaning across the railings opposite Thames House, pretending to look at the river, but actually keeping an eye on the two Asian men across the road.

"Let's walk a bit," Mordred said. "If we make our way to Pimlico tube station, we can confirm they're following us."

"Why don't we just climb over the railings?" Alec replied. "We could be away in a flash. No, hang on, that's a stupid idea, sorry."

"If they've got reinforcements," Mordred said, "That's likely where they are, some of them. They'll be anticipating us. Besides, I wouldn't want to slip halfway across."

"Plus, we want to find out who they are. Laugh."

They both laughed uproariously at nothing. According to the manual, one of the best ways of putting shadows at ease when you were in company.

"Now what?" Mordred said.

"Let's go with your plan. But we'll walk at a reasonable speed, see if they keep pace."

"Maybe Pimlico isn't such a good idea," Mordred said. "Maybe St James's Park or Victoria. Somewhere a bit more crowded."

"Okay," Alec agreed. "I don't like the way the park comes out south either. Let's double-back then and head north then west at the roundabout. Hang on. Look right, look left. See anything?"

"Nothing suspicious."

They had another laugh and set off, building up speed gradually.

"Well, this is fun," Alec said. "I hope we're not going to get our heads kicked in."

"If only Annabel was still with us. She's got a black belt."

"That's dedication. I've a brown, second *kyū*. What colour's yours?"

"Green," Mordred replied, "but I hardly ever wear it."

"*Green?* That's pathetic."

"I prefer to solve disputes by mediation."

"I definitely wouldn't ask her out then. She'll snap you like a twig."

They rounded the corner into Horseferry Road and slowed to give their pursuers time to catch up.

"See anyone else?" Alec asked. "Possible accomplices?"

"Not yet. No one obvious."

"You mean you can see possibilities? Where?"

Mordred shrugged. "Those men over there by the taxi?"

"Don't be ridiculous. They're nothing. Look, wait till we're past St John's Gardens and take a sharp left. We'll ambush them."

"How? It's not like we're carrying guns."

"We trip them up and you put your finger in your coat pocket and point. In my experience, these guys will believe anything."

"What guys? We don't know anything about them."

"Yes, but they know we're secret agents. They saw us come out of Thames House. People make assumptions. How are they to know we're just glorified office workers?"

"They're not going to believe we'll shoot them dead in Horseferry Road!"

"Slow down, we'll have passed the bloody park in a minute. In fact, stop. So what's *your* plan, smart arse?"

Mordred shrugged. "Call the police?"

"Brilliant."

"What's wrong with it?"

"It's the sort of solution a *castrato* comes up with, that's what."

"Oh."

"Come on, think. Tripping them up's a good first – hang on."

The two Asian men hadn't stopped coming. In fact, they'd accelerated. Mordred turned to face them, ready to fight, and sensed Alec do likewise. In a flash, however, it stuck them that, whatever else the two men were, they weren't aggressive. Then Mordred recognised one of them. Bloody hell, Mr Sharif.

"Nice to see you again," Sharif said, slightly breathless. "May I introduce Hanif Mubarak, Bidisha's father?"

Mordred hesitated for a moment. His heart was still on high alert. He shook hands noncommittally, as indignation succeeded relief.

"You're probably wondering how I knew you worked in MI5," Mr Sharif said.

"I'm more interested in why you think it's a good idea to follow us through London at midnight," Mordred replied. He wasn't going to introduce Alec until he'd got an explanation.

"We've got a very serious situation," Mr Sharif said. "I've booked us a hotel room nearby because we need to talk urgently. I fully appreciate you can't allow us into the world's biggest spy-centre."

Alec laughed. "I take it you've never heard of Langley, Virginia,"

"Or looked across the Thames," Mordred added.

Sharif called a black cab and they all got in. Hanif Mubarak was about the same age and build as Alec, with wispy eyebrows and a roman nose. All his clothes were black: jumper, jeans, jacket, even shoes and socks. He was expertly dressed for following a couple of spies through London. He looked depressed throughout the journey to wherever they were going, and stared at his knees. Sharif gazed out of the window, apparently equally glum. No one spoke.

Ten minutes later, they pulled up outside the Apple Fair Inn on Jewson Street. Sharif preceded everyone in. He spoke to the receptionist, picked up the key and led them all along a long corridor to a ground floor room with a single bed, *en-suite* and a dressing table but no window. He closed the door behind them. They all sat down.

"Never mind how you worked out I was in MI5," Mordred said. "It's irrelevant now. Let's get to the point. What's all this about?"

Hanif Mubarak cleared his throat. "This afternoon, one of your operatives – I assume it was yours – came round to my house to install some kind of spy camera in my daughter's computer. I'd taken the day off work, so I could help keep a lookout, in case she came home from school early for some unforeseen reason. We couldn't afford for her to find out. Too much family tension already. You probably know the background. We've reason to think she and her friends Fatima and Mariam may be contemplating a one-way trip to Syria."

"I'm fully familiar with the case," Mordred said.

"Anyway, we noticed something was wrong with Bidisha tonight. She's been a bit withdrawn recently anyway. I mean, more than normal. You try to talk to your children, but they're not children any more at fourteen. They've gone off you. Sorry, I'm rambling. I wondered if she knew. About the computer-camera thing. But I came to the conclusion she didn't. If she knew, she'd have been angry at us. But she wasn't. She just seemed … scared."

"Scared?" Mordred said.

"It turns out that when she was on her way home, a man came up to her and told her not to go on the internet at all tonight, or until further notice. He knew the police had been round, you see. And that's not all. He's one of a team of men who've been watching our house – and, I understand, Miriam and Fatima's houses too – since Aisha disappeared. They're desperate to find her for some reason."

"Why didn't your daughter say anything earlier?" Mordred said, although he'd already guessed.

"Death threats. I don't mean just against her, although that's apparently how it began. I mean against my wife and I too. I can't speak for the other girls, but these men have been terrorising my daughter. She broke down tonight. She couldn't take any more. They've got our house surrounded. She took me upstairs to the bedroom window. She showed me some of them."

"They want to find out where Aisha is?" Alec said. "Haven't they read the posts from Umm Ibrahim?"

"I don't know. I couldn't ask Bidisha about that. She'd know we'd been to the police about her computer."

"Do you think her decision to run to Syria may have anything to do with these men?"

"I'm sure it has. She actually told us she'd been thinking of running away. She didn't specify, of course. Syria's probably the one place she thinks it would be impossible for them to find her. She said she'd given up the idea since the men started making threats against Raananah and I."

"Except, of course, for the fact that she thinks Aisha's there."

"But you're right," Mubarak said. "If these men are looking for Aisha, why aren't they put off by what Umm Ibrahim's saying? Surely that proves Aisha's in Syria."

"Except she's not," Mordred replied. "We saw through Umm Ibrahim almost immediately. These men will have done the same."

"But why do they want *my daughter?"* Sharif burst out. "What are they going to do to her? *What do they think she's done?"*

"We don't know yet," Mordred said. "We didn't know anything about these men, by the way."

"I'm Alec Cunningham," Alec said. "John's colleague. Could you describe them, Mr Mubarak?"

"I only saw about three or four, but Bidisha tells me there are more. Two white men, two black. Heavy build, shabby clothes."

"What about the man who approached her today?"

"A black man with an accent," Mubarak said. "Not European, she doesn't think. But there have been others. Two white, three black. Five separate people. And the other two girls, something similar, I believe. I actually had to sneak out of my own house tonight, Mr Cunningham, under cover of darkness. That's why

I'm dressed as I am. I'm pretty confident no one saw me. They may not even have been watching, but that's hardly a given. I went straight to Yousaf's house, and he brought me here to see you. Now, of course, I've got to re-enter my house the same way I left."

Mordred put his palms together in front of his nose and thought for a second. "It sounds to me as if whoever these men are, they've done to your daughters' computers exactly what Tariq did to them yesterday. Put some sort of spybot in. How else could they be monitoring their social networking? They must have anticipated us. Mr Mubarak, did your daughter mention being given anything to insert into her USB port, or anything like that?"

"There can't be anything suspicious there," he replied, "or the police would have found it. Unless it wasn't obvious."

"More likely they've bullied their passwords and usernames out of them," Alec said, "and if they're in the locality, they may have access to their provider, and be using it to create a makeshift network. That's where their access will be."

"And of course, they daren't change their passwords," Mordred said.

"And day and night, they'll be bombarding my daughter with *where are you* messages," Mr Sharif said. "In the guise of her friends. My God!"

"She must know they're after her," Mordred said. "That's the only explanation. She must know who they are and what they're up to. Otherwise, she'd have replied."

"So what do we do now?" Alec asked.

"We've a range of options," Mordred said. "We could scramble the local internet signal, keep it down so long, they simply get fed up and leave. Or we could set a trap of some kind."

"Why don't you just surround the surrounders?" Mubarak asked. "Take them in for questioning?"

"Because a good lawyer will have them out on bail within a week," Alec said. "And in the meantime, they'll be replaced by others. And there may be reprisals."

"Not if they know the police are watching!"

"They'll bide their time. Likelihood is, the only way you'll get rid of them permanently is if you're prepared to up sticks and move house, and maybe even assume new identities. Because this sounds like a pretty serious outfit. You don't put a whole bunch of men on a stake-out across three houses, over this length of time, unless something pretty big is at issue. For all we know, they'll do whatever's necessary to protect their secret. They've already done a lot. It may be too late to back down now."

"But this is outrageous!" Sharif yelled. "That we can't do anything about something like this in a free country!"

Someone in the next room banged three times on the wall.

"Sorry, sorry!" he called apologetically.

They sat in silence for a few seconds.

"That's the problem with free countries," Alec said quietly. "As a rule, they're reactive, rather than proactive."

"So what are we going to do?" Mordred asked.

"First up," Alec said, "we're going to have to get Mr Mubarak back inside his house. Then we probably need to find out where these men have their base. If we can discover that, we can probably find out who's paying them."

"What about Tariq?" Mordred said. "I'd completely forgotten about him. He's going round to all the houses tonight to get their phones. Could he be in danger?"

"Highly unlikely," Alec replied. "They're not going to jeopardise their cover by attacking someone they probably think works for the police. They'd have to be stupid."

"Put it like this," Mordred said. "Whoever's watching the houses now knows they've lost the advantage of surprise via the girls' computers, otherwise, they wouldn't have warned them against going online. Once we've installed something in their phones as well, that's their last line of access gone. If Aisha then gets in touch from, say, Edinburgh, we're always going to be able to get to her before they can, because no one in this country's ever more than ten miles from a police station."

"Bloody hell, I hadn't thought of that," Alec said.

"Killing or wounding the principal technician might give them breathing space," Mordred added. He took his mobile out and called Tariq. No answer. He looked at Alec and shook his head.

"Who went with him?" Alec asked. "I'll call base." He put his phone to his ear. "Hello, yes. Alec Cunningham. Get me a secure line to Outreach. Yes, it's urgent. Hello? Brian, yes, long time no see, we must catch up sometime. I'm ringing because I've just come into information that gives me cause for concern about one of our agents … Tariq al-Banna … When was he due to report back?" He looked at Mordred. "An hour ago. He should have rung in after the first job, okay. Could you call the second address on his itinerary and confirm he's arrived? I see. And he hasn't. Yes, I think that's a good idea." He put the phone back in his pocket. "He's issuing a missing persons report to the police, plus his number plate."

"They'll make it look like an accident," Mordred said. "Bloody hell, why didn't we think of it *sooner?*"

Alec grimaced. "Come on, John, how soon *could* we have thought of it? Matter of minutes? We've done all we can. Come on, Mr Mubarak, we'd better be getting you back home. Where do you work?"

"Halycon Pharmaceuticals in Teddington. I'm a managing director."

"I'll come to see you at work tomorrow."

Chapter 13: Watching the Watchers

An hour after Mr Mubarak left the Apple Fair Inn, he led Phyllis, Ian and Gina stealthily across his back garden and in through his back door. With Mrs Mubarak's help, the guests took up residence in the front upstairs bedroom, behind a thick net curtain, to watch the watchers. Over breakfast, Hanif Mubarak introduced them to his daughter. She seemed quietly relieved and pledged confidentiality. That day, a total of twenty-three more agents on foot, on bicycles, in vans, and on public transport, passed and re-passed the houses of all three girls, gathering a hoard of data on the encirclement. Officers in cars took telephotographs of the men who approached them on their way to and from school. Via the magic of Interpol, names were matched to faces; by the science of deduction, shifts, behavioural patterns, working relationships and hierarchies were deduced. By 7pm, a good picture had emerged of who the authorities were dealing with. All that remained to discover was their HQ, but the confident expectation was that it was only a matter of time. Hours, at the outside.

After leaving the Apple Fair Inn, Mordred went straight home to bed. He received a text from Ruby Parker at 6am telling him to sleep in, take that day off and report for duty at midnight. In the meantime, the team could comfortably take up the slack. His insight had simply been that there was no time to lose. Those who'd taken it upon themselves to hijack the lives of Aisha's best friends knew their grip was loosening. The assault on Tariq had been meant to buy them a little extra time – at the time of his car crash, he'd completed one of three jobs - but they'd realise it wasn't much. They'd be torn between wanting to see some return on their investment and the need for caution. Once they saw Tariq's replacement arrive to do the remaining two jobs in the early hours of the morning, that dilemma would become acute. They couldn't arrange another 'accident' for another computer technician exactly twenty-four hours later – could they?

Clearly, no one knew where Aisha Sharif and Sebastian Chewton were, but equally obviously, the search was also a race. The police and MI7 against ...? Filling in the blank was an integral to winning. It wasn't yet clear which of the two teams was in pole position. Even then, the finish-line was still shrouded in obscurity.

At 2am, twenty-four hours after the Apple Fair Inn conference, a grey Renault Clio pulled up outside the Mubarak's house, a semi-detached with a small front garden surrounded by a picket fence. Tariq al-Banna's replacement, a bearded man with a slight limp, parked leisurely against the kerb, allowing himself several tries to get exactly flush, then switched off the engine. He checked to see the replica gun was still in the glove compartment and picked up some wires from the passenger seat. He got out, opened then closed the gate as if he was in no hurry, and knocked on the front door. Mrs Mubarak answered. There was no light on indoors, as agreed. She looked around the street as if scanning for danger, and let the caller in.

"You must be Mr Mordred," she said, when she'd closed the door.

"Call me John," he replied. He removed the stick-on beard that Phyllis had insisted he wear and put it in his pocket.

"Your friends are upstairs. They were most anxious to observe the street when you arrived, so I thought it best not to disturb them. Would you like a cup of tea?"

"That would be very nice. Thank you."

"Bidisha's in the kitchen. We woke her up in case you had any questions. Can I take your coat?"

He gave it to her. "There was no need to keep get your daughter out of bed, really. I'm sure my colleagues will have spoken with her already. She's probably tired."

"Yes, but she wants to meet you. You're 'the mastermind', apparently."

He detected Phyllis's keen sense of irony here, but kept quiet. It didn't do to let the public glimpse the mutual subversion rampant in MI7. She led him through into the kitchen, a small, windowless room with an oven, a table and a fridge, but otherwise choc-a-block with cupboards. Bidisha sat at the table in a hijab, opposite her father. She wore glasses and a dressing gown and had a mug of hot chocolate beside her. She and her father held hands. When she saw Mordred, she stood up.

"I'm John Mordred," he said.

"I'm Bidisha Mubarak," she replied nervously.

"Come and sit next to me, John," Mr Mubarak said. Bidisha's mother sat next to her daughter and whispered for her to sit down.

"She wants to know if you'd like to ask her any questions," Mr Mubarak said.

"You probably need all the sleep you can get," Mordred said, speaking directly to the girl. "My colleagues should have debriefed you fully once you got in from school. Our aim was to make this as nonintrusive as possible."

"Thank you," she said. "It was a huge weight off my mind when I decided not to go to Syria. Nearly anything would be better than that, but I thought Aisha was there, and those men …" She started to cry and wiped her eyes hard with the base of her thumb.

"They know they've got nothing to gain by hurting you," Mordred said, "and they're professionals, from what we can work out. They'll almost certainly be gone within the week. And once that happens, they won't come back."

"He's not saying don't be *careful*," Mrs Mubarak said. She got up and put the kettle on. It started boiling almost immediately.

"They gave us all new phones today," Bidisha said. "They took our old ones off us. They told us to pretend the new ones were ours, so that when you put something in …"

"Did you explain that to Gina?"

"Yes. She said not to worry. But they'll be trying to get Aisha to get back to them, pretending to be us, won't they?"

There was a knock on the door. Gina entered, looking as if she was a candidate for well-dressed office worker of the year. She was about the same age as Mordred, but had weathered better: fresh complexion, brainy eyes, lips that looked like they were used to discharging sensible, useful and encouraging sentences. She wore a freshly-ironed blouse, pencil skirt and kitten heels, and had fully compliant hair. Didn't any part of her know what time it was? "We've diverted the numbers," she said. "Sorry, I couldn't help overhearing. If Aisha tries to ring you at any stage, we'll pick up and they won't even know. We're keeping an eye on all your social networking sites back at base."

Bidisha grinned. "How embarrassing."

"Don't take this the wrong way," Mordred said, "but I really think you ought to be getting back to bed. It's a school day tomorrow."

She stood up. "Well, I've enjoyed meeting you."

"Remember, don't switch any lights on when you get upstairs," her mother said, putting Mordred's tea down gently in front of him.

"Is it really true that you're called 'the mastermind' at work?" Bidisha asked him.

"Did Phyllis tell you that?" he asked.

"Yes."

He smiled. "She must know something I don't."

"It *could* be true, though?"

"Well … I hope so."

She said good night again and left the kitchen.

"If you don't mind, John," Mr Mubarak said, "my wife and I should be getting to bed now too. You'll probably want some time to confer with your colleagues."

"With Phyllis, certainly," he said.

They laughed politely and left the kitchen. Gina smiled. "I thought you handled that very well," she said. "You didn't undercut Phyllis – even though, God help me, she probably deserved it

– and you didn't come across as an arrogant bighead. Going by what I've just seen, you've a real way with children."

"It's not because she's a teenager. It's because she's a girl. I've got four sisters."

"I bet they all idolise you."

He laughed. "Not likely. I'm the runt of the litter. They think I'm a travelling machine-parts salesman."

"My parents think I work for Avon. At a high level within the company, of course. I have to be able to explain the travelling."

"Should we go up and see Phyllis and Ian?"

"Phyllis is coming down here. You need light to see what we've picked up, and we can't switch the one up there on. Don't be too hard on her. She was only having a laugh. She's bored a lot of the time, so she says."

"I thought it was just me."

"Oh *no*. All spies are more or less permanently bored. It's an occupational hazard."

"Anyway, I'll let you into a secret. I'm actually scared of Phyllis."

"Hush, I can hear her coming!" She raised her right hand, wagged her fingers in a stylised goodbye and let herself out of the kitchen.

The weird thing about Gina was it was impossible to spend more than two minutes in her company without feeling inadequate. And without wanting to cancel that feeling by seeing much, much more of her; without falling in love with her, effectively. She made being thoroughly conventional seem like the world's most attractive life choice.

Phyllis came in with an upmarket shopping bag full of what looked to be documents. As usual, she was dressed like someone out of *Tatler*. In fact, when he thought about it, Gina, Phyllis and Annabel were all very good adverts for MI7, sartorially speaking. Even Alec looked well-dressed most of the time. He, Mordred, tried to keep up, but kept sliding back to Ian's level. Ian looked like a hard-up undergraduate, circa 1957: chiefly jackets, jumpers and ties in various stages of crumpledness.

"I understand you told Bidisha Mubarak I'm known as 'the mastermind'," he said.

"Because that's how *I* think of you, John," she replied. "And I know I'm not the only one."

"Right." Pointless challenging her about the false beard then.

"Anyway, let's to business, shall we?" She took a folded piece of A1 paper from her bag, spread it out on the table and surrounded it with large black and white photos of men taken from a distance. In one, a giant in a black leather jacket and three-day stubble leant over Bidisha, his hand on her shoulder.

"This is the Mubarak's house," Phyllis said, pointing to the map, "obviously, here in the centre. That's George Street; Altamont Avenue; Collins Drive; Shoeman's Lane. We've got three cars in all: here, here and here, two men apiece, and there are never less than two cars at any one time. They seem to be working in eight hour shifts from what we can tell. One car's due to leave tomorrow morning, 9am. Rush hour, so we'll be able to tail them unseen. Hopefully. That's at all four houses."

"Four? Not five?"

"The Sharifs house, yes, but there doesn't seem to be anyone watching the Chewtons' house. And no one monitoring his social networking. And, as far as we can tell, no one watching his school."

Mordred took a raft of air in, and let it out slowly. "Doesn't bode well."

"Anyway, that's why I made you don a false beard and affect a limp when you came here. It's possible someone out there remembers you calling at the Sharifs' house. Or did you think I was just making fun of you?"

"It had occurred to me."

"Well, I'm not."

"Whatever Sebastian Chewton and Aisha Sharif have got in their possession, it must be pretty bloody valuable for these guys to go all this trouble. It must be something to do with JMCB. It *must* be!"

"I think we're all in agreement about that now. But we can't do anything about it without hard evidence. Meanwhile, for reasons unknown, Cranenburgh Bradley is trying to erase internal company data."

"Bloody hell, really? And we're just going to sit and watch?"

"We put the firm on GCHQ's watch list just after your little brush with Terence Dimbleton. It's quietly siphoning off and salvaging what it can. The bottom line is, however, any firm's legally entitled to delete its own data, providing it's not breaching an injunction."

"You and Annabel were supposed to be on the case."

"Well, thanks to you, I had to ditch that and come here. I tend to follow orders, thank you. As for Annabel, she's been understandably distracted by what happened to Tariq. She tried to make an appointment to see Dimbleton, bless her, but he's out of the country at the moment, and he won't be back for at least a week."

"Where's he gone?"

"Morocco, on business. Rachel and David are working on it back at Tracy Island, but we've a lot of agents tied up here, John. I don't know what you're having a go at *me* for, anyway. I'm not in charge."

"Sorry, I didn't mean to come across like that. I was just asking questions."

"Ask nicely then."

"The men outside. They haven't twigged we've got them under surveillance?"

"Almost certainly not, otherwise they'd be a lot less casual. It's been fairly easy to get food and other sundries into the Mubarak's house without them seeing, so we're more comfortable than I expected. What I don't understand – and you might be able to tell me, since you're the mastermind – is, why don't they make any direct online threats against Aisha Sharif? 'If you don't come back, we'll kill your parents', that sort of thing?"

"Because that's the sort of thing that gets the police heavily involved. And it doubles as evidence in court. So far, they've kept it very low-key, by which I mean, nothing incriminating in writing. Nothing whatsoever."

"And of course, that may change as they become more desperate?"

"Possibly, possibly not. We're agreed that whatever Sebastian Chewton stumbled on, it was something important. Whatever's going on now may be just the first stage. That would explain why discretion's absolutely *de rigueur*."

"Pretentious phrase."

"Moi?"

"Now, pay attention." She pointed to the black and white photos. "This is Abdiweli Barkhad; this is Mukhtar Arte; this is Mahmood Jawari. We got their names from the French police. *Irrégulières*, and we've no record of them entering this country at all. Likewise with the other three, all white. One, we've been unable to identify, although he doesn't seem to be important. The other two are Rolandas Brazauskas, a Lithuanian, and Mircea Voronin, Moldovan. Again, no record of them coming here. Brazauskas belongs to the *Lietuviu Tautos Sajunga,* while Voronin's been linked to the *Noua Dreaptă,* both far-right political parties in their respective countries."

"Could just be coincidence."

"There are a lot of grubby fascists outside the other houses too. Too many for happenstance."

"I wonder what the connection is?"

"I don't know," she said. "Let me finish."

"Sorry."

"Now, we've got Barkhad and Arte in this car, a red Ford Fiesta; Jawari and Voronin sit here in a grey Fiat 500, and here are Brazauskas and the unknown guy, in a welded together Vauxhall

Corsa. Here's Brazauskas, approaching Bidisha this evening, after school."

"A hell of a lot of men just to find a runaway teenager. And there must be a fair number more to cover rest-breaks and co-ordinate shifts."

"We've identified an organiser, but not by name. Tall, thin, black. He has his hood up all the time, so we've been unable to get a clear shot of him. We've adjusted positions to accommodate, so tomorrow we may be luckier. He's been round to all four sites, apparently issuing instructions, asking questions, gathering information."

"I don't think we've much time left. I told Bidisha Mubarak they'll be gone soon and I don't think she'll see them again. What I didn't tell her, is that I think she and her friends are already free of them."

"Oh? How come?"

"They know we've got access to the girls' computers, so they can't steal a march there, and now, they've got their phones. In other words, these men think they've closed down, or come into possession of, all the means by which Aisha Sharif can contact her friends online. They don't need the actual girls any more. I'm assuming, of course, they don't know the phones have been diverted. If I'm right, the only thing that's keeping them here is the slim chance that she – or Sebastian, assuming he's still alive - will turn up in person. But that's much more likely at the parents' houses. I'm guessing that they've also got a surfeit of manpower, and they're under contract, or between jobs. Otherwise, they'd have scaled back already."

"See, this is why everyone calls you 'the mastermind'. Or should do. How long do you think we've got?"

"Unless we've been unusually careless and all four tails nose-dive tomorrow morning, it doesn't matter. Once we've found where they're based, we can take it from there. Until they abandon wherever that is – which they probably will, at some stage - we'll have all the time we need."

"It takes time to disband a small army. Which is what this looks like."

"The one thing we can be pretty certain of is that they have no idea where the two runaways are. Sitting outside her friends' houses all day is what you do when you're clutching at straws. I understand we've persuaded the Sharifs and the Chewtons to cancel their joint press-conference?"

"Apparently, although I don't know why. Personally, I thought it was a good idea."

"Let's say it works and it persuades Aisha Sharif and Sebastian Chewton to break cover, yes, there's probably a ninety per cent chance we'll get to them first. But it's not a given. It depends who comes forward with information, where and how. If someone posts a report of a sighting online, for example, and we don't see it in time. It happens. A better short term strategy is to find where these men have a base, find out what they know, if anything, and see if putting it together with what we know makes any difference."

Phyllis laughed. "As I recall, we don't know anything. And, as you've just said, *they* can't either, otherwise they wouldn't be sitting round all day, farting into their car-seats."

"In that case, we break the organisation up. As you've just said, most of these men are illegals. We can take them into custody for a long time, and then plonk them back where they came from. Then we can do the press conference."

"Time frame?"

"Two days. I'm guessing. We can't afford to hang around. Just like I can't. I'm the technician. I'm supposed to be here for an hour at the most."

"Good, because I'm dog tired. It's quite cramped upstairs and there's only one bed. Luckily it's a double. I never thought I'd utter this sentence, but I've been sleeping with Ian."

"Don't tell your boyfriend."

She laughed. "I haven't even told Ian yet."

She began putting the documents away. Mordred put his false beard back on, let himself out of the house and went back to his car. He started the engine. He had the curious sense of a plan about to materialise.

Chapter 14: Get Off the Phone, John!

If you ever get the curious sense of a plan about to materialise, you should act on the first whisper of inspiration, that was the rule. He was being watched from both sides, so what better way of setting everyone at their ease than with a casual phone call? There was no telling whether the men watching the house would try to force him off the road, later on, like they'd done with Tariq. Nothing could be gained by their doing so, and the general agreement was that they were 'professionals', which meant they ought to know it was pointless, but still, they were probably thick, so nothing could be ruled out.

"John?" came Annabel's voice. "Where are you? I thought you were on a job tonight?"

"I am, but it's over now. How's Tariq?"

"He's right here actually. I'll put him on."

"Hi, John," came Tariq's voice, world-weary and slightly aggressive. "You never give up, do you? I guess you thought I'd be in hospital, eh?"

"Well, I - "

"So you could ring my girlfriend at three o'-bloody-clock in the morning, and ply her with your smoothie, phone version of pillow talk! While the cat's away, the mice will play - "

" *...that!*" Annabel. The tail end of 'give me that'. "Sorry, John, Tariq doesn't know what he's saying. He's had a big bump on the head, and he's about to get another one. I'm not your *girlfriend*. We just went out for dinner together. That doesn't make us man and wife!"

"Maybe I should call back later," Mordred said.

"What did you want? Because I'd prefer not to talk about last night. I said things I shouldn't have, and I'm sorry if I misled you. Unfortunately, that's what happens when I get rat-arsed."

"It's all forgotten. Water under the bridge. I knew it was just the whisky talking. The bits I can even remember. I apologise for getting you drunk."

"Oh," she said. "That's good then."

"It won't happen again."

"Right. So … so what did you want?"

"Remember that burglary we did a while ago in the pursuit of more and better intel?"

"Sir Malcolm Rhys-Dwyer's flat? Yes?"

"Well, I wondered if you wanted to do another. I'm thinking of crashing Terence Dimbleton's London residence. We may never be lovers, but I do still think of you as my burglary buddy."

"That's sweet. Do you even know where Terence Dimbleton's is?"

"No, but I can find out at base."

"And you've run this idea by Ruby Parker, have you? And she's agreed?"

"No, but obviously I will, and I'm pretty confident about the outcome. I'm just offering you first dibs, that's all. Phyllis and Gina are tied up at the Mubaraks' house, Alec's over at the Wilsons', and, well, you'd be my first choice anyway, but it so happens that you're available."

"Yes, I am available."

"In that case - "

He heard Tariq objecting in the background. Something about 'he's flirting with you'. She snapped back. Tariq replied.

"Sorry, John," she said calmly, "I've got to hang up. I'll call you back in a second."

He put it down on the seat. Two seconds later, it rang. He picked up without looking at the screen.

"For crying out loud, John" – Phyllis's voice – "who the bloody hell are you on the phone to? Don't you realise, those men are watching your every move? You're making them jumpy! If you get into trouble, and we have to come and help you, it'll all be over, and it'll all be *your fault.* Put your bloody foot down and get out of there!"

"Don't be ridiculous. They're not going to get the jitters because I'm on the phone. What could be more normal?"

"Don't argue. I outrank you, and I'm giving you an order. Scoot!" She hung up.

It rang again.

"Who were you just on the phone to?" Annabel said.

"My other girlfriend, Phyllis." He waited for the laugh, but it didn't come. "Joke," he said.

"Listen, John, I asked whether you knew where Terence Dimbleton's London residence is because I wanted to find out how up to speed you are. The fact is, I'm sitting outside his flat now, with two other agents in different positions. Ruby Parker put us on stake-out about six hours ago. Tariq's not meant to be here, but I thought what the hell, he's a member of the crew and he got injured in the course of duty, *so I brought him along out of pity,*" she almost shouted. "We've got two or three agents staking out Dimbleton's Edinburgh holiday home, and his place in Marbella. There's no possibility of burgling any of the three, I'm afraid. Especially since he's got men in, house-sitting. We're trying to establish a connection between them and the men parked outside your teenage girls' addresses."

"Fair enough. Some other time then."

"Okay, speak to you tomorrow."

He hung up and suddenly the idea that had been hanging round on the mental street corner ran into the middle of the road and started waving its arms. He switched his phone back on and went to a Lithuanian website. He read the first two pages in his head, then out loud, trying to imitate a Lithuanian newsreader he had on DVD at home. After about thirty minutes, he went to a Romanian website and did the same thing. His phone rang. *Alec.*

"Are you bloody mad? Phyllis has just told me what you're doing! What the hell are you up to, just sitting there like a bloody rabbit caught in the headlights? And don't tell me 'nothing'!"

"I was going to ring Annabel, but you'll do just as well. Listen, I'm going round to the Wilsons'. I'd like you to keep your phone switched on."

"Except you're *not* going round to the Wilsons', because Tariq went there last night! Have you been drinking or something? Or are you ill? My God, have they done something to you? Wait there, I'm coming to get you."

"No - " Too late. He'd hung up.

Time to get moving then. He started the car, drove to the end of Shoeman's Lane, and turned left. He saw the Vauxhall Corsa pull out behind him. It followed him at a distance until they reached the main road into London, when it turned its full beam on and started tailgating him. He tilted the rear-view mirror to anti-glare. He slowed down and put his hand out of the window, pointing for them to pull into the hard shoulder. He saw them exchange quizzical looks.

He pulled slowly to a halt and they pulled in behind him, almost touching his bumper. He took the replica pistol from the glove compartment, got out and slammed his door hard.

"Get back in the car!" he screamed in Lithuanian, *"NOW!"*

They were burly with shaven heads and small eyes, and dressed in crumpled black. They put their hands up slightly and got back in their car.

"For God's sake," he said, under his breath, as if he was having difficulty restraining his temper, "you're supposed to let me into the back seat first, Brazauskas, you bloody moron."

He got in, put the gun away and started shouting again. "It*'s taken me nearly TWO YEARS to get where I am today! Nobody suspects ANYTHING! Then you two clowns come along and start flashing your headlights! Don't you guys realise there are cameras all over this city?* I'm being paid a hell of a lot for my help, but I doubt you can compensate me for losing my job. *Or maybe you can! Maybe you can afford a couple of hundred thousand, because that's what's it going to cost you!"*

"I don't understand," the unknown man said.

"I've been putting the diversion-switches in, stupid, as agreed! We've got exactly four hours until the police work out what's going on. In that time, I've got to get to base and reel Aisha Sharif in. *That's what I'm being paid for, and if it doesn't happen, there's a very good chance I'll get a serious salary cut!* Comprendez? *So I'd rather not spend the next two hundred and forty minutes sitting in a layby, chewing the fat with you two jerks!* Now let me get back in my own car, and you lead the way. *And don't pull in again for ANY reason? Got that?"*

They nodded, maybe only half-convinced, but becoming more so. Brazauskas got out of the car, and pulled the front seat forward for him to get out.

"I'm going to have to call my bosses now, explain what I'm doing here; *how I pulled you into the side and gave you a good telling off, understand?"*

They didn't look at him. He put his hands in his pockets and walked to his Renault, and rang Alec.

"Don't hang up. I've found a way inside. Track my mobile and wait for a hotel reservation. Get everyone there and wait for Aisha Sharif. I'm serious."

He hung up, thrust his phone into the gap in the upholstery designed for just such emergencies, and gestured impatiently from the window for them to get a move on. They pulled out. He set off in pursuit.

Chapter 15: Andrius Paksas, Pleased to Meet You

Mordred and the car he was pursuing left the main road and slowed for the speed cameras. They meandered through a housing estate until they turned into an industrial park, where they stopped in front of a windowless, corrugated steel workshop. A metal staircase led to the single entrance door on this side. The two men got out of their car. Mordred put the replica gun back in his glove compartment and followed them up the stairs. They knocked and the door opened an inch. A man of roughly the same age and build as Brazauskas and his friend looked out.

"What you are doing back early like this?" he asked, in what Mordred recognised as English with a Slobozian accent.

"I picked them up and got them to accompany me," Mordred replied in Romanian. "Andrius Paksas. I believe you're expecting me. Let me in and get me a computer. There isn't any time to lose."

The door opened and he found himself face-to-face with five very apprehensive looking men, all of whom looked like they breakfasted on pit bulls and barbed wire.

"The diversion switches are in place, as arranged," he said. "Who's in charge here?"

"I am," said one of the men. Downstairs, Mordred could see a group of black men huddled around an electric fire.

"I'm Andrius Paksas," Mordred said. "I've been paid by JMCB to help you smoke out Aisha Sharif. In my day-job, I work for metropolitan police information technology. I've just been round and put diversion switches on the Muslim kids' computers plus the wire they've put in her phone. That means whoever's watching them won't see what I'm about to do. But I've only got a narrow window."

"Who sent you?"

"Terence Dimbleton. Call him if you like, although I'm warning you, there's a wire in his phone too, so you probably won't get much sense out of him. Look, I'm only here to get you the girl, then my job's done. Do you want my help or not? Because I'm very expensive, and nothing would suit me better than for you to send me away so I have to come back a second time, and pick up another fat cheque. Although there might not be a second time, once the pigs find out what I've done. In that case, it's on your head, Mr ...?"

"Petru Ghimpu," the man said, extending his palm for a handshake.

"I need the use of a networked computer, and unregistered phone and a complete list of all Aisha Sharif's passwords. Leave the rest to me. You can watch if you like, but please don't interrupt."

"I *will* watch," Ghimpu said. "Anything else?"

"Right now, I'd like a cup of tea if possible, and something to eat."

Two men took him to an office with a desk and a computer. They pulled out the chair for him and switched the computer on. The phone and the tea arrived together. A few men brought chairs in to watch him work.

Best to start with a direct text message. *Aisha, we have lost patience. Arrange to meet us within three hours, or your parents will die. Text back as soon as you receive this, for their sake.* Send.

Which made him feel like a monster, but omelettes mean broken eggs. His biggest fear was that she wouldn't be there to receive it. With Sebastian probably dead, she might be living rough in a barn or something. She might even have lost her phone. She definitely hadn't texted her parents or any of her friends, though they'd been bombarding her.

"Now we wait," he said, as confidently as he was able.

"I thought we were only supposed to mug her," Ghimpu said. "This is a pretty big change of tactics. It gives us away. Are you sure you've thought it through?"

"I know what I'm doing."

He sipped his tea and tried to look unconcerned. The next thirty minutes passed like someone had squeezed a decade into each second. He could feel his heart thumping harder and harder.

Finally, a ding, as of the incoming. It read, *Please don't hurt my mum and dad*. Ghimpu translated it aloud into Romanian, and everyone in the room grinned and cheered.

Now, he had to organise somewhere for her to go, and get her a ticket.

"Text back!" Brazauskas exclaimed. "Don't let her get away!"

You need to meet us, he replied. *We won't hurt you. We just want to meet.*

Where? she texted back

Tell me where you are, and I'll make arrangements for you to get to us. He still didn't know for sure that Sebastian Chewton was dead, but no one in the room had even mentioned him, which seemed fairly persuasive. *Bring anything of Sebastian's,* he texted.

I haven't got anything of his. Whatever you want will either be at his house or where you buried him.

"Forget about that," Ghimpu said irritably. "We just want the girl."

"Where's he buried?"

"Why do you want to know?"

"Because we're missing evidence and Dimbleton thinks he may have swallowed it."

Ghimpu shrugged. "So why don't you ask Dimbleton where we buried him?"

"Because he's in bloody Morocco and his phone's wired! For crying out loud, we haven't time to play games! JUST TELL ME!"

"Great Yarmouth," Ghimpu said sulkily, all his resistance finally broken. "North. Just above the high tide level."

"Thank you!"

Back to work. *Where are you?* he texted.

Birmingham, she replied.

He went to the advance tickets website and typed in the station name and paid for a non-stop train on his account.

I'm sending you an electronic ticket, he wrote. *7.45 tomorrow morning from Birmingham Moor Street. Don't miss it. If you do …*

I understand, she texted back.

Next, he went to *mystayinlondon.co.uk*.

"What are you doing?" Ghimpu said. "You're booking her into a fancy hotel? Why not just get her to come *here?* That would be simplest."

"We need to gain her confidence. Asking her to come to an unheard-of industrial estate in the London hinterland is hardly going to do that. If she thinks she's coming to a five-star city centre hotel, in the daytime, she'll be okay. We can have a car waiting outside the doorway. Or even get her while she's in her room."

Ghimpu shrugged. "Okay."

He booked the hotel room using his credit card and got them to send the details to Alec's phone with *Aisha Sharif* in the 'guest's name' slot.

"What's that number you've just entered?" Ghimpu asked.

"I've an account at this hotel. Problem?" Best way of pre-empting is always to get straight back on. *I've reserved you a room at the Elmbank Hampton in Piccadilly,* he texted. *Get a Euston Station Cars taxi as soon as you arrive in London. Give them the name Sharmila Mallick. Tell them it's paid for.*

"It isn't paid for," Ghimpu said.

"Well, it will be," Mordred said. "Because that's how I work. One thing at a time, rather than ten things simultaneously. And it's my money, by the way. No one's asking you to stump up." *Do you understand, Aisha?* he texted. *This is very important.*

I'll be there, she replied.

"A job well done," Mordred said. "Even if I do say so myself. Well, I suppose I'd better be getting back to my real workplace now. It was a pleasure meeting you guys."

Everyone got up and shuffled out of the office. Mordred tried to join the general exodus, but Ghimpu put his arm in front of him. "You stay here," he said.

Mordred shrugged. He'd half-expected this. "As you wish," he said. "But they'll notice I'm missing, and if I go down, it'll jeopardise the whole operation. The police may not be able to find you, but Dimbleton will."

The office was empty now, except for him and Ghimpu. Ghimpu closed the door. "How much do you actually know?" he asked.

"Enough not to speak about it."

"Because I know hardly anything at all. The Somalians probably know more than me."

"It's probably best to keep it that way. If anything goes wrong, you can deny all knowledge, and look credible."

"What are we going to do with the girl?"

"I don't know. It's not up to me."

"I'd rather not hurt her," Ghimpu said. "She's just a kid. One of us should knock her out – quick blow to the head from behind – then we should put a pillow over her face. She won't even know it's happened."

"I can't see we have to do anything really," Mordred replied. "If she had information, she'd have gone to the police."

"Kids always think no one will believe them. And Dimbleton's got a track-record of making problems go away. She'd say her piece, the police would be a bit like, 'well, I suppose we'd better humour her', Dimbleton would go ballistic, and a couple of weeks later, she'd be knocked down crossing the road. End of story."

"I wonder what her 'piece' is."

"That's the thing, I don't think she's even got one. Her boyfriend didn't. He'd got fragments but really, you couldn't put them together. We should never have threatened him in the first place, if you ask me. All the time and energy it's wasted. He'd have probably forgotten about it by now."

"Whatever it was."

"Something about ISIS and an oil company and a bunch of nationalists in western Europe. Made no sense to me, and I was the one charged with finding out. Didn't make me proud, by the way, doing what I did, but orders are orders. That's why I don't want to hurt the girl. Gets in your head, all that screaming."

"Figures."

"Would you like a drink? I've a bottle of whisky in my locker. Don't mind sharing it."

"I'm driving. But thanks anyway."

"You seem like a nice guy, contrary to first impressions."

"I was slightly nervous, to tell the truth. Teenagers aren't really my forte."

"Tell me about it. I've got two daughters. My oldest, Sophie, she's just a bit younger than Aisha Sharif. I'll show you a picture. You might as well stay till the morning, mightn't you? Tell them you got a flat tyre or something."

Mordred shrugged, trying to maintain his insouciance. It had suddenly hit him that if he left now, he'd have no pretext to come back, and none to be there when they attempted to grab Aisha. "Okay," he said, "but no alcohol. Not for me. You can."

Within an hour, Ghimpu was asleep. Mordred had stayed in bed late the previous morning with the anticipation of starting work at midnight, so he didn't feel very tired.

He wished he'd brought his phone in here. No one had searched him. He could have texted Alec. Maybe. Instead, he was forced to sit and think. Which meant worrying. Maybe she'd have second thoughts; maybe one of Ghimpu's mob would attack her; maybe the police would get things wrong, and a hostage situation would develop; maybe there'd be a shootout; maybe, maybe, maybe – every one bad. A million ways things could turn nasty, and only one way for them to turn out well. It might even have been better to leave her where she was. Now, she was in mortal danger and he was totally responsible.

They didn't move from the office and there was no clock. After what seemed like an hour, he shook Ghimpu awake. He'd had an idea. "We need to keep an eye on the time," he said.

The Romanian looked at his watch. "Five," he said.

"I'm going to switch the computer on and get the number of the taxi firm. If she sets off at 7.45, she'll arrive with the first wave of tourists after the commuters are done. We'll need to make sure nothing goes wrong. That means arranging things way in advance."

"Yeah, okay." He went back to sleep again.

Mordred went to the Euston Cars website, stared at the contact details without taking them in, and phoned.

"Who is this?" Alec said.

"I'd like a taxi in five hours' time from Euston station," he said.

"*John?* Are you okay? … Go ahead, yes. I'm listening."

"I've got a fourteen year-old girl arriving at Euston railway station at about 9.45am, unattended, name of *Sharmila Mallick*. I need you to take her to the Elmbank Hampton hotel in Piccadilly. And I'd like to pay in advance by credit card, if I may."

"Bloody hell, you're a genius. We'll have people waiting on the platform, don't worry."

"My number is: 5529, 4204, 5061, 5464 … Certainly. That's 5529, 4204, 5061, 5464."

"We put a track on your mobile, like you suggested. We've got your industrial unit surrounded with armed policemen."

"Mr Andrius Paksas. A-N-D-R-I-U-S-P-A-K-S-A-S, that's right. The sixth, sixteen … Absolutely, yes. Four-eight-three."

"Is anyone armed in there?"

"Nine forty-five is when she'll be getting in. Sharmila Mallick. Asian girl, probably a little dishevelled."

"I'll take that as a yes," Alec said. "Okay, we'll wait till you come out."

"Thank you." He hung up.

Ghimpu stirred slightly and smiled. "I've got your credit card details," he teased. "I've got a memory like an elephant."

"You'll have forgotten them in a few hours' time," Mordred said, back in Romanian again. "I guarantee it."

All that remained now was to wait. At seven fifty-five, he finally got the text that meant everything was going to be okay. *I'm on the train, like you said.* He showed it to Ghimpu, who nodded solemnly. He texted back: *As soon as you get to London, go straight to the rank outside. Get a Euston Cars cab. Tell them you're Sharmila Mallick and you want to go to the Elmbank Hampton hotel in Piccadilly. I'll be waiting for you. We only want to talk, that's all.*

"Genius," Ghimpu said.

"It's nearly eight o'clock," Mordred said. "You'd better get some men together and we'd better get over there. Rush hour's already started. And don't bring any guns. They can't conceivably help."

"How many men do you think we'll need?"

"Make it eight. That usually covers all entrances and exits."

Ghimpu left to make arrangements. Two minutes later, a Somalian beckoned Mordred from the doorway. He went out and got in the first of three cars. Astonishing, the way they just expected him to leave his here, as if he wasn't already expected back at work.

Not really, though. They could probably only cope with one consideration at a time, and they weren't big on empathy. Their little convoy left the industrial estate and turned left onto the road. It was immediately surrounded on all sides by police cars and armed marksmen shouting at them to get out. Mordred could already see the firearms units entering the building he'd just left. He stepped out with his hands in the air.

Chapter 16: Perhaps Just Slightly Identical to James Bond …

The rest of that day was given over to making police statements and sifting the avalanche of discoveries into 'evidence' and 'other'. Aisha Sharif was reunited with her parents. Sebastian Chewton's body was disinterred in Norfolk. Two further corpses were discovered nearby, both of middle-aged men. They were identified as two of the persons who had been to see Sir Ronald Chewton, posing as JMCB employees. In fact, they worked for one of JMCB's legitimate private equity rivals, Quinion, Frederic & Seabright. The mock-cyber attack on JMCB had thus begun life as a routine exercise in industrial espionage. Four senior managers at QFS were arrested. Three unconnected eastern European men were charged with the murder of Sebastian Chewton, and a further twenty with conspiracy to kidnap using menaces. A warrant was issued for Terence Dimbleton's arrest.

"But of course, we've still no real idea what he was, or is, up to," Ruby Parker said the next day. She sat at the head of a large table, first floor Thames House, whose other points of interest were Annabel, Gina, Phyllis, Alec, Ian and Mordred. "John," she continued, "you mentioned ISIS, an oil company and various nationalist movements. We've been unable to find a whiff of any of that in the data GCHQ recovered from JMCB's epic data cull."

"Aisha Sharif must know something," Mordred said. "It's just a question of waiting till she's recovered a bit, then asking her."

"She's already cooperating fully. She's a tough little nut, I'll give her that, but unfortunately, unable to give us much more than your friend Ghimpu did. Terence Dimbleton is involved in a plot with ISIS to dot-dot-dot backed by an unidentified oil company and several unnamed far-right political parties. Unless we can fill in the blank and supply the monikers, we're nowhere. Still, that's important enough. It was apparently worth killing Sebastian Chewton for, and forming a firm intention to murder Aisha Sharif."

"Where was she hiding?" Gina asked.

"A hostel for homeless youngsters in Birches Green, Birmingham. She wouldn't give them her name. She kept her bag with her at all times and charged her phone in the local library, beneath the computer terminal desks when the staff weren't looking. When you got in touch with her, John, she was ready to throw in the towel. She just wanted to – in her own words – 'get it over with'. She fully expected to die."

"How did they find the Chewton boy?" Alec asked.

"They had bugs in Sir Ronald's house. We didn't check because we had no idea who we were dealing with at that point. They learned about his appearance in Great Yarmouth from his parents and sent someone up there. Two and a half hours' journey, but of course, it was the seaside, and a nice, sunny day, the two adolescents had just been to the bank, and they thought they were safe."

"How very, very sad," Gina said emotionally.

"We've got some new pictures back of the man who was apparently coordinating the stake-out of the four houses. Quite clear this time." She passed the photos round. "I want you to take a good look, and remember that face. He's not among the men we arrested at Enterprise Park yesterday, so he must have slipped through the net."

Mordred was at the bottom of the table, but they were passed round quickly. Everyone would be getting their own copies in a few hours' time. Mordred took one look and a sharp breath.

"Someone you recognise, John?" Ruby Parker said.

"His name's Musa Farole. As far as I know. He's the man whose leg I nearly broke at Canary Wharf that evening after I upset Terence Dimbleton. His bodyguard."

"Are you sure?"

"He did walk with a limp," Phyllis said. "Which would fit."

"I'm surprised he's walking at all," Alec remarked, "after what you did to him, John. Pretty impressive. I read your report and thought, 'There's hope for ol' Green Belt yet'."

"You've only got a *green belt?*" Phyllis said.

Alec shushed her. "Don't tell Annabel."

"What's it got to do with *me?*" Annabel said.

Ruby Parker held up her hands. "Enough. John, that's good. It's enough to tie Dimbleton to what happened to Aisha Sharif so securely that even he can't wriggle free of the knots. All we need do now is to find him."

She thought for a moment. No one spoke. "Phyllis and Annabel and Ian," she said at last, "I'm sending you to Morocco. John, Gina and Alec, I want you to stay here, help sift through the evidence this end."

Alec put his hand up. "John's our resident languages expert. With respect, wouldn't he be best deployed abroad?"

"It's reasonable to suppose that Musa Farole followed his employer abroad," she said. "If that's the case, sending John over there may place him – you: sorry, John – in unnecessary danger."

"I have a false beard," Mordred said.

Phyllis laughed.

"There's another reason I need you to stay," Ruby Parker asked. "Aisha Sharif has asked to meet you. I'm not sure how, but information about your role in all this has reached her ears. It may be she worked out it was you who persuaded her to get on the train from Birmingham. Her father's probably mentioned you, and it could be that she's put two and two together. Either way, it'll do no harm to see her."

"Is she angry?" Mordred asked. "I mean, I did threaten to kill her parents."

"I don't know," she replied. "Not if she's sensible. But, of course, she's probably still feeling the effects of her ordeal, and she's probably confused, to say the least, and she's a teenager."

"I think it would be wisest to assume she's fuming," Alec said.

Mordred sighed. "Where is this meeting going to take place?"

"We've arranged for you to meet over afternoon tea at the Dorchester. Two PM today. Her mother and father will be accompanying her."

"How long does it last?"

"A couple of hours. Sandwiches, then tea, then cakes, then more tea."

He put his head in his hands. Bloody hell. "Okay."

"Gina, I'd like you to go too. Mr Sharif expects him to bring someone. He's paid for five people, and I know you're very much at ease with this sort of occasion. You'll be able to get the best out of John."

"Good luck with that," Alec said.

"Let's go up to the canteen, John," Gina said, when they were coming out of the meeting. This was the bit where she bought him a jam doughnut or something and grilled him, gently but firmly, about his clothes. *But, no, John, you can't wear those to the Dorchester!* He'd itemise his wardrobe, and she'd try to envisage it from his descriptions, and if nothing caught her fancy she'd suggest a quick shopping trip. Because she was Gina, it would all be very gentle. Afterwards, he might even feel grateful, because that's how good she was.

The canteen was fairly quiet at this time of day; one or two arch-spies enjoying a Bakewell tart and a latte, but so well distributed you could always be sure of privacy. There was a strong smell of tomato soup.

"What would you like, John?" she asked. "I'm paying. You choose a table."

"A jam doughnut, please," he replied. "And a cup of Earl Grey. Milk, no sugar."

She smiled. "You sound like James Bond when you say that." She imitated Sean Connery. "*Earl Grey. Milk, no sugar*."

He laughed. "Right."

"A kind of semi-retired James Bond who never ventures far from his office in Hemel Hempstead."

"I'll go and sit down."

"While you're waiting, think about what you'd like me to wear this afternoon. Because I don't want to embarrass you."

He chose the table by the window, farthest from everyone else. He took his phone out and went to the Littlewoods catalogue. Then *occasion wear*. He had to look like he was taking this seriously. He chose a dress at random.

"Wow," she said, when he showed her. "I can tell you've got sisters. That's perfect and, as it happens, I do have something very similar at home. Not identical, obviously, but a pretty fair approximation. I'll wear that, shall I?"

"Okay." Damn.

They sat in silence for a few moments. Obviously, she'd know he was going to break. Probably most men couldn't hold out against her for more than a minute. Beads of sweat appeared on his forehead. She looked out of the window.

"Lovely day, today," she said, in a disappointed tone.

"What would you like *me* to wear?" he blurted out.

She gave a relieved laugh. "Let me just get my phone," she said.

They arrived at the Dorchester at ten to two, gave their names at the desk and waited. She wore a black and white pencil dress with a matching hat and shoes. She looked super, but nothing like the woman in the Littlewoods catalogue. It was a completely different outfit in a completely different colour. He wore a tan suit and tie, and matching brogues, all of which she'd persuaded him to buy an hour ago from Ted Baker on Regent Street. He actually felt uplifted, which was odd considering how much money he'd spent. He was in love with her, that's why - against his will, to be honest, but that was how it was. He should probably be in love with Annabel instead. Which he was. But Annabel didn't want him. He had a headache.

She reached in her bag. "Two paracetamol," she said. "Don't let anyone see you take them."

"How did you know?" he asked.

"I'm psychic. And you've had a very stressful morning."

He put them discreetly on his tongue and gulped them down. "How are we going to handle this?"

"What do you mean?"

"I mean, are you going to take Mrs Sharif and Aisha, while I concentrate on the father?"

She laughed. "It's supposed to be a treat, John, not a police raid on a two storey building. Besides, Aisha's here to talk to you, not me."

"I guess so."

"It's sweet that you're so nervous, by the way. We must go out socially again. I'm really enjoying myself."

He might as well strike while the iron was hot. "Where would you like to go?"

"There's a race meeting at Goodwood next week. That would be nice. We'll see, shall we?"

He got it now. She was warning him. *We'll see how well you do today*. But Gina wasn't dishonest, everyone agreed that. If she said she wanted to go to Goodwood with him, she almost certainly did. Wow.

The Sharifs arrived. Mr Sharif wore a suit almost identical to Mordred's, his wife a blue polka dot dress and pink shrug, and Aisha wore what looked like a child's party-dress: white and frilly with four big buttons down the front. She had a ribbon in her hair and pumps on her feet. She looked unhappy to be here, and didn't smile when her father introduced her to Mordred. Once the formalities were complete and pleasantries had been exchanged, the group followed a smiling young man called Alexis to a narrow pair of sofas facing each other with a low table in between. He gave them the list of teas. Everyone chose something they'd probably never heard of before in an attempt to make the most of the occasion. Alexis smiled, deftly retrieved the list and actually clicked his heels before departing.

Mrs Sharif and Gina complimented each other on their outfits. Mordred and Mr Sharif talked about the journey over here, and Mr Sharif tried his hardest to engage his daughter with *didn't you, Aisha?/ weren't you Aisha?/ couldn't you, Aisha?* solicitations, to which she either nodded or shook her head, without making eye-contact.

But there was only so long this could go on. It was obvious Mr Sharif was becoming more and more annoyed and his wife was becoming more and more embarrassed, and this was gradually getting in the way of the conversation. The tea came and went. The sandwiches came and went. More tea was served.

Mordred started to feel responsible. Which might not be reasonable, but he was the one who'd threatened to kill her parents, and it was obvious she still hadn't forgiven him. It was the heffalump no one dared picture.

"I met Bidisha," he told her. "She seemed very nice."

"She is."

"Look, I'm really sorry you went through what you did. If there had been any other way of getting you home, I'd have done it. I was in a warehouse full of people who wanted you dead when I messaged you. If they'd known who I was, they'd have killed me too. I originally told you to come to the Elmbank, but then I realised you might be in danger, so I told my colleagues to meet you at the station."

No one spoke. She looked directly at him for a moment, as if none of that was remotely important or even interesting, and suddenly he saw clearly. She was grieving. Probably no one outside the police had spoken to her about Sebastian. She was back home, that was supposed to be the important thing, and her family had never met him; as far as she was aware, there was no prospect of ever meeting anyone who'd known him. She was utterly alone.

"I went to Rheeming Hall as part of my investigation," he said. He saw something come to life behind her eyes. "I spoke to Mr Bolam, Sebastian's headmaster, and Dale and Graham, his friends. They all spoke of him with very high regard. They all knew he had a girlfriend, too, and that he was thinking of converting to Islam. We can talk about him for a while, if you like. Not in a 'police-y' way, just … what he was like. Not here; not in front of your parents; I understand you may not want to do that. But there's a spare sofa over there. You wouldn't have to say anything. I could just tell you what I know about him."

She was crying now, but not so she'd lost control. Gina and Mr and Mrs Sharif regarded him as if he was mad.

"I *would* like that," she said, wiping her eyes. "I'd like it very much. Mummy, Daddy, is that okay? We won't be long."

"No … no, of course not," Mr Sharif said, recovering. "Absolutely not."

Two hours later, Gina linked arms with Mordred outside the Dorchester and they waved the Sharifs' taxi away. "I was very proud of you today, John," she said. "Not for the first time in my life either. Mr and Mrs Sharif think you're wonderful too."

"Gosh."

"So what's happening with Aisha?"

"Ruby Parker willing, I'm going to drive her and her father to Rheeming Hall on Friday, and I'll set up a meeting with Sir Ronald and Lady Chewton a day or two later."

"Isn't that likely to be rather tense?"

"On the contrary. They know now that he was running away because of something he did to upset JMCB. That would have happened with or without Aisha. All she did was stand by him in his hour of need. They're actually desperate to thank her."

"So all's well that ends well."

"Maybe. I've a strong feeling there's something she's not telling us."

"Quite possibly. But I'm sure there are lots of things. Are you sure it has any connection to the case?"

"I don't know."

"Now, haven't you something you want to ask me?"

"Er, what would you like me to wear for Goodwood?"

She smiled and took her phone out. “Excellent.”

Chapter 17: Maybe Even an Ovaltine

He got back to Thames House at five to find Alec sitting in front of a computer with a cup of coffee beside him. The older man looked up and scowled when Mordred came within range.

"How were the cucumber sandwiches?" he asked.

"Yummy," Mordred replied. "And to make matters even better, I'm taking Gina to Goodwood racecourse a week on Saturday."

He rolled his eyes. "*Très* droll."

"No, it's true. What have you been doing all afternoon?"

"Festering with envy and resentment."

"Apart from that."

"Apart from that: using the JMCB databases to track down its former employees. I've a long list of potentially useful people to interview here. We're going to see them tomorrow early, so get ready to do some work for a change."

"Well done indeed."

"I don't 'bring out the best' in you, apparently."

"I'm sure Ruby Parker didn't mean it like that. We're friends. You're not about reforming me."

"Whereas Gina is, I take it."

"Er, yes, obviously. I'm hardly good enough for her as I am."

"Granted."

"Whereas I *am* good enough for you."

"I'm not sure whether you've making a dig," Alec said, "and frankly, I'm too depressed to care. Did you bring me any cake back?"

"No, sorry. I simply didn't think about you at all."

"That's good. That's grist to my self-pity. Thank you."

"Doing anything tonight?"

"No."

"Me neither," Mordred said. "Want to get together and watch a vid?"

"No."

"Just testing. Well, good night. See you tomorrow morning."

"Yeah, bye."

He took a report form from the stack in the stationery cupboard. He'd fill it in manually on his way in tomorrow morning. Tonight was going to be great. He'd go to the shops, buy a carton of soup – mushroom, probably, though he was prepared to be flexible – and watch a bit of telly – *The Good Wife*, maybe, or *Kimmy Schmidt*. Go to bed at about half ten. A bit of a book beforehand: perhaps the one by that Costa prize-winning woman with the fez and the golden armlet? Maybe even an Ovaltine.

The next morning, he was on his way across the foyer on his way in, when Alec caught up with him. "Sorry I was a bit tetchy yesterday afternoon," he said.

"That's okay," Mordred replied. He paused to post the report he'd completed.

"I'd better brief you and we'll get a car over to our first interviewee, a Mrs Gemma Cummins, forty-nine. She worked in JMCB's personnel division."

"How many people did they have working for them in all?"

"Two hundred. Mostly junior, interns and zero hours, though; unlikely to know anything."

"How many top bods have we got?"

"None. We've got mid-level bods, that's all."

"Why?"

"Because no one at the top's talking, except to the police, and even then, only with their solicitors present. And the police are simply trying to build a conspiracy case: kidnap and murder. What *has* happened, in other words, not what is happening."

"And certainly not what's going to happen."

The car came round and they got in. Alec and Kevin exchanged greetings, then Mordred asked Kevin how he'd been getting on since their last meeting, and silence snapped down. It lasted until they reached their destination in Lewisham, a 1970s terraced house with a white plastic bib and heavy net curtains. Gemma Cummins wore a tartan skirt, a Fair Isle jumper and thick black tights. Her hair was short and thin and she wore tortoiseshell glasses that made her eyes look huge. "Come in," she said. "I've no idea what you're after, though. I didn't know anything about those poor children. If I had, I'd have gone running to you straight off. I'd never have waited for you to come to me."

They followed her into her living room and sat down. A large golden retriever got up and left the room like it had been discreetly informed they needed privacy. They heard it slump down in the kitchen. Mrs Cummins bade them sit down on the sofa, and she took the armchair half-facing them. The TV was on mute, and four bars of the gas fire blazed, although it was warm outside. "Ask me anything you like," she said.

"When you were working for JMCB, did you ever notice anything odd?" Alec asked. "Anything that made you think, 'I wonder why that's happening?' or 'I never expected that'? Anything at all?"

"Personnel wise? Not really. We used to get a lot of African men in. I don't know why. They didn't work for us, not officially. They certainly weren't on the payroll."

"Do you think they were here illegally?" Mordred asked.

"I used to imagine, probably," she said. "Obviously, you get a lot of foreigners coming in to work most places nowadays, but mostly eastern Europeans. Africa's not part of the EU, though. It's a whole different continent. I always thought, if the bosses want extra workers in, foreigners, why not just get Poles or Czechs?"

"Did you ever get the sense that JMCB's private equity transactions might have had a political dimension?" Alec asked. "Obviously, I'm not asking you in your role as head of personnel here. I'm just asking about office gossip. Ever pick anything up to that effect?"

"Way beyond my depth, that question. I don't know anything about politics."

"I was granted an interview with Terence Dimbleton shortly before he left the country," Mordred said. "He introduced his bodyguard to me. A Somalian, called Musa Farole. Does that name ring a bell?"

"Called what?"

"Musa Farole. F-A-R-O-L-E."

"Never heard of him. He certainly never received a pay packet through my office."

Alec and Mordred looked at each other. "That'll probably be all," Alec said. "Thank you for your time, Mrs Cummins,"

"Told you I didn't know anything," she replied cheerfully.

"Well, that was a complete waste of time," Alec said, when they were outside. They walked along the road to the bus stop. Alec sat down on the bench inside the shelter. It began to rain.

"Is there anyone on your list who had a hand in the business side of things?" Mordred asked.

"It's probably a waste of time. Put it like this. JMCB deleted all relevant data. They were prepared to kill to stop information leaking. How likely is it that Bob from Accounts is going to have anything worthwhile to divulge? No, they'll have covered their tracks."

"What about the bank statements?"

"A lot of money's been withdrawn, but I don't think JMCB's stumping up the cash for whatever's going down. It's a private equity firm. It's probably acting as a middleman. I wouldn't be surprised if there's an element of *hawala* in there."

"Of what?"

"It's a means of making international payments through the honour system, without actually moving any money. Mostly middle-eastern, but also in north Africa and India. If we're talking ISIS and Somalia, it's more or less a given. In which case we're likely to find zilch."

"We are anyway," Mordred said.

"I think we need to go back to Thames House and put our heads together. I was too busy seething about you and the Dorchester yesterday to get any proper work done. Like the big baby I'm ashamed to admit I actually am. What a waste of an afternoon."

"Don't be too hard on yourself."

"It's because you were with Gina, probably, and I was jealous."

"But wait a minute. I thought you were in love with Cecily."

"Gina doesn't count."

"Why not?"

"Because everyone's in love with Gina. She's, like, the perfect human being who just happens to be a woman."

"It's lucky she's on our team then. Why didn't we bring her along?"

"She's got the morning off. I don't know why. Good behaviour, probably."

"Let's bring her in for the afternoon then. See how good she really is."

"Done."

Three hours later, they all met in seminar room C33, first floor Thames House. Gina wasn't keen on meeting in the canteen, because the smell of onions got into her clothes.

"I think you may be looking in the wrong place," she said. "Alec's right. No one left behind by JMCB is going to have anything worth telling us. The mother ship's upped sticks and left town, but not in such a hurry it wasn't able to delete files, and probably destroy hard drives."

"There is some forensic evidence of that," Alec said.

"So talking to people like Gemma Cummins is likely to be a waste of time," she said. "It's exactly what they'd want us to do."

"The alternative seems to be doing nothing," Alec replied gloomily.

"Did we keep Sebastian Chewton's computer?" she asked.

Both men had a moment of mingled revelation and awkwardness. "Why didn't we think of that?" Mordred said.

"That's why MI7's all about teams," Gina replied.

"It should still be in the basement with Tariq," Mordred said. "I haven't heard of it being released. I don't even know what they do when they've finished with them."

"They certainly won't have finished with this one," Gina said. "This is an ongoing case, remember?" She was on her phone. "Hello, Tariq? Gina Fairburn here. Hi, lovely to speak to you again too. How's your brother? ... Oh, God, yes. Mind you, I couldn't possibly comment. I've never actually seen it. Heard about it, yes ... About three weeks, I understand ... Yes, we must catch up sometime. Listen, I'm ringing about something very specific. Sebastian Chewton's computer. We need a new analysis of his hard drive. We're looking for any hidden files, probably not on the computer itself, more likely on the cloud, but to which the computer may contain access-details. Does that make sense? ... Yes, I'd love to. I might learn something. I'll just wind up here and I'll see you shortly."

"He wants you to go down there and sit with him," Alec said.

"What's wrong with that?" she asked. "He's good company, and a capable teacher."

"What are John and I going to do? We'd like to learn things too."

"It would be rude to just turn up with you so I'll ring him back. I take your point. It's much better for the team to learn together."

She pressed 'Call' and 'Speaker' and put her phone on the table. They listened to it ring twice, then Tariq's hello.

"Hi, Tariq, it's Gina again. Is it okay if I bring John and Alec with me? We might all benefit."

"It's a bit cramped down here," Tariq said, "but as you wish."

"You don't sound very enthusiastic," she replied.

"John and I aren't getting on particularly well at the moment. He keeps trying to steal my girlfriend."

Gina's eyebrows rose. "Really? I didn't even know you were in a relationship. Anyone I know?"

"Annabel Gould."

"Annabel?" Her features seemed to harden. "Well, I had no idea. And John's trying to steal her away, you say?"

"Getting her drunk while I'm not there, ringing her all the time when I am: if that's not trying to steal her away, I don't know what is."

"Did he actually *ask* her out?"

"… Well, no, not in so many words."

"And did *she* say he was?"

"No, but then she probably wouldn't."

Her eyebrows furrowed. "Where was she when John got her drunk?"

"Down here, in the computer room."

Alec rolled his eyes. "Reality check," he said lethargically. "It was actually me who got all three of us drunk. I came to keep John company when he had to watch three PC screens for six hours, and we shared half a bottle of scotch to kill the boredom. Next thing you know, Annabel turns up out of the blue. So we offer her a drink. Seemed only polite. She didn't want one, but we persuaded her because there's nothing worse than being slightly smashed in the presence of Sober Joe. Yes, she got a bit tight, but not remotely what I'd call slaughtered. We had a good time, and she got a taxi home at about midnight. There's an edited version in John's report for the fourteenth. It was the night we met Messrs Sharif and Mubarak in Horseferry Road."

"I – didn't know that," Tariq said.

"John rang you when it was in full swing," Alec said. "I invited you to come over and join us, if you recall."

"It was the night I crashed my car. I *can't* recall. That's the point."

"John's going out with *me,* Tariq," Gina said. "I don't mean to sound harsh, but I'd be grateful if you'd refrain from making sweeping accusations unless you've proper evidence. You scared me."

"I didn't know you two were an item. I apologise. If John's there, tell him I apologise to him too."

"Let's let bygones be bygones," Mordred said, feeling like someone had just lifted him high above London on a downy cushion. *John's going out with me*! "Is it still okay for us all to come down?"

"Looking forward to it, guys!" He hung up.

"Nice bloke, really," Alec said. "Just insecure, that's all."

"There's no reason for him to be," Gina said. "Listen, Alec, would you mind going down ahead of us? I just need a quiet word with John."

Alec looked from side to side, as if he thought something like this might be on the cards, but couldn't believe it had happened so quickly. "No problem," he said. He put his hands flat on the table, eased himself out and left.

Gina took Mordred's fingers. "Sorry."

"For what?" Here it came: *I've built your hopes up unforgivably*.

"I said we were going out together, and I haven't even really asked you."

"Well, the answer's yes."

Against all his expectations, she beamed. "I hoped it would be. I didn't want to be presumptuous. But before we get too carried away, there's something you should know about me, and I quite understand if it puts you off … Well, I won't *understand*, but I'll 'understand', if you see what I mean."

He hadn't the foggiest idea. "Go ahead."

"I'm a Christian."

He laughed. "Okay."

"And I don't believe in sex before marriage."

He smiled. Was this it? *This* was what she considered might be an obstacle? "Let's not get too heavy. I mean, we've got a date to go to Goodwood, but we don't have to make long-term decisions."

"This *is* a long-term decision, John. For me."

"We'll just go out for a while and see how we get on. No sex until we're married. Not that that's a given, of course: getting married, I mean, not the no-sex thing."

"Are you a Christian? Just out of interest?"

"No, although I am sympathetic."

"An atheist?"

"No."

"Good, there's hope for you yet." She smiled to show she was teasing.

"Let's say we go out for a while and I decide I want to marry you," Mordred said. "Do *I* have to become a Christian?"

"Not necessarily. But you would have to make allowances for me. I go to church every Sunday and I've got lots of friends there. As my husband, you'd have to spend time with them. Unless you did that, it's difficult to see how we wouldn't grow apart. And of course, I'd have to bring up our children as Christians."

"Okay."

"That's not intolerant. It only sounds it because most modern people don't have beliefs. They only have appetites and preferences. You see it on TV and in novels all the time. If you truly believe something it means you have to reject something else. That doesn't mean you refuse to tolerate it."

"Of course not."

"It's never easy for me to have this conversation, John. It scares the hell out of most men. But it's for the best. I was very impressed by the way you dealt with Aisha Sharif the other day. I'm not bothered about looks or physique in a man. Well, I am a bit: I don't want to marry an old guy. What I want is someone kind and thoughtful. Even if he isn't a Christian."

"I understand that. I'm a secret agent, by the way. I don't get scared."

"It's horrible to come across all 'terms and conditions'-y at the start of a relationship – before we've even been on a single date. But I wouldn't do it if you didn't think you were worth it.

Now, listen: I'm sure this has given you an awful lot to think about. I don't want an answer yet. Get back to me in a few days. If you still want to go to Goodwood, I'll be delighted. If not, I'll understand."

"Done."

"We'd better go and find Alec. He'll be wondering where we've gone."

They got up and made their way to the lift. When they reached Tariq's floor, he was waiting to meet them. He looked anxious.

"Is anything wrong?" Mordred asked.

"Ruby Parker wants you in UF1 for an emergency conference. Alec's already on his way over there."

They exchanged quizzical looks. "Any indication what it's about?" Gina asked.

"I've only heard the rumours," Tariq replied, "but I'm pretty sure they're true. I'm surprised you haven't heard anything – but – but of course: he was your friend, wasn't he?"

"Who was?" Mordred said. "What's going on?"

Tariq lowered his voice. "You're not going to believe this – it's surreal - and you definitely didn't hear it from me. It's Ian. Ian Woodward. He's gone to Syria."

Chapter 18: So Long, Ian, We Hate to See You Go

They went straight to Underground Floor 1, where Ruby Parker was waiting with Annabel, Phyllis, and Alec, seated around a table. She glowered at them as if they were late. They sat down without offering excuses.

"As you may have heard," she said, "sometime yesterday evening, Ian Woodward boarded a flight from Heathrow to Ankara. An hour ago, he saw fit to inform us that he's in northern Syria, in company with the YPG, preparing for an assault on Rojava. The YPG are the Kurdish People's Protection Units. Rojava is held by ISIS. I'm assuming – I dearly hope - no one here knew anything about his intentions beforehand."

"I can't believe it," Alec said after a deathly pause. He almost laughed. "I'm in shock. Ian. *Ian Woodward*. I literally can't believe it!"

"You'll all be asked to sign formal declarations to the effect that you weren't aware of his plans," Ruby Parker said. "So if any of you feel that's likely to pose a problem, you'd better speak up now."

Silence. Everyone except Alec looked glum.

"You don't look or sound terribly saddened, Alec," Ruby Parker told him.

"I'm not saying I'd do anything similar," he replied, "but I can't help thinking it's admirable. Sorry if that's controversial, but I might as well be honest. I'm not going to tut-tut just because everyone else is."

"How dare you?" Phyllis burst out. "You know *nothing* about what anyone else here's thinking!"

"All that strikes me," Gina said, "is we've lost a friend."

"To a noble cause," Alec replied.

Ruby Parker drew herself up. "We're not here to discuss the ethics of it. We're here because I'm required to issue you with a formal notification. As of the conclusion of this announcement, you are *not* permitted to discuss the matter with anyone else in this building. Including each other. Obviously, if anyone outside MI7 contacts you about it, you're to report that fact straight to me. Do *not*, under any circumstances, respond with information, and absolutely not an opinion."

"With respect," Alec said, "we're spies. If we want to talk about it, we're probably going to find ways."

"I didn't hear that," Ruby Parker replied witheringly.

"Is he likely to be prosecuted when he gets home?" Annabel asked.

Ruby Parker sighed. "Annabel: 'With anyone in this building' includes me."

Alec put his hand up. "Sorry, I will just say this one thing, because I misjudged the mood earlier, and I'd like to make up by setting everyone's minds at rest. The YPG isn't a proscribed organisation in this country and it's not a terrorist group. The Kurds are just normal guys trying to defend their villages from genocidal rapists. Since Britain's actually aiding them, weapons-wise, the Crown Prosecution Service is going to find it very difficult to build a case against good old Unmentionable."

"And I don't expect to hear another word on the matter," Ruby Parker said. "On pain of suspension. John, go home and pack your suitcase: you're going to Morocco in Ian's place. Your plane leaves tomorrow morning early. Phyllis will brief you. Alec and Gina, you'll continue following up domestic leads. Any questions?"

"With respect, I'd like to be excused from Morocco," Mordred said. "I promised to take Aisha Sharif to meet Sebastian's school friends, then his parents."

"Surely, Gina can do that," Ruby Parker replied.

"She trusts John," Gina said. "I'd be no substitute, really. Besides, I've never met Sebastian's friends, nor his parents."

"I'm not trying to get out of going to Africa," Mordred added. "But I made a promise and, in this particular case, I feel bound by it. If it helps, I think there's something she still hasn't told us. I'm not saying it'll ever surface, but I know it definitely won't if I disappoint her."

"What sort of a 'something'?" Ruby Parker asked.

He folded his hands together. "My instinct is, it's case-relevant."

"Then it's settled. In any case, I think she's had enough disappointment for one lifetime. Gina, you'll go to Morocco. John, you look after Aisha Sharif and see what you can find out. Alec, you follow up whatever leads you were working on this morning. If there are no further questions, I hereby declare this meeting closed."

"I'll let you into a little secret," Alec said at the King's Head, that evening. They'd come all the way to Canning Road to avoid other spies. The pub was busy – every seat was occupied, and there were people standing, and a group playing darts - but it wasn't packed. Alec and Mordred leaned on the bar; Gina, Phyllis, Annabel and Tariq sat around a table on the other side of the pub, in the corner. "Ian didn't go alone," Alec continued, holding up his empty glass. "Two more porters, please, Tim."

"Who went with him?" Mordred asked.

"Thelma, his girlfriend, and Angela, both from White."

"I don't think I've met Angela. I've heard of Thelma …"

"… Goodvibes. Not her real name, obviously."

"Does Ruby Parker know?"

"I think everyone does. Another department, though, so she's not obliged to dispense gagging orders. Remember, if you're caught: no one said we couldn't discuss Thelma and Angela, only the big 'I'. The latter just came up incidentally."

"Do you think Ian persuaded Thelma or the other way round?"

"I doubt any of the three was press-ganged. The Kurds are perfectly happy with women in the front line. Some of their best fighters are female. Did you see *Unreported World* the other week?"

"At work, with Emily and Jeff, just before clocking off. Jeff had popcorn."

"Typical Jeff. How bloody original."

"You're talking about the battle for Kobani, that one? With that thin lady?"

"Kiki King, yes. Made me laugh when it said ISIS think they'll go straight to hell if they're killed by a woman. They all seemed to love that in Kurdistan."

"I wonder what Ian's doing now."

Alec laughed. "Polishing Thelma's rifle, probably."

"I'll miss him. I didn't know him terribly well, but well enough."

"I'm always surprised more people don't go and fight ISIS. But no one in our society believes in anything any more. Well, some people do, but mainly nutters."

"I had a similar conversation with Gina earlier."

"Yes, sorry about that, by the way. I did my best to give you two a shot. You heard me. If I hadn't spoken up, Tariq's paranoia would have carried the day."

"We're still on. She's a committed Christian with all that that implies, so she's allowed me to decide."

"What? Whether you want to go out with her? She's actually saying she's game if you are?"

"That was the gist."

"Good God, you didn't bloody hesitate, did you?"

"She wants me to take time to think about it."

"What? Just because she's a Christian?"

"Keep your voice down! It means, er … no sex before marriage."

"Ah." He nodded mournfully. "I see."

"Obviously, I'm still going to say yes."

"So would I. I mean, you've got no sex *now*. This way, you'd have still no sex but with the bolt-on prestige of a glamorous, high achieving girlfriend."

Mordred sipped his porter. "I'm not sure that's the point, but hey."

"You'd have advanced a peg."

"You know Gina better than I do. I mean, you worked with her before I arrived in MI7."

"The question is?"

"It just seems strange that she suggested Goodwood, that's all. Gambling. And look, she's over there with a pint of Guinness."

"Odd, I admit. Probably a hangover from her previous life. She's become a lot more religious fairly lately. Guess what denomination she is?"

"Baptist?"

"No."

"One of those new churches where everyone puts their hands in the air and talks to Jesus like he's a Garage DJ?"

"Greek Orthodox. The good news is, her parents brought her up that way." He sipped his drink. "Because never get involved with a convert, John. They're always fanatics."

"And that's your explanation for why she likes a flutter and a drink. 'She's not a convert'."

"Bloody hell, she's *normal*, John. Thank your lucky stars! If she was a puritan, I'd say, yes, run a mile. But look at her: nice clothes, nice make up, nice laugh, nice perfume, nice big glass of stout. Christian she may be, but she's no prig. Put it another way. She's a spy. She must have to do morally dubious things from time to time, we all do. But she's not looking for another job."

"I take your point."

"Play along with her for a while. If you treat her properly, you might find the no-sex thing's as much up for grabs as the no-gambling thing or the no-alcohol thing."

"So long as I don't make that my reason for going out with her."

"You're highly abnormal, John, so I don't suppose that's likely."

"How are you getting on with Cecily, by the way?"

Alec spluttered slightly into his beer. "My God, of course! We could start going to church together! I mean, just until I move back in with Cecily and you start sleeping with Gina: we don't have to make it permanent or anything."

"A bit too cynical for my liking."

"Mind you, church has a way of doing that to you; sucking you in."

"What denomination is Cecily?"

"Pentecostal. Fair point, I hadn't thought of that."

"I wonder if it's right to burn my bridges with Annabel."

"Annabel doesn't want you. She was just using you to make Tariq jealous, and got carried away. Forget about her. She probably doesn't drink much, and when she does, she goes straight to stage nine."

He glanced in her direction. She had what appeared to be a tall glass of still orange in front of her. She and Tariq seemed to be getting on famously.

Phyllis came over. "For God's sake, we're supposed to be having an office night out! Gina and Annabel and I are going to be seeing each other *all day* tomorrow. We came here so you could say goodbye and buy us lots of drinks, instead of which, *this*. You're both useless."

"What are you talking about over there?" Alec asked.

"Ian, of course. You?"

"Ian."

"So much for super-injunctions. Come on, or do I have to drag you?"

The next day, Mordred arrived at the Sharifs' in the Kevin car. He was so used to not being spoken to now, he didn't even try to start a conversation. He wondered if Aisha or her father would be any more successful.

He got out and knocked on the front door. Aisha answered. She wore a plain blue dress and fringed plimsolls. She held an empty ceramic mixing bowl under one arm and leather handbag over the other. Her face appeared different to when he'd met her at the Dorchester, more make-uppy and older. Her father stood behind her.

"Dad's not coming," she said. "Is that okay?"

"It's fine with me," Mordred said. "But does your father ..."

"This is something Aisha has to do on her own," Mr Sharif said sheepishly, as if he'd learned a script. "We've talked about it, don't worry. I can see she's right."

Mordred understood. She'd been given up for lost, and she was found. She was likely to get her own way a lot from now on. He hoped it wouldn't ruin her. Not that it was any of his business.

He hesitated. Front seat with Kevin, or back seat next to Aisha? The latter seemed preferable. He was supposed to talk to her, and he couldn't very well be expected to crane his neck the entire journey.

Any awkwardness was obviated when she held the back-seat door open for him. He thanked her, got in, and was in the process of shifting across, when he saw her going round the car to take her place up. He shifted back again and saw Kevin smirk in the rear-view.

"We're going to Rheeming Hall first," she said, when she was settled. "Is that right?"

"That's correct."

"What's the driver's name?"

He smiled. "Why don't you ask him?"

"Excuse me," she said, leaning into the front slightly. "What's your name, please? I mean, what would you like me to call you, if we have to stop?"

"Call me Mr Jones," he replied reluctantly.

"Because I feel very nervous," she went on, trying to address him and Mordred both at the same time. "I've been sick twice this morning. And I couldn't even eat any breakfast. I think it'll probably happen again on the way there. Mostly, just a bit of dry retching, I expect. If it's okay, I'd like you to turn away while it's happening."

She rolled down the window. Her father passed a big box of paper tissues in, and a wad of what looked like polythene sandwich bags. "You'll need these, Beauty."

"Thank you, Daddy. I might get a nosebleed as well," she told Mordred. "It happens."

He wondered how she'd survived on the road so long, given her apparent fragility. More probably, she'd just become like that recently.

"What would you like to talk about?" she asked as the car pulled away. "I don't mean to be a burden, but a conversation might make me feel less nervous."

"What else are we going to do if not have a conversation?" Mordred replied. "It'll be a pretty boring drive if we just listen to the radio, or sit here swiping our phones and moaning to Mr Jones that there's no signal."

She laughed politely. They talked about her GCSEs, her school friends, her family, what it was like on the run, how happy she was to be home, her future plans. Every so often she filled with embarrassment that all the talk was of her, and she asked a question or two about him, but, with his connivance, it came back to her again. He never felt 'burdened', because she was interesting. He liked the way she looked upwards when she became serious, as if getting precisely the right words was absolutely crucial. The sort of thing adults ought to do more. She didn't mention being sick again.

"Is this – is this Rheeming Hall?" she asked when the car turned into the school grounds. "Oh, God."

"It's going to be all right," he told her. "Just be yourself."

She turned to him and smiled sadly, as if to say, That's right, it's not really about me. She put the bowl down and looked as if it wasn't nerves she was struggling with any more, but emotions. When they got out of the car, she seemed to have withdrawn into herself. She didn't speak.

They gave their names at reception and sat side by side on two cushioned chairs facing the school secretary. Five minutes later, Mrs Pierce arrived with Dale and Graham, both looking no less solemn than Aisha. Hands were shaken, names proffered.

"You can go up to the canteen, if you like," Mrs Pierce said. "It's empty at this time of the day. Or you can take a walk round the grounds in the sunshine. You'll probably want to be alone, so take as long as you like, and let the school secretary know when you've finished. Aisha, if you'd like to come back again sometime, that can be arranged too."

"Thank you," Aisha said.

"Where would you like to go?" Dale asked her. "The canteen or the lawn? Or anywhere."

"It's your choice," Graham added. "We're here for you. You can ask us whatever comes into your head."

"We might question you a little too, if that's okay," Dale said.

Mordred felt more touched by this than by anything he'd experienced in a while. The blatant civilisation of the entire event, made more impressive because they were supposed to be still practising to be adults. Maybe there was hope for the human race yet.

In the end, they chose the lawn, because it was such a nice day. They walked away talking softly, and sat under an oak tree.

"They're really grieving, those two," Mrs Pierce told him, when the teenagers were safely out of earshot. "This is probably the best thing that could have happened for all three of them right now."

"It was good," was all Aisha said when she got back in the car. They didn't speak on the journey back. She seemed absorbed in her own reflections and looked out of the window most of the way. They stopped at a service station halfway along the M2 for cheese and potato pasties – she was a vegetarian, just like him - and coke. She ate slowly and smiled absently when they made eye contact. When, after another hour, they arrived in front of the Chewtons', she seemed to recall where she was.

"I'm sorry I haven't been talking," she said. "I didn't realise the time. Is this it? Is this Mr and Mrs Chewton's house?"

"It is."

She picked up the bowl and retched several times. Mordred pretended to look out of the window. When she'd finished, she wiped her mouth with the tissues, then round the bowl. She put the tissues into a sandwich bag and tied it. She blushed furiously.

"I can't go in yet," she said miserably. She put the bowl in her lap and held her hands up. "Mr Jones, could you drive us somewhere so I can wash these? I'm really sorry. I'm so sorry. You can open the windows. It smells. Sorry for being so *gross*."

Mordred smiled. "To be fair, I wasn't really ready to go in yet. And I happen to know Mr Jones is desperate for a wee."

She laughed and wept at the same time.

They arrived back at the Chewtons' another hour later, after two more tries. Mordred's big fear was that Mrs Chewton might not have taken her tablets, but if so, it wasn't evident. Sir Ronald shook Aisha's hand and Elaine hugged her, and they sat down to eat cakes and sandwiches and drink tea, just like the Dorchester. Mordred hadn't known in advance, but the three had already met briefly at the funeral. The parents spoke of their son and showed his photos. Aisha related things he'd said and kind deeds he'd done and what Dale and Graham had told her about him, then showed some pictures on her phone. They promised to stay in touch.

On the way home, she clutched the bowl, not as if she was about to be sick again, but as if she knew she was going home now, and didn't want to lose it. Mordred remembered she had something more to tell him – or he thought she did. They probably wouldn't see each other any more, but he couldn't pressure her. She'd had enough of the police, and re-introducing investigation-type enquiries at the parting would ruin her day.

When they arrived in Richmond, she phoned her parents.

"I'll be back in a few minutes," she said. "Don't come out to meet me. There's something I need to tell Mr Mordred … Yes, three times. I didn't get any on my dress, though … It was good, yes. We'll talk about it when I get in. I love you."

She looked straight ahead after she'd hung up. Two minutes later, the car pulled up on her drive. She thanked Mr Jones and got out. "Come on," she told Mordred.

They walked a few paces, and stopped halfway between the house and the car. She turned to face him. "I won't say I've enjoyed today," she said. "It's been emotional and sometimes very embarrassing. But it would have been mostly unbearable without you. You made it something I can look back on it without shuddering. Thank you."

"You were good company."

"I know you're a secret agent," she told him. "Don't ask me how, because I don't want to get anyone else into trouble. I also know where you work. Is that a problem?"

"Er, not if you don't tell anyone."

"Bidisha knows too. She told me, not the other way round. But we won't let on, I promise."

He smiled. "All's well that ends well then."

"I'd like to see you again – not in a 'romantic' way, obviously – but I know what you'll say if I ask you: blah, blah, blah, child protection act, blah, thought to be inappropriate, blah, so I won't bother. But you will see me. I thought it only fair to warn you."

She put the bowl down, grabbed both his arms and stood on her toes to kiss his cheek. Then she scooped it up and strode into her house without looking back.

Chapter 19: The Deadly Threat of Peregrine

The following morning, Alec and Mordred sat in front of a computer terminal on the first floor of Thames House, both reading copies of Tariq al-Banna's report on Sebastian Chewton's computer. A single sheet of A4.

"So Sebbo 'may have been storing whatever he had in the cloud'," Alec read. "But if so, 'it's been deleted'. Very helpful. Means we're back to square one."

"The date of the deletions tallies roughly with his estimated time of death," Mordred said.

"Which sounds portentous, but doesn't help. And you didn't get anything out of the girl?"

"Afraid not, but she was a bit cagey when I dropped her off at home. 'You'll be hearing from me again'. Words to that effect."

"Like a baddie, or like she might have a crush on you?"

"Neither."

"Come on, John, it must be one or the other. There's no middle ground."

"If only Gina was here, instead of Morocco, she'd know what to do. I thought they needed a two-women-one-man team over there. I know I couldn't go, but why not send you?"

"Leaving you and Gina alone at last."

"That wasn't what I meant."

"Did you take her any flowers to the airport?"

"I thought about it. For about a millisecond."

"And?"

"I didn't want to embarrass her in front of Annabel and Phyllis. We're at work. It didn't seem right."

"You'll lose her. She'll go back to that horsey man."

"What horsey man?"

"Polo player, muscular. She was quite serious about him, from what I heard."

"Really."

"'Peregrine', that's it."

"I'll just have to take my chances. Besides, I trust her. She said she'd give me time to decide. She's not going to go off with Pezza in the intervening."

"You say that, but think about the gambling and the alcohol."

"Waste of time, trying to make me paranoid."

"Just one last point before I leave you alone then. It may be time to start eating meat. And I'm deadly serious this time."

"I don't know what you mean."

"She's angling for you to become a Christian, right? You'll find resistance a lot more difficult if she becomes a vegetarian, because it could look like a fair exchange of compromises. Be careful, is all I'm saying. Eat a bacon sandwich in her presence occasionally, so she's got no point of entry."

"That sounds quite reasonable on the surface. It's only when I look closely that I have to remind myself: 'Alec's got a warped view of human nature'."

"Ten years' time, you'll look back at this moment and weep."

"Was Peregrine a Christian?"

"I never met him, I just heard about him. In my experience, it's only possible to tell whether a person's a Christian if they tell you directly."

Mordred's phone rang. He took it out, looked at it, and answered.

"John, where are you right now?" Ruby Parker asked.

"Upstairs. First floor. Reading through Tariq's report with Alec. Why."

"I'd like you to go to any river view window and look down into Millbank."

"The street?" Stupid question: it wasn't like there was another. He had the feeling he was in trouble, that's why.

He did as requested.

Ah. Aisha Sharif together with Bidisha Mubarak. Bidisha wore a hijab and held an umbrella – a storm was raging – and Aisha clutched a bunch of dilapidated flowers.

"I see them," he replied. He felt Alec slap him on the shoulder and heard his chuckle.

"I've just had security on the phone," Ruby Parker said. "This is the tenth time they've walked between the pier and the roundabout. And they always slow down the closer they get to the entrance. Almost like they're waiting for someone to come out of the building."

"I'll deal with it."

"Be polite but very firm." She put the phone down.

"Would you like me to come?" Alec said. "Remember, I've got a teenage daughter. I'll be tactful."

He hesitated. "She doesn't know you."

"Best of British then."

He went down the stairs and across the foyer. Colin Bale stood dourly behind the reception desk, a bald, slightly oversized man with impressive ears, looking to poleaxe unauthorised visitors.

"Hi, Colin," Mordred said. "Do you have an umbrella I could borrow?"

"Well, we don't …"

"It's in the line of duty. Ring and ask Ruby Parker if you don't believe me."

"I could lend you mine, I suppose."

"Would you? Of course I'll buy you a new one if it turns inside out, or I lose hold of it and it flies into the Thames."

"That's very generous of you, John. Thank you." He reached down and provided his brolly. Heavy-duty, black and expensive-looking.

Mordred exited the building via the grand arch. Aisha and Bidisha saw him immediately and waved. He returned the gesture mechanically - probably everyone in the building was watching now. He descended the steps and crossed the road to meet them. He didn't have to hurry: they were running towards him. Something in Colin Bale's umbrella seemed to snap and it turned inside out. He cursed under his breath.

"John, what a nice surprise!" Aisha said. "I've brought you some flowers to say thank you for yesterday!"

He accepted the bouquet. He was set to scold them, but they were drenched to the skin and obviously freezing, and his heart melted. "Do your parents know you're here?" he asked.

"Not exactly," Bidisha said miserably.

"Shouldn't you be in school?" he persisted.

"Come under our umbrella!" Aisha exclaimed. "You'll get wet! There's plenty of room!"

"You should go straight home," he told her. "You're soaking. You'll catch pneumonia!"

"I need to talk to you, John!" she replied. "There's something I haven't told anyone, and I have to tell you! Only you! I promise you won't be sorry!"

So here it came. But he couldn't just do the Cynical Spy thing, grab the info and run. "Fine, but we need to tell your parents where you are first."

"That's okay, but you've got to tell them not to come and get us. I want *you* to accompany us home."

"Why?"

"Because I … we want to talk to you about our work experience week. It's not for another year, but we're supposed to be making preparations. Bidisha and I want to come and work in Thames House."

He smiled, even as the rain smacked his face. "I'll see what I can do. We had some *Blue Peter* kids here a while back. Who knows?"

The girls looked at each other as if *of course* their dreams had been realised, because their plan had been so ingenious.

"I'm not promising anything," he said. "I'm not in charge."

He took his phone out and phoned Ruby Parker. "Aisha says she has new information," he said. "I need somewhere dry to talk to her and Bidisha, and a new set of clothes for each girl, and someone to ring her parents."

"Tall order. Are you sure she's not bluffing?"

"They're drenched and they're freezing."

"Harsh though I know it sounds, we're not Social Services."

"I realise that." He suddenly – no reason at all – had a vision of hundreds of Syrian refugees, children some of them, just like these two, being turned away at the gates of what was supposed to be civilisation. "But, well, let's be nice."

It turned out they actually had a room for just such emergencies, in the foyer, just opposite reception. It had hardly been used since the Cold War, and a large framed picture of a young Shirley Bassey hung inexplicably on the wall facing the door so that, for a moment, as you entered, it was all you saw. It was cold, and the furniture and fixings were grim: a stack of 1970s-style plywood chairs with stark metal frames, a single lightbulb in the middle of the ceiling, a clunky desk-cum-interrogation table with a piece of folded paper under one leg. Mordred took the girls inside and returned to reception. He hadn't been able to find a bin in Millbank. Colin Bale flinched when he saw his obliterated brolly.

"I'm really, really sorry," Mordred said. "I'll get you a new one as soon as I've finished with the girls. Today, obviously."

"That was from *Harrods*!" Colin Bale replied. "It was an Alexander McQueen Small Skull!" He looked close to tears.

"Like I say, I'm really sorry. How much was it? Twenty? Fifty? I'll have one delivered."

"Three hundred and ninety-five pounds!"

"*What?* Bloody hell. Okay. I haven't actually got that amount on me at the moment, but I can go to the Harrods website and pay by credit card. I'll do it in a moment when I come out. I'll get same day delivery while I'm on. And I'll buy you something else to make up. Maybe not Alexander McQueen, but some chocolates or something. Promise."

Colin Bale gave him an I'll-believe-it-when-I-see-it look and blew his nose. Amber Goodings – a stout forty-nine year old with diamante spectacles - arrived from the first floor with two changes of clothes and batch of towels over her arm. "Just stuff I rustled together at short notice," she said. "Probably won't be perfect fits, but should do."

"That's really kind," Mordred said. "Could you just see if there's any kind of fan-heater? It's colder in there than it is outside. And maybe some blankets? Quite a lot, if possible. Please."

She smiled. "Sure. Back in a mo." That was the great thing about Amber. Nothing was ever too much trouble.

He left the girls to get dried and changed. Amber came and took their clothes away for a swift dry-clean while he went on the Harrods website from his phone and ordered a new brolly and a box of Belgian chocolates. They didn't do same-day delivery which meant he'd have to go and pick them up in his lunch break. If he got one.

"I may not be able to go and pick them up today," he told Colin Bale. "Depending on what happens in the next half hour. Is next day delivery okay?"

"I suppose it'll have to be, I just hope it's stopped raining by clocking-off time. It's a long walk to Pimlico without a brolly."

He went to the *Kensington Cabs* website and booked a taxi for five-thirty.

"Where do you live?" he asked.

"I don't want anything delivering to my house," Colin Bale replied. "I'm never in when the post-person arrives."

"I meant, so I can get you a taxi from the tube to your house."

"Oh, I see. High Wycombe. But for goodness sake, John, don't go booking another cab."

"Fair enough."

"Cash would be much easier. Twenty pounds or thereabouts."

Mordred suppressed a desire to leap over the reception desk, pick up the PC and use it to batter Colin Bale to death with. "There you go," he said.

"Thank you, John. And if anyone should ever ask me, I'll tell them you're an honourable man."

As he walked back to the Shirley Bassey room, he calmed down. People were probably always borrowing things from Colin and either not returning them, or bringing them back in bits. He was 'just' a receptionist, not something important like a spy. He probably got in trouble if he withheld his personal property from The Realm. That was how the class system worked. Maybe they'd be friends from now on.

He knocked on the door. "One sec!" from inside. Amber.

He sat on one of the chairs near the building's entrance. In the gloomy cold, listening to the wind howling in the grand arch, he felt like the seventy-seventh earl of Gormenghast. Eventually, Amber emerged. "All ready! Let me know when you're done, I'll bring their own clothes down."

He went in. Amber – or maybe all of them – had set the table in the middle of the room with a single chair this side, and the girls shoulder to shoulder facing it on the other. They looked as if they were waiting to be interrogated, except that they were swaddled in blankets and continental quilts, and wore this-is-the-best-day-out-ever grins. The fan heater buzzed in the corner, but it was still cold in here. He sat down.

"Ask us anything you like," Aisha said.

"We're nice and warm in here," Bidisha told him, as if it might console him.

"My toes are still cold, though," Aisha remarked.

"Would you like me to bring the fan heater a bit nearer?" Mordred asked. Fine interrogation this was turning out to be.

"Yes, please, John," she replied.

He got up and brought it as close as the wire would go. He pointed it at her feet. Both girls were wearing fluffy slippers. God knows where they'd come from, but that was another of Amber's skills: able to procure anything at a moment's notice.

"When we were outside," he went on, "you said you had something important to tell me."

"Das stimmt," she replied. "I've still got to get my head back together, but I'm getting there, thanks to you."

"I'm glad," he said.

Bidisha's hand emerged from her wrappings and went up. "Aren't you supposed to put a tape-recorder on?"

"I don't want a tape-recorder," Aisha said.

"It's not really necessary," Mordred told her. "But thank you for reminding me."

Aisha swallowed. "I didn't know whether I could trust you at first. I mean, not that I believed you worked for *them* or anything, but I did think maybe you weren't, like, a good person. I don't mean I thought you were a bad person. I just didn't know. Maybe if I gave you information, it wouldn't necessarily benefit anyone, and the whole thing might just kick off again and the next thing, I've got twenty people chasing me, and no information this time to give anyone; nothing to make me worth saving."

"We certainly didn't save you because we thought you had information," he said.

"*You* didn't."

"No one did."

She sighed as if he was quibbling about nothing. "Anyway, the point is, I have got information and lots of it. Sebastian gave me his USB stick. I'm pretty sure it's what they were looking for."

His heart sped up. "Where is it?"

"Buried. In the Peak District."

"What's on it?"

"I don't know. Something you're probably aware of already. He didn't have much idea himself. He just knew it was something illegal."

"How?"

"Because it mentioned ISIS. Like in a good way, as if they're not a clapped-out bunch of complete defectives."

"What else?"

"An oil company. Something with three or four letters. And Eritrea. And a few political parties. Sebastian looked them up. They weren't very important ones. Look, John, why don't we just drive up there and *find* it? Then you'll know everything there is."

"You haven't told anyone else about it, have you?"

"I'm not stupid. Until I met you, I was prepared to just forget it existed. But I want to help, don't you see?"

There was a knock at the door. Amber put her head round. "Aisha, your mother's outside in the car. She wants to see you right away."

"Tell her I'm assisting John with a matter of national security," she said.

Amber stayed where she was. "I'm not sure I can stop her coming in if she wants to."

Aisha turned to Mordred. "I thought I said: stop her coming to get us."

Mordred laughed. "I'm sure we tried, but she's your mother. She loves you, and she's probably still suffering the after-effects of thinking her daughter was dead in a ditch somewhere. She's not obliged to take instructions from complete strangers. Would you like me to come outside with you?"

"Please." She laughed nervously. "I'm warning you, though, she is *so* going to do her nut. This is going to be majorly embarrassing."

"We'd better get changed," Bidisha said. "Mrs Goodings, could we have our clothes back, please? We can wring them out. It doesn't matter."

"It so happens they're here and dry," Amber said, coming in and putting them in two neatly-folded piles on the table. "John, we'd better wait outside."

They left the room. "How angry is she?" he asked, "on a scale of one to ten?"

"Eleven."

He went to sit back on the Gormenghast chair and wait. Aisha and Bidisha emerged after two minutes. The three of them exchanged looks but didn't speak.

Mrs Sharif's car was parked on the double red lines against the bollards. Colin Bale was remonstrating with her through the open passenger window, telling her she had to move, the police were on their way. Since he didn't have his brolly and the rain hadn't abated, he was already soaked, which was called Karma.

When she saw Aisha and Bidisha, she got out, slammed her door hard and came round and threw open the rear passenger door. *"Get in!"* she screamed.

They didn't argue. Mrs Sharif spotted Mordred and went over and began pushing him along the pavement with both hands, crying as she yelled. *"What the – HELL – do you think you're – PLAYING AT? – Why can't you leave us – ALONE? – What have we – DONE? – Haven't we – SUFFERED ENOUGH? – Just go – AWAY – ALL OF YOU! – Just leave us – ALONE!"* They were both as drenched as Colin Bale now. Before she could do anything else, Aisha got out of the car. She and her mother had a yelling match that ended with them slapping each other's outstretched hands. This seemed to bring them to a mutual understanding. Mrs Sharif grabbed the wet rope of hair that had swung across her face, thrust it back into place, then turned, strode away and got back into the driver's seat. Aisha followed her onto the back seat next to Bidisha. The car screeched away, its hazards still flashing. At the precise moment, it turned right onto Lambeth Bridge, a police car appeared at the opposite end of Millbank, its siren blaring.

"I'll leave you to explain," Mordred told Colin Bale.

Chapter 20: Coming Down With Something

After Mrs Sharif had pushed him the length of Millbank, Mordred went downstairs to see Ruby Parker. In a way, it was like going to see his mum after an encounter with the school bully. He actually felt sorry for himself; she might help. He knocked on her door, went in and sat down. She wore reading glasses. She took them off to look him hard in the eye.

"Don't tell me," she said disdainfully. "It was a waste of time. She's developed an adolescent crush on you and she's stringing you along. You really do need to cultivate a little more worldly wisdom, John. Being 'nice' isn't what this organisation – MI7: the one you belong to - is about. We seem to be re-visiting - "

"She was in the process of giving me valuable intelligence, for your information. You were supposed to *stall* the parent, not encourage her! For all I know, we've lost a very important lead now, and all because you insist on making assumptions!" He didn't know where it had come from, but obviously he'd been angry all along.

She recoiled a little, but recovered. "Okay, now you have my attention."

"Does the word 'Eritrea' mean anything to you?"

"Keep going."

"One thing we all noticed when we started observing the houses was how many Africans there were. Somalians, we thought. Now, to my knowledge, that's internal information. There's absolutely no reason Aisha Sharif would know it. But let's say she did. She'd relay it to us verbatim, yes? If she was 'stringing us along'? According to her, she and Sebastian had a conversation in which he mentioned an oil company, a few political parties – 'not important ones', as he put it – and Eritrea. Next door but one to Somalia, though I hardly need tell you. But of course, that's just me being immature and gullible. There's no reason whatsoever to think it might be a significant lead."

"There's no need to be sarcastic, John."

"I'm sorry, but I'm only human. I've had bloody Colin Bale on my case about his stupid umbrella, thanks to which I'm five hundred pounds the lighter; I've been soaked to the skin; I've been patronised by everyone in the building over Aisha Sharif; I've been pushed through central London by an hysterical parent, and to cap it all, I come in here and you start giving me the immaturity speech. I'm sorry. I'm sorry I'm angry, but sometimes you just can't help it, you know?"

"I want you to take the morning off. I apologise for the little speech I made a moment ago. I didn't ask to see you: you came to me, and in hindsight I should have let you speak first. You may well have been on to something after all, and this isn't the first time I've underestimated you. It seems to be becoming a bad habit. Secondly, I'll reimburse you for the umbrella. Thirdly, we'll get Aisha back. I had no right to imply you'd been anything less than one hundred per cent professional in your dealings with her."

"Thank you. She says Sebastian gave her a USB pen with all the relevant data on. She buried it somewhere in the Peak District. If we can get it, we can probably solve the case."

"Good God. And she'll lead you to it, will she?"

"That's – it *was* – the idea."

"I've been a complete idiot."

"We're all fallible."

"It's obvious you're not the only one in this room who needs a rest. I'll retrieve the situation, since it's my fault. Keep your phone switched on."

It was one of those days where you knew going home wouldn't help. You'd be trapped in between four walls with rain outside and nothing to do inside but watch telly or read a book or brood. And whichever of those three you chose you'd end up doing the last.

So he didn't go home. When he left Thames House, he wandered the streets for a while. The unfairness of it: that's what irked him. He'd done nothing but try to help. A whole day devoted to taking Aisha to deepest Kent and back. Not that he resented her, she was a nice kid. But her mum – what the hell was she thinking? That he was somehow stalking her daughter? Because that's what it felt like. He could still feel her pushing him. He ducked into the Barley Mow on Horseferry Road and leaned on the bar. "Strong cup of tea," he told the barman. "Milk no sugar."

Normally, it'd be Charles serving, a Yorkshireman in his early forties. Mordred would request an Earl Grey, then another. He never needed a third, but always made the pretence of ordering just so Charles could do his, Don't-you-think-you've-had-enough-sir, and Mordred could go, Tea-I-must-have-more-tea and Charles could threaten to call security. Neither had any idea why they persisted with it, except that Mordred liked two cups of tea.

Outside, he bought a flimsy brolly for 99p. He needed a church right now, or a library. Somewhere in the city where he could sit down in silence and commune with the old and grey. Musty smelling books, pews, claustrophobic shelving, stained glass windows. Or maybe something to eat would cheer him up. He didn't feel hungry, but then he hadn't felt angry either, down in Ruby Parker's office. *Know thyself.* Something he was rubbish at. Maybe he *did* come across as a stalker. How would he know?

He bought a spinach and ricotta pasty in *Top Drawer Comestibles* on Elverton Street, but it was a poor specimen, and he fed it to the pigeons in Vincent Square. They said you shouldn't do that, but it was better than putting it in the bin. Besides, the threat of feral birds was overestimated. They wouldn't need to mug you if they weren't hungry most of the time. Thinking about it, he was actually *staving off* an Alfred Hitchcock-type apocalypse.

He'd had enough now. He was cold and depressed and at home he could at least be watching a comedy. Why had she pushed him so hard? With such vehemence? That was what was upsetting about it. The outright venom. *Modern Family*, that was quite funny, or even a few episodes of *Frasier*, for old times' sake. Or *Father Ted*. DVDs. He could watch those. It wasn't like he could even have fought back.

He was about to descend the steps to Victoria tube station when his phone rang. Ruby Parker. "Hi," he said. It hit him he was freezing cold.

"Mrs Sharif would like to apologise," she told him. "To you in person."

"Spontaneous, or did we twist her arm?"

"The police followed up and they contacted us. I've just this minute been in touch with her. She does sound genuinely sorry."

"Because a fake apology's not going to get us very far. I'm talking pragmatically. I don't mean my hurt feelings."

"I appreciate that. I said I'd speak to you, but that you weren't around at the moment. My view is, this sort of situation, it's best to let people stew for a while. If she's going to apologise, she'll have to come to us."

"Thank you for letting me know."

It struck him on the tube that what he was feeling wasn't normal. Mingled paranoia, self-pity, lassitude and depression. He was coming down with something. When he got in, he went straight to bed and shivered violently. He got up, took two paracetamol and drank a glass of orange juice. He returned to bed and slept. He woke up in the dark and looked at his phone. 8pm. He'd been out for a good seven hours. *One missed call*. Bloody hell, Hannah, his older sister. He couldn't hold his end of a conversation up, and that would mean admitting something was wrong, and in turn that he was ill. Then she'd come over and he'd have to endure being micromanaged with Lemsips and thermometers, and perpetual jibes about 'man-flu'. He texted that he was in the middle of something and he'd call back tomorrow. He took two more tablets and finished the carton of orange juice and returned to bed.

He seemed to lie wide awake for a long time, although when he looked back on it later, he must have been asleep otherwise he couldn't have had such odd thoughts. Hannah was coming to get him. She was at the door and he couldn't muster the energy to answer it. Gina, and the flowers he should or shouldn't have sent to the airport. His lust for her. Peregrine the horse man. Annabel. Aisha, and how the adult world always let you down. How he was letting her down. 'I'm ill'. 'I don't believe you, John.' 'No, I am.' 'Try and forget what my mum did.' 'I already have, but I'm unwell and I can't get out of bed, I'm trapped.' What Amber must think of him. Colin Bale's brolly. The further adventures of horsey man in Morocco. Gina: she'd never said any of that stuff, he'd just dreamed it. Alec: Best of British. The scars on his chest from Mrs Sharif's red-hot fingertips.

He fell asleep and woke up properly at five am. He was sick. He'd have to ring in as such, but how could he, with so much work to be done? So much relying on him?

But if he did go to work, he'd spread it around. He put his alarm on for eight o'clock, and sat up when it went off.

He used introspection to discover whether he was better or not. Yes, he was. A miracle, but that was how strong constitutions worked. Yet when he swung his legs over the side of the bed, the nausea returned, redoubled. He called Ruby Parker and told her he wasn't fit to make it in today.

"Do you need anything?" she asked. "I can ask Kevin to do a quick shop for you if you're stuck for provisions."

"I should be fine, thank you." The thought of The Man Who Never Spoke picking groceries for him was almost enough to induce another level of delirium. "I should be back in tomorrow."

"From your description of the symptoms, I very much doubt it. Give it at least another day. I won't expect to hear from you tomorrow unless you're better."

"What about Aisha Sharif?"

"You're hardly going to be doing her a favour if you give her whatever you've got. No, I'll put her and her mother off."

"Fair point."

"Mrs Sharif is genuinely sorry, by the way. She has no idea what came over her, except that she just 'snapped'. I believe she's bought you a present. I don't know what it is."

Normally, he would have made some quip, but nothing came. It was only three hours later as he was getting ready for a trip to the shops that the answer came to him. *I expect it's a bullet proof vest*. Or maybe just: *a bullet proof vest?* The fewer words, the funnier, that was the general rule. He pulled his socks on and tried both versions out loud. Did the general rule apply here? There were always exceptions. He opened all the windows, to let some fresh air in. Were either of the two versions funny? There was a knock at his front door.

He froze. Bloody hell, Kevin. Could it be? He pulled on his trousers and went to look outside through the little spy hole.

No, it was worse. A tall, thin woman with long blonde hair, and a raven-ish looking man in a trench coat. Hannah and Alec. He opened the door. Alec held up a full carrier bag. "Orange juice, milk, and a few cabbage pies to keep you going. Anything else you need?"

"Alec tells me you're ill," Hannah said irritably. "Why didn't you tell me?"

"Because I'm twenty-nine. Don't come in. It's probably catching."

"I'll see you back at work," Alec said. "I've specific orders from the boss not to effect entry." He turned round and descended the block stairs. Hannah pushed into the flat. She tied her hair up. "What needs doing?" she asked.

"Nothing. I'm fine."

"You're ill. You'd be at work if you were fine."

"I don't need looking after. I know you're four years older than me, and that makes you my mum, but it's not bubonic plague, just a touch of flu."

She sighed. "Let me see what Alec's bought." She took the bag from him, removed the contents and started putting them away. "He's a good friend. You're lucky to have him, you know that? Most travelling salesmen, their colleagues are their rivals. They don't want them to get better, because it means less of a market-share."

"We're not gay, if that's what you're implying."

"So what if you are? There's nothing wrong with being gay!"

"Obviously, but you're going to start modifying my Christmas and birthday lists."

"Just shut up and go to bed, John. You're delirious. Oh, look, you're right out of paracetamol and aspirin. I'll go and get you some."

"I'm dressed. I was about to go out and get them myself. I'm not wholly incapable."

"Except that you've left all your shirt buttons undone. You look like an advert for a men's fragrance."

"That's very flattering."

"*Farmer's Market*, it's called. Now get undressed again and go back to bed."

He did as he was told. He heard her rooting about in his drawers, looking for where she knew the key was. Then the door slam. If he pretended to be asleep, he wouldn't have to speak to her when she got back. Cruel thought. But fair. He looked at his phone. 11.15am.

The first thing that struck him when he opened his eyes was that the light was slightly different. His mobile had gone, and there was a glass of orange on his bedside table with a note taped to it.

Your phone's on charge in the kitchen. The new paracetamol and the aspirin are in the drawer where you normally keep them. Call me if you need anything. I'm at work all day tomorrow and I'm in New York over the weekend on business, but if you leave a message, I'll get Tim to come round. DRINK LOTS, EVEN IF YOU DON'T FEEL LIKE IT. Love you. H. xxxxxxxx.

Something was up. She hadn't mentioned man-flu once. She must think he was really ill.

Maybe he was. But they were running out of time. He had to get back to work.

Chapter 21: Stalkers Again

When he thought about it later, he may have gone back to work slightly too early, but at the time it seemed the right thing to do, and nothing else mattered. He put his suit and coat on, texted his sister and sent her some flowers, then rang Ruby Parker. She didn't try to dissuade him. He arrived at work at five to nine. Everyone watched him as he went to his desk, and when he got there, someone had e-mailed him an attachment. A video of him being pushed along the road by Mrs Sharif to *Hit Me With Your Rhythm Stick*. He smiled, aware of the vast number of eyes on him. Right underneath was an e-mail from Ruby Parker to all staff: anyone found in possession of, or playing, said MP4 would suffer immediate suspension with full loss of pay. He downloaded it to his phone for something to laugh at when he retired to Riga with a gunshot wound and a wheelchair, and deleted it from his PC.

His phone rang. "We need to meet," Ruby Parker said, "A lot of water's passed beneath the bridge since you fell ill."

He went to her office, entered on command, and took the single seat facing her.

"As it turns out, your illness was a stroke of luck," she said, after welcoming him back. "Had you taken Aisha Sharif to the Peak District on the day she came here, it would probably have been a disaster."

"I think her mother made that pretty clear."

"I'm not talking about Mrs Sharif. I mean, Aisha's being followed."

"Again?"

"We still haven't found Terence Dimbleton and it makes perfect sense for him to keep trying until he gets what he wants."

"In that case, why are they pussyfooting around? I mean, why not just kidnap her and torture her, like they did Sebastian Chewton? Come to that, why didn't they threaten her like I threatened her during Round One?"

"Both good questions. And I can answer them, because luckily, one of the men you helped capture has talked."

"Finally."

"He doesn't know the full picture – or even a quarter. All he knows is that it's wide-ranging. It 'may' involve members of the government of this country in some capacity."

"What difference does that make?"

"Yousaf Sharif was a junior minister. The law is supposed to treat everyone equally, but we both know that the murder of the teenage daughter of someone that well connected would set the hounds of hell loose. The culprits would get a lot more than they bargained for. No, they're 'pussyfooting around', as you put it, for a reason. It was just a good job the Sharifs never held that press conference we pencilled in for them. That would simply have upped the stakes."

"That only makes sense if there's more than one route to the truth. If the USB stick's the sole road in, once it's destroyed, game over. In that case, they wouldn't stop at anything. They must be worried we'll approach it from another angle."

"There's always more than one route to the truth, John. According to our source, they didn't discover Aisha Sharif was involved until they'd dispatched Sebastian Chewton. He told them exactly who she was as well."

"They removed his toes with a bolt cutter. I'd have told them."

"'We were only supposed to mug her'. That's what Ghimpu told you."

"What about it?"

"You must surely have thought, why go to all this trouble just to fake a mugging?"

"Yes, but then I decided a better explanation was that 'kill her' got lost in translation."

"Apparently not. The truth is, a bogus mugging would allow them to search her and take whatever she had. Then she'd go to the police. They'd find Sebastian's corpse. There would be a murder enquiry, an unconnected investigation into an assault, and a disturbed teenager's yarn about a mysterious conspiracy detailed on a USB pen that doesn't exist."

"You're suggesting it didn't occur to them that she'd have hidden it somewhere in the big, wide world?"

"Why would she do that? She would only come home if she thought it was safe to do so. If her aim was to keep the pen secure, she'd bring it with her. After all, there are always lots of hiding places in your own house."

"Yes, that makes sense."

"Back to the present then. According to her mother, Aisha's pretty certain she's being watched again."

"What are we doing about it?"

"First, we had to be sure she was right. Take a look at these." She spread six black and white stills across the table. They showed the exterior of Thames House, with the date and time at the bottom, and Aisha and Bidisha sheltering under an umbrella at different positions along Millbank. The same white car appeared somewhere along the road in each.

"Ten minute intervals roughly," he noted.

"We also have one of the same car pursuing Mrs Sharif after she came to pick up the girls. At speed."

"And we've traced it, I assume?"

"Stolen. And Aisha's house has been burgled."

"Er, hang on. Burgled? How does that tally with them not wanting to draw attention to themselves?"

"Perhaps that's the wrong word. Unknown individuals have entered the Sharifs' house and searched it without unsettling anything much. They did it so well, that in the normal course of things, their activity would have gone completely unnoticed. But naturally, context creates new fears. When you've been through what the Sharifs have, and something's not put back exactly right, or there's an odd smell, or an inexplicable jumble, or all three, you're less likely to dismiss it unthinkingly."

"CCTV?"

"We're looking for a white Transit van with a muddied-out number plate and a man in a hoodie, roughly five foot ten."

"Brilliant. And he's not been back, I take it."

"Not yet."

"I take it we're looking to tempt him back, though."

"Not necessarily. We've already rounded up one set of individuals. Now we've got another. If we round them up too, we'll have a third, and they'll be yet more careful."

"So what's the plan? As if I didn't know."

"We've been keeping a very close watch on Aisha. We're meeting her and her mother this morning so mum can apologise – she insists – then you're going off on a treasure-hunt in the Peak District."

"Who is?"

"Mrs Sharif, Aisha, Bidisha, Fatima, Alec, you and Gina."

"*Gina?* I thought she was in Morocco?"

"I recalled her. I had a word with Alec. I asked him if you had a girlfriend."

He grinned. "I see."

"Sorry, John," she said, "but in this organisation, even the most searching enquiries into your personal life can sometimes be justified. I'm still worried that Aisha Sharif is developing a crush on you. You could find yourself exposed if you're both wandering round the English countryside together. We're bringing in her friends, her mother, and your girlfriend, with a view to putting a healthy distance between you."

"And Alec. Do we really need that many people?"

"Yes, because she can't remember 'exactly' where she buried it. My view is, you could be out there a long time, and I'd rather have seven people out there for one day than one for seven. Call me a pessimist."

"It must have occurred to you that she might attempt to string it out a bit if she thinks we're all having a good time."

"Yesterday afternoon, I saw both her and Bidisha in one of our ground floor offices, re their work experience placements. I impressed on them the importance of *having a good memory* for the sort of work we do."

"You're not seriously thinking of putting them to work here next year?"

"As a one-off, I don't see why not. Given sufficient notice, if we can't ring-fence things we consider ultra-sensitive, even within this building, then I don't think we should be here. Besides, I see no reason to dampen their enthusiasm. They're intelligent girls and proud to be British."

He cleared his throat. "On a slightly different subject, can I ask what Alec told you about me and Gina?"

"He simply said you and she were 'exploring possibilities'. It may or may not be relevant, John, but I don't necessarily discourage workplace romances. It's important to find someone who understands the sort of pressures we sometimes face. In any case, the point is, regardless of the true state of affairs, for the purposes of this trip to the Peak District, Gina 'is' your girlfriend, understood?"

"I can manage that."

"She's flying straight to Manchester. Alec's already in transit. Once you and I have seen Mrs Sharif and Aisha, Kevin's going to pick them up. He'll already have Bidisha and Fatima. He'll then lose whoever's tailing them, and drive to Biggin Hill, where a private jet will be waiting to take them to Tatenhill Airfield in Staffordshire. We'll have another car and another driver waiting to take them to their destination."

"And me?"

"There's a fairground on Wandsworth Common at the moment, and a man advertising helicopter ascents. At the time you arrive – midday – there'll be a 'closed for refuelling' notice in place. Have a wander round the stalls, try for a few prizes – that always puts the jitters in any shadow - and Gerald will find you. Just follow his instructions. You should be in the Peak District in under an hour. Amber's already taken care of all you need in terms of clothing, etcetera. You're booked in under the name of

Michael Henderson. None of you are going by your real names, of course."

"Okay."

"Alec will have a laptop with him at all times. The minute you find the data pen, upload it on to the MI7 website, wait twenty minutes for confirmation and then destroy it. Alec's got full instructions concerning the destination folder. We'll make separate arrangements for you to get back."

"It seems odd to have to begin with an apology from Mrs Sharif. Wouldn't it be best to wait till we get there?"

"You're not one party in the Peak District. There's you and Gina, there's Alec and there's the three teenage sisters and their Auntie. You don't know each other. Outside in the open, of course, that may have to alter – it probably will - but be cautious."

"If Gina and I are partners, does that mean we're sharing a room?"

"Don't get carried away, John. Gina has her convictions, and you need to respect them."

"Obviously. I was just thinking, that's all."

"There are ways of sleeping together without 'sleeping together'. I'm sure I don't have to explain."

He smiled. "No, I expect Gina will do that."

Mrs Sharif and her daughter were waiting for him in *Café Stilfuld* on Erasmus Street, just round the corner from Thames House. It housed six tables – five of them empty - and a stainless steel counter with a big window and spotlights to show the cakes. It hissed with espressos being pressured and squeezed and concentrated like oranges. A board on the wall showed items and prices in swirly chalk lettering, and an old woman sat behind a till. She got up and smiled when she saw Mordred come in.

Mrs Sharif waved sheepishly, then stared straight ahead. Aisha held her hand on the table without looking at her. How was this meant to go? Neither mother nor daughter had a cake in front of them, only what looked like empty coffee cups. Normally, he'd have asked them if they wanted a refill, but this was meant to be The Apology in neon lights, so he wasn't sure it was appropriate. Bloody hell, he didn't want or need anyone to say sorry! What Mrs Sharif had been through – he realised with a stab of anxiety that he'd either forgotten her first name, or had never asked it: which was worse? – justified anything really. Yes, she'd pushed him down the street and his colleagues had turned that into a twenty-second music video, but there were worse things.

To hell with it. He went over. "Would either of you like a coffee?" he asked.

"Mr Mordred," Mrs Sharif said, "please sit down. I've taken the liberty of ordering. Ms Parker said you like tea. It'll be here in a minute. We'll have cakes too."

"There's absolutely no need to apologise," he said. He slipped into the one seat opposite and midway between them. If he looked directly ahead, all he saw was a gap, but he couldn't move it without appearing to prefer one over the other.

Mother and daughter exchanged looks. "You have to," Aisha mouthed. "I know," Mrs Sharif whispered. She welled up.

"Please," Mordred said. "I know how much you've both suffered. An apology will only make me feel bad. Besides, it was quite funny really, seen in the right light. It made my colleagues' day." He thought about showing them the video on his phone, but decided not to. This was the wife of a junior minister. She wouldn't see the funny side, not if she cared about her husband. Show some respect.

Mrs Sharif sighed. "I'm a devout Muslim, Mr Mordred. At times like this, though, I almost wish I wasn't. A little 'Dutch Courage' might have helped. But it shouldn't ever be necessary for a true believer ... like myself. Just doing the right thing should be enough. I did wrong. You're a very, very good man, and I publicly humiliated you. I'm sorry." She wept.

He realised the time of resistance was gone: she wanted to say this, and he shouldn't object, because it was for her as well as him. Aisha picked up her mother's hand, kissed it, and wiped both their tears with a napkin. The two women looked at each other. The tea arrived in a kind of timelessness. Mordred poured it out. The old lady behind the till brought them a whole lemon drizzle cake. Aisha cut it into sixths and told them to eat up. Mrs Sharif laughed at the words 'eat up'. She ate daintily.

They talked about Islam. Mrs Sharif gave him a present – what looked like a long, thin rod, wrapped in gold paper. When he opened it, it was an Alexander McQueen Small Skull umbrella. "I heard you broke yours," she said. After about ten minutes, she got up to go to the toilet. Kevin was due any minute. While she was out, Aisha looked at her plate for a while, then wiped her eyes. She looked desolately at Mordred.

"I – I thought we might never see each other again!" she said.

Chapter 22: Gina the Revealer

Mordred had no sense of being followed when he left *Café Stilfuld* at 11.15. Only when he reached Pimlico, three minutes later, did he sense someone, and when he boarded the tube, he saw him: a thirtysomething in a chullo and plain grey T-shirt, pretending to read a *Metro*. Mordred made no attempt to evade him. When they changed at Victoria, they were joined by another man in a baseball cap, stocky looking, in red jeans. The two acknowledged each other with infinitesimal nods. They pursued him onto the Northern Line; they followed him out at Balham. Eleven minutes later, they split up to keep both sides of the fairground under observation. When the helicopter took off, Mordred gave them a little Be Seeing You wave.

An hour later, he and Gerald touched down in a field somewhere in the Peak District. He transferred to an idling car where Gina awaited him on the back seat. She gave him the gift she'd brought him from Marrakesh - a box of hand-made mint chocolates – and they exchanged pleasantries. Five minutes later, they took their suitcases from the boot and checked into The Black Labrador, a half-timbered Tudor guest-house with six picnic benches scattered in front. Their room had a double bed, a small armchair, and a sofa. A pair of leadlight windows gave a view of the street below and the hills in the distance. The décor was Gloomy Victorian. Gina took her clothes from the suitcase and put them methodically into the wardrobe.

"I'll take the sofa," he told her.

"There's no need. It'll be very uncomfortable on there. And I trust you. I'm going for a shower now."

"Would you like me to go out for a while?"

"There's a door between here and the bathroom, so no."

"Thank you. I won't look."

"I like you here. Did you think about what I said, by the way?"

"It didn't take me long to reach a decision, if that's what you mean. Yes, I definitely think we should formally inaugurate a serious romantic relationship."

She took his hand. "I'm so pleased."

She didn't look it. Her eyes were elsewhere.

"You get changed," he said, "then I'll shower and change, then we'll go for a walk together before everyone else arrives."

"That sounds nice."

"I've a feeling there's something you want to tell me."

Her mood changed. She stopped pretending and the solemnity broke the surface. She put her arms round him and kissed him, then drew back an inch and looked into his eyes. "You're one of the most sensitive men I've met in a long time."

The sort of thing you'd probably say to console someone if you were about to deliver bad news.

Peregrine. It had to be.

Mrs Sharif and her teenage 'nieces' arrived thirty minutes later. Mordred watched them enter the building and stooped to tie his shoelaces. Gina was ready now. She came to the window to see what he was looking at, but they'd gone inside.

"It's a lovely view," she said. "Probably even nicer on a sunny day."

He didn't reply because she didn't seem to expect it. He couldn't imagine any way in which sunshine could improve what was about to happen: the *do you think a man and a woman can ever just be friends* question, with all that it entailed in terms of exhaustive unpacking and minute application and bitter disappointment. It was a stupid question anyway, especially for a man with four sisters. *But that's exactly the point, John: I want to be your fifth sister.* Afterwards, he'd phone each sibling to ask if they'd be willing to accept a new one. Majority vote, or should it be unanimous? He almost laughed, despite his gloom.

They left the hotel and walked down the road to the village green. A large duck pond lay beneath a willow tree and in between four benches. They sat down on the bench farthest from the road. She held his hand.

"I'm very confused," she said. "Sometimes, I think no one knows the real me."

Maybe he should short-circuit it, get it over with asap. "Is this about Peregrine?"

"What?"

"Peregrine."

"Peregrine *Henderson-Thomas?* Who told you about him?"

"Alec."

She laughed tetchily. "You've been talking about me to Alec?"

"Not in the way you think."

"How many ways are there?"

"Fair enough. I mentioned that I might be taking you to Goodwood. He asked if I'd sent any flowers to the airport the other day when you were going to Morocco. I said no, I'd thought about it, but I didn't want to embarrass you in front of Annabel and Phyllis. He said I should be careful, because I might lose you to Peregrine. He didn't know his last name."

"Being Alec, of course he'll have told you how much *in love* with Peregrine I was."

"Not in so many words."

"Well, I wasn't."

"Oh." He nodded for want of anything else to do with his head. "Right. Good."

"You said earlier you wanted us to have a relationship. You must have a pretty low view of me if you think I'm only asking you because I'm on the rebound."

"Even if I knew you were, I'd still say yes. I've liked you a lot for a long time."

She looked at him in silence for a moment and laughed. "Wow."

"What?"

"You're forgiven."

"Are you – you're being serious?"

"That was exactly the right thing to say. It means you like me unconditionally."

"Of course I do."

"Why didn't you tell me before?" she asked.

"I was waiting till I'd completed the self-improvement course."

"What 'self-improvement course'?"

"Life, it's called."

"So left to your own devices, you'd probably *never* have asked me out?"

"That's not necessarily true. For example, I might improve dramatically over the next year."

"Thus making you worthy."

"It's the chivalric ideal. Don't knock it."

"You're not going to put me on a pedestal, are you? I'm definitely not too good for you, and nothing positive can come of you treating me as if I am."

"You're already there. You're on everyone's pedestal. Alec called you 'the perfect human being'."

"Really? Alec said that?"

"How can you expect not to be on people's pedestals if you're intelligent and good looking and well dressed and you go round being nice to everyone? You brought it on yourself. Don't blame me."

She smiled. "I don't want this conversation. I'm seriously starting to fall in love with you, and it's too early. Shall we start again?"

He laughed. "Given what you've just said, no."

"I need to have a serious conversation with you, John. Just not the one you were imagining."

"Okay. I'm listening."

"I said a moment ago that no one knows the real me."

"This time, I'm not going to guess what that means. Carry on."

She sighed. Then sighed again. And yet she was no drama queen. Whatever it was, it was obviously important.

"John, if you loved me – let's say we were to fall in love – would you follow me anywhere?"

"Up to a point."

"What do you mean?"

"Sometimes, you don't follow the person you love. You stop them going. If you think they're going to hurt themselves, or what they intend is wrong. But I'd do one or the other, yes."

She eyed him anxiously. "How much do you – know about what I'm going to tell you?"

He laughed. "We won't find out until we get there." She wasn't amused. "Nothing, as far as I'm aware," he added.

"It's not funny, John. What did Alec say to you about Ian? Because I know you've talked about him. We all have."

"He went to Syria with two women. Angela, his girlfriend, and Thelma, I think it was, from White. Known for her pathological cheerfulness."

"That's right."

"Is this about Ian?"

"In a way."

The connection between Ian and Peregrine – could there be one? Could she have a thing for Ian? No, because she'd already told him -

"It should have been three," she said. "Three women. I was meant to go too."

Aha, a joke. She was joking. But -

"I backed out at the last minute," she added.

It whooshed down on him like a tub of cold water. "Bloody hell," he said. "Why?"

"Look at me. 'Goody Goodwood Gina'. No one knows the real me." She laughed, bitterly. "Christians and Muslims have lived together in harmony in that part of the world since the time of Jesus. Now, the churches are being demolished and the people are being exterminated or expelled."

"What were you going to do when you got there? Join the Kurds?"

"The Lions of Royava, it's called, no. That's where Ian and Thelma and Angela went. I was looking to link up with Dwekh Nawsha. It's a Christian militia group."

"I can't picture you holding a rifle." Stupid comment, but he had to keep the conversation going.

She shrugged. "I thought I'd better tell you. It's only a matter of time before Ruby Parker finds out, then I'll have to leave MI7. I'm not worried."

"What will you do then?"

She said nothing. The sun broke through the clouds and went in again. "I don't actually know," she said. "In order to answer that question, I'd have to know why I backed out of going to Syria."

"How close were you?"

She showed him a millimetre between thumb and index finger. "It wasn't cowardice," she said. "It was … When Phyllis and Annabel and I were in Morocco, we got talking about it. Why is there all this killing? Phyllis thinks it's men, pure and simple. God created Eve, Adam corrupted her, then Adam re-wrote the whole thing. Because God's a woman, she's prepared to let it go, because, well, you know how blind women can sometimes be about their boys, we're our own worst enemies." She put her hands in her hair and groaned. "We were a bit drunk at the time, obviously. But – but it put into words what I felt. I don't want to become a man. An eye for an eye – that's not the right way. It's not what I should be!"

"Do Phyllis and Annabel know about you and Ian?"

"I've never had any secrets from either of them. I also know that Annabel said she was in love with you, by the way."

"She was full of scotch."

"'I can't picture you holding a rifle'. That's it in a nutshell."

"Wanting to help doesn't mean that. Why not become a charity worker? I could leave MI7 and we could go out to Syria together."

"You'd do that?"

"Why not? I'd only try to stop you if I thought it was wrong."

"But we could get killed."

"I don't think death's the end anyway."

She smiled. "Yes, I forgot that about you. Anyway, it's a non-starter. If we joined a charity, we'd have to have skills – medical, probably – and we wouldn't get away with laying down terms and conditions to the effect that we've got to be deployed in Syria. There's suffering everywhere. That means we could be sent anywhere."

"Why is that a problem?"

She shook her head. "Because – because … I don't know!"

"I mean, if a person's suffering - "

She stood up and put her hands on her temples again. "My God! You're right! I don't know whether I want to talk to you any more, John. I began this conversation to try and clear my head. Now I'm even more confused. You're right. Why should I care any more about a suffering Christian in Syria than I do about a suffering Muslim in Burma or a suffering Nepali in Rasuwa? Of course I shouldn't! It's all too big!"

"Don't fall into the trap of imagining you're just thinking too much."

"What?"

"It'd be easy to do. 'I should have just gone with Ian while I had the chance. I shouldn't have over- deliberated.' I think you'd have been wrong to go with Ian."

"Do you think Ian himself was wrong?"

"No. But that doesn't mean I think he was right. Killing ISIS people is just the lesser of two evils in that situation."

"Put it another way then. Do you think he shouldn't have gone?"

"I don't know. If I say he should, I'm committed to the idea that everyone should. That's what it is to make a moral judgement rather than just, say, express a preference."

"So? What's wrong with that?"

"It's essentially the same as saying we ought to invade Syria."

She sighed the thousandth of ten thousand sighs. "I'm glad I talked to you. I'm a long way from where I was at the beginning of this conversation. But I do feel a bit wiser. Thank you, John."

It wasn't the most romantic conversation he'd ever had and he didn't know where it left him – or her. As they walked back to the Black Labrador, he was aware of the hard crenelated tower of the local Anglican church louring at them over the rooftops. They played backgammon when they got in, then sat in the lounge reading. They saw Mrs Sharif leave with the girls just before five-thirty, and come back just after six-thirty. She made brief eye-contact with Mordred and shook her head. At seven they ate dinner and at ten they went to bed. They slept under the covers without touching. She approached it as if it was the most natural thing in the world. At two o'clock in the morning he awoke in darkness to an odd noise. He knew immediately where he was, but for a few seconds couldn't place the sound. He reached over to warn Gina, but she wasn't there.

Then he realised. It was her praying.

Chapter 23: Crunch Time

The next morning, he and Gina arose at six, went down to breakfast an hour later and left the inn with a packed lunch at seven-thirty. They were dressed in full hiking gear. Clouds hung low and grey over black-looking hills, and the sky spat rain. A taxi picked them up from beneath the village sign and took them to Grindslow Knoll in the Dark Peaks. They walked a short distance through wet countryside and sat down beneath a tree to await the others.

"Have you seen Aisha since she arrived?" Gina asked.

"Not to speak to."

"Would you be able to tell from examining her face whether this is a wild goose chase? You're supposed to be good at that sort of thing."

"I was the one she originally told. I definitely didn't get the feeling she was lying. Anyway, there must be something. She's had burglars. Very discreet ones."

"She also has a crush on you, so I've heard."

"I doubt that. It's just an explanation everyone's come up with because she's a teenage girl, I'm a young man, and it fits. It's sexist."

She hooted. "What's your explanation?"

"She thinks I can help her, and that I've got enough of an overview to be effective."

"Keep your guard up, though."

"That's what you're for. Besides, even if she did have a crush on me, she'd realise it had no future. She's highly intelligent; she's not an idiot."

"There are lots of different types of intelligence, John. Logical-mathematical and emotional are completely different animals."

"It's academic."

She smiled. "I suppose so. I don't care, anyway. I'm enjoying myself. Part of me hopes she is playing a prank. But I wouldn't want to see her get hurt."

"Here they come. Look busy."

"Incidentally," she said, "I didn't get any sense that we were followed here."

"Me neither. I think we're safe."

"Where's Alec?"

"On the other side of the hill. They'll meet him in about thirty or forty minutes." A car drew up. It deposited Mrs Sharif and four teenagers on the grass verge, then sped away. Mordred nodded to them. They came over.

"Good morning, Mr Mordred," Mrs Sharif said. "Good morning, Ms Fairburn."

"John and Gina," he corrected her. "Where should we begin?"

Aisha gave him a drawing. It showed what looked like a single stone half buried in grass with hills in the background. "This is what it looks like," she said.

"You're pretty sure it's round here?" he asked her.

She nodded. "This is where my phone said I was before the battery died. I saved the location, but it's not exact."

He pointed to the picture. "Okay. This is the stone's surface. Is it vertical?"

"That's right. Sticking out of a bit of a mound of earth covered in grass. About this high" – she flattened her palm about two feet from the ground – "and the whole ground going up slightly."

"Whereabouts exactly is it buried relative to the stone?" Gina asked.

"I didn't have anything to dig with," Aisha said, "so what I did was poke my finger in between the top of the stone and the soil. Mostly, it was grass roots, and when I'd put it in, it sprang back. You couldn't tell anyone had ever done anything."

"What were you doing here anyway?" Fatima asked.

"Looking for Bamford Manor," she replied. "I just wanted to see it one more time."

No one asked. Mrs Sharif put her arm round her.

"You must have come from a road or joined one at some point," Mordred said.

"And I guess it must have been this one," she replied. "But don't ask me how far I was, or whether I came from it or left it or both. I can't remember."

"Okay," he replied. "Let's get started. Make sure your phones are switched on."

Gina linked arms with him and they walked away. The four girls and Mrs Sharif set off in the opposite direction and split up just enough to comb their path without losing sight of each other. Alec would be on his way to meet them now.

"She doesn't have a crush on me at all," Mordred said, when they were out of earshot.

"How do you know?"

"When you asked where the USB pen was relative to the stone, she didn't bat an eyelid. Not in any way grudging, not over-eager. You're just another person. Just like me."

She smiled. "Part of you must feel a little disappointed."

"None of me. Not remotely."

They split up. After five minutes, he went to autopilot: there just weren't that many stones like the one she'd drawn, and she might have misremembered the details anyway. In half an hour, he found two, more horizontal than vertical. He ran his fingers round the edges of them and pulled them out. A few insects, not many because they were both so tightly lodged, otherwise nothing. He replaced them, being careful not to hurt the insects, and drew an X on them with a short chalk stick.

Strange how she'd been unfazed by Gina, especially given her 'I thought we might never see each other again'. She was probably mixed up at the moment in all sorts of ways.

More worrying was Gina. She was about to do something momentous and probably didn't even know it. Given the intensity of her nervous energy, there was no telling where she might end up. Three weeks ago, had anyone told him she was a Christian – well, he wouldn't have been surprised exactly: mostly, Christians tended to keep their beliefs to themselves nowadays. Sometimes you were surprised: someone you considered pretty unpleasant turned out to be one. But on the whole, they came across as excusably respectable: after all, maybe they quietly gave a lot of money to Oxfam; that was supposed to be the Christian way.

He didn't want her to go to Syria. She'd be okay handling a gun, obviously. It was part of her training. But she probably wouldn't be okay killing people. Being in MI7 wasn't like being in the army. It was mostly acting, sleight of hand, detective work and, if you were unlucky, an act or two of heinous betrayal. It wasn't trench warfare and shooting people. Besides, she was going for ideological reasons, which meant she'd probably die running into no man's land to rescue one of her comrades. If you already took orders from your conscience, no way were you going to let some half-baked Battalion Commander share precedence. She wouldn't last a week.

But a second attempt to leave for Syria was almost certainly what she was thinking of. In not so many words, she'd admitted it. *I don't actually know what I'll do now. First, I'd have to know why I backed out of going to Syria.* But of course, her options were limited. She wasn't going to join a charity: she'd made that clear. And she wasn't going to settle down to a 'normal' job – the City, or interior design, or marketing, or whatever she'd qualified for at university. That didn't leave much to choose from. And the call of 'duty' is sometimes irresistible.

He had to stop her. Or go with her. One or the other.

What would he be like in Syria? He wasn't particularly a Christian, and he probably wouldn't be much good as a soldier. And war wrecked you. It always threw up situations where there was some *good thing* you had to do at the almost certain cost of your own life. So you either tried to do it, and you perished, or you didn't – sometimes you couldn't, but 'couldn't' was always an on-the-spot matter of personal judgement here - and you came back haunted for the rest of your life. If you were very lucky, you'd only encounter one such situation. That was why men came back from wars and refused to talk about them. Because they were 'guilty'. In their own minds, they were. They were scared you'd find out. His own grandparents, *Las Brigadas Internacionales*. Both romantic and noble on the face of it, you'd think they'd be proud, want to reminisce, discuss, pass the idealistic flame down the generations. But no. Not a word, either of them. And sometimes, you'd see them staring desolately into space. And in the end, her suicide, no note.

His phone rang. He jumped and pulled it out. *Gina*.

"I've found it," she said.

He was the last to arrive. A shallow valley bisected by a stream, a fenced field to the east, and a hawthorn hedge extending from the summit to halfway downhill where it mysteriously petered out. Sheep grazed on its far side. The rain had stopped and the clouds were thinning a little. Alec sat alone on a rock with the laptop on his knee, presumably uploading as instructed. Gina stood talking to Fatima and Mariam. Aisha and Bidisha sat with Mrs Sharif on a transparent piece of plastic sheeting whose edges kept billowing noisily.

"All done," Alec said. "We've still got to wait for confirmation, but it looks like we can all go home now." He took the USB stick out and handed it to Mordred. Blue, plastic casing with a little 'S.C.' etched into the side, pitted with mud now. They were supposed to destroy it, but looking at Aisha, it didn't seem like a good idea. She looked as if she was going to vomit.

"Case closed," Gina said. She crossed her fingers. "Hopefully."

Alec came over. "So who's going to smash it?" he asked. "Two rocks, put it on one, hammer it with the other? That's all I can think of out here."

"Maybe we should ask Aisha," Mordred said.

"I don't think that's a good idea," Alec replied.

"What if she says she doesn't want it destroyed?" Gina asked. "She might want to hang on to it for sentimental reasons. We can't allow that."

"I don't want to stand here like a bloody caveman smashing it between two rocks while she's sitting there looking ill. It feels very wrong. Like we've used her somehow."

Alec rolled his eyes. "For God's sake, Mordred, you're hopeless. Have you never read a John Le Carré novel in your entire life? We're *supposed* to be bastards. Give it to me. I'll look after it."

"No."

"So what are you intending to do? Go over there and say, 'Excuse me, Aisha, we'd like you to do the honours'?" His laptop pinged. He opened and closed it, "Confirmation. Time's up."

Mordred handed it over. "Let's just wait till she's gone."

Alec shrugged. "Fair enough. There's no hurry. And we don't want to upset her unnecessarily."

Aisha stood up and came over. "Could I have the USB pen, please?"

"We've orders to destroy it," Alec replied.

"I understand that," she said. "I'd like to be the one to do it."

He swept a panicked look to Mordred but handed it over gingerly. Bidisha was carrying a boulder. She put it down on the plastic sheet and stood back and put her fingers in her ears like there was about to be an explosion. Mrs Sharif took a claw hammer from her pocket. She handed it to her daughter. Aisha put the pen on the boulder and smashed it with a single blow.

"If it hadn't been for that stupid thing," she said sadly, "Sebastian would still be alive now. Good riddance. I suppose it's time to go home and get on with my life now."

Officially, they were meant to 'await orders' via the laptop - Alec had been charged with receiving and disseminating them - but they assumed it was merely a formality. The discovery of the USB could mean nothing other than the end of their visit to the Peak District. After Aisha destroyed it, they went back to The Black Labrador. Their suitcases were already half-packed. Mordred sat with Alec in the lounge and read the morning papers, Gina went into the village alone, and Mrs Sharif and the teenagers took a bus to Heights of Abraham.

Two hours later, Alec's phone vibrated. He went to his room and returned ten minutes later. Although there was a TV in here, the lounge was obviously built for quiet: thick dark carpet, William Morris wallpaper and gilt framed portraits of Victorian worthies. "Not exactly the message I was expecting," he said.

Mordred folded his paper up. "And …?"

"We're to stay here for a few days, just in case anything happens to the Sharif party. They've decided to make a mini-holiday of it. Gina's to report to London immediately."

His heart sank. "Sounds ominous."

"She's probably asked to go back to Morocco. Too erotically tempting, spending another night with Mordred the Magnificent. Nothing happened did it?"

"We only slept together in the sense in which it's not a euphemism."

"Her leaving's a sign that she's throwing in the towel, then. She's weakening. Which means she may be amenable to persuasion. I'd see if I could talk her out of it if I was you. I'm sure you can make a good case. Tell her you're still scared of Aisha."

"Maybe I should."

"Of course you should. Then I can go to Morocco instead."

He went upstairs and knocked gently on their door. No answer. He went in. No one. So she still wasn't back from the shops. He paced up and down for a moment, taking deep breaths to fuel his brain. Bloody hell, he had to think of something. Ruby Parker would sling her out on her ear, and that would provoke the very outcome no one wanted. A week later it'd be on *News at Ten:* first British woman killed in Syria in anti-ISIS militias. He could see each step already fully realised, like the generic storyboard of every Greek tragedy ever written. He had to forestall it somehow.

But how? He couldn't talk to Ruby Parker because, well, what if he was wrong? What if Alec was right, and it was simply about Morocco? What if it was something neither of them suspected? The only possibility was to talk to Gina herself. Knowing Ruby Parker, given the seriousness of the charge, she'd have called Gina directly. She'd have ordered her to go straight to the station and not talk to anyone. *You are not permitted to discuss the matter with anyone else in this building, including each other*. That was obviously how she worked. She might even have sent a car. So worst case scenario, Gina might even be already on her way to London.

He pulled on his coat, charged down the stairs, out of the hotel, and emerged onto a country road of driving wind and rain. The village – yes, that way. He set off at a sprint.

Half a minute later, a convenience store, a post office, two hairdressers, a dry cleaner's, bookshop, butcher's, grocer's, bank. If she was still here, the first or the second were best bets. He went into the store, walked down the aisles at speed and emerged without buying anything. The Post Office was small enough to scan through the window. She wasn't in there either.

Now what?

The church. That was it! That had been it all along! She hadn't come shopping; she'd come out for another round of prayer. He laughed with relief. That was the great thing about God's house: you had to switch your phone off. Ruby Parker was probably cursing into her … whatever she ate for lunch. No time to lose.

He didn't know exactly where the church was, but you could see the tower from everywhere. He followed it behind two sets of houses, then along a tarmac path that led to a lych-gate and from there, a cobbled path through an ancient graveyard overshadowed by a Yew. It took his eyes a second to adjust in the dark of the porch, then he switched off his own phone, lifted the latch and went in.

Norman in design, probably. Three huge stained glass windows at the far end, and a number of pillars supporting Romanesque arches. Gina knelt with her head bowed in one of the middle pews. As far as he could tell, they were alone in here with the scent of wood polish and the thick solemn silence. As quietly as he could, he went to sit next to her.

She finished what she was saying and opened her eyes to look at him. "John," she said happily. "How did you know where to find me?"

"I have to talk to you."

She got up and took his hand and kissed it. "What about?"

"You've been recalled to London."

She drew air in hard, but quickly regained her composure. "It was inevitable, I suppose. I was going to confess all, anyway, soon as we got back. I assume it is about *that*."

"I don't know. Alec and I have been ordered to stay here. The Sharifs have decided to make a vacation of it. We're to keep an eye on them."

"I suppose their being here *is* our doing." She smiled. "I say 'our'. MI7's."

"Forget about them. I'm worried about you. I think we should get married."

She laughed. *"What?"*

"It's not like we've only just met. I've known you for a long time, and you've known me. We like each other and we share the same values. That's what matters. If our deepest principles are the same, we can weather anything. We're perfect for each other. Do you realise how rare that is?"

"Our convictions are only superficially the same," she said. "Yours are moral, mine are religious. They may look the same – even to God, I think – but they're not."

"I'll convert."

"Not because of me, you won't. I love you too much for that."

"Say that again."

"I mean I'm *falling* in love with you fast, that's all. I'm not good for you, John. You've got a brilliant future in the service, and you've already got your own convictions. You can't subordinate everything to me. I won't let you."

"But none of that matters. People matter, not jobs or promotion - or even ideals."

"Put it this way. Fifty years ago in this country, women were expected to give up their identities and take on their husband's values, likes and dislikes. It was wrong. It was wrong for women and it's wrong for men. It's wrong for me and it's wrong for you."

"Just think about it."

She put her palm on his cheek and looked into his eyes. "No. I won't."

"Please."

"No." She switched her phone back on and smiled. She showed him the screen. *5 missed messages.* "All from Ruby Parker. I'm going to leave now." She stood up and sat down and grabbed him and buried her head in his chest and gasped. "Yes, yes, I *do* want to marry you! I know what you mean about everything you've said! It's all true! But I *can't!* Sorry I'm being such a bitch! I just thought it would make it easier! Don't get up. *Stay here!"*

She disengaged herself, stood up and strode out of the church.

He knew enough about relationships to realise he had to obey. He'd catch up with her in London for Round 2. He would put his sisters onto her, that would wear her down. Then he'd pick her up and introduce her to his parents – women liked that. He'd be her slave, whatever she wanted, but not too servile, because women didn't like that. She'd said she loved him. He'd won the first battle, turned the tide just as it looked like he was going to be routed. There was still the war to be won, but he stood on the battlements and felt confident. Men's metaphors, pathetic ones. For all he knew, she'd go straight from being sacked to boarding a plane to Istanbul. That was how she struck him right now. Energised. She had something in mind, and it wasn't him. He'd have to go after her. Bloody hell, he hoped the Sharif's extended sojourn wouldn't be a long one. Please God, let them long for London.

He sat in the pews for a moment, to give her chance to exit the village without him hanging on her skirt. This was bloody Primorye all over again, when he thought about it. Dao-ming Chou, as he now remembered her. The love of his life, supposed, who'd just disappeared into thin air. Just like Gina seemed to be about to. *Once is bad luck, twice is careless* – who said that?

He counted to two thousand, then got up and trudged through the rain back to The Black Labrador. It wasn't until he walked into the hallway that he realised he was dripping wet and freezing. Alec stood next to the lounge door, apparently waiting for him, with a face like thunder.

"Where the bloody hell have you been?" he said. "I've been trying to ring you."

"I went into the village to find Gina. She's on her way to London, I'm afraid."

"Forget Gina. We've an emergency on our hands. Aisha Sharif's been abducted."

Chapter 24: In Which We Finally Learn What's On That USB

"What do you mean, 'abducted'?" Mordred said.

Alec grabbed his arm and pulled him into the lounge. "Keep your voice down. We need somewhere to talk, and you need to get a change of clothes. Your room."

They took the stairs two at a time and shut the door behind them. Alec sat on the bed. Mordred stripped down to his boxers, hung his clothes up to dry and towelled his hair.

"The police are on their way," Alec said. "They want to interview us. Ruby Parker's been in touch with them, so they know we're not suspects."

"What can we possibly tell them?"

"What the hell did you say to Gina, by the way?"

"What do you mean?" Mordred replied listlessly.

"She came back here, packed her stuff in about thirty seconds, them kissed me on the cheek and said good-bye like we'd never see each other again. Not 'goodbye'. 'Good-bye'. With a ten foot hyphen. What did you do to her?"

"I asked her to marry me."

Alec looked nonplussed then guffawed and slapped his thigh. "No, I shouldn't be smiling, not with what's happened to the Sharif girl, but that's so typical *you*. The Mordred kiss of death. Haven't you ever heard of One Step at a Time? Bloody hell, talk about off-putting. Married!" He laughed again. "That's the great thing about you, John: you're always good for a roll in the aisles."

"I'm in love with her."

"Sure, yes, of course you are. Even so," he went on, as if he was addressing an imbecile, "you're supposed to play your cards one at a time. That's how mating rituals work. Look at the animal kingdom one day and take a few notes. Bloody hell."

"She's not going to Morocco. She's being expelled from MI7. Probably."

"Er, what?"

"When Ian left this country, she planned to go with him. She backed out at the last minute."

"Gina?"

"And now Ruby Parker's found out."

"Gina?"

"That's what she's called, yes. Surname: Fairburn. Date of birth, sometime in 1987. Aqua McGina of *Stingray* fame. That one."

"I can't believe it."

Mordred shrugged. He pulled a dry shirt on. "Conversation kaput then."

"I knew she'd become a lot more religious lately – I mean, I don't think she was religious at all when we all went to Primorye – but I never thought she'd become radicalised. Bloody hell."

"She's not 'radicalised'."

"What would you call it then?"

"Standing up against genocide?"

"Don't try to muddy the waters. If she's doing something that's a massive departure from the norm, she's doing something radical. That's what the word means. If it's because she's caught the ideology bug, then she's become radical*ised*."

"Okay, so she's become radicalised. But there are good radicals and bad radicals. Gandhi good, Hitler bad; MLK good, Bin Laden bad. If no one had ever been radical about anything, we'd still be living in mud huts."

"She's been brainwashed, probably. It's only a matter of time before she tries to get back to Syria. Once these people have got their claws into a person, they don't give up. We've got to stop her."

"I've tried and I can't. It's up to Ruby Parker now."

"That's true. She'll have her watched twenty-four-seven, especially her internet activity. Miserable existence, but she's probably safe."

"I hadn't thought of that. You're probably right."

"Unless that's not what Ruby Parker's recalled her for. Maybe she really is going to Morocco. That would be a disaster."

"Gina said she was going to confess all, anyway, once she got back to London."

Alec sighed miserably. "That's okay then. I'll really miss her, though. Not just because she was so easy to look at either. She was a genuinely nice guy."

"What a bloody horrible mess this case is becoming. You wouldn't think we'd almost cracked it and it was over. Have we heard back about what's on the USB pen yet?"

"Ruby Parker's going to speak to us by MI7 Videocom at eight tonight. I guess that'll give her time to sack Gina. It'll mean she can include the *never mention her again* speech. Two birds, one stone."

The phone on Mordred's bedside table rang. He fastened the last button on his cardigan and picked up.

"The police are here to see you, sir," the receptionist said.

The Sharif party had returned from Heights of Abraham and carried on past the village where they were staying to Peak Cavern, hoping to squeeze in one more local attraction before dinner. When they came out, Aisha went to the toilet and never returned. After a few minutes, they all went in a group to find her, then reported her missing to the site manager, who, after a quick call round to his employees, contacted the police. Ten minutes later, the attraction was sealed off so all visitors could be identified and questioned before they left. Four separate witnesses recalled a teenage Asian girl apparently leaving the site in a hurry, accompanied by two bearded men in their early thirties, white, brown hair, casually dressed. One saw them all get into a white Renault. CCTV footage confirmed it.

Mordred told the police what he knew, while Alec did the same on the other side of the lounge. Ruby Parker had been in touch by e-mail to let him know he was still Michael Henderson, and that they were fast-tracking the USB analysis. The Sharif party was still at the police station. The families of the three remaining girls were on their way to collect them and take them home. Yousaf Sharif was also in transit. The police interviewed him by Bluetooth as he drove.

Mr and Mrs Sharif arrived at the hotel an hour after the last police officer had gone. She went straight upstairs without making eye-contact.

Mr Sharif came over and shook hands with Alec and Mordred. "She's looking for someone to blame."

"We shouldn't have let them out of our sight," Mordred said. "We still don't know how they found us."

"If it's any consolation," Alec said, "we're going hell for leather on the data stick. If it's got anything worth having on, we should be able to make a few arrests. That might persuade them it's not worth holding on to her. Once they know the game's well and truly up."

"Or they might use her as a hostage to gain traction," Mr Sharif replied. "Try and get whoever's arrested out of police custody in exchange for her. That's another possibility, but it wouldn't have to be Aisha for that to work. It could be anyone. Why *her?*"

"They must think we haven't found the USB yet," Alec said, "and that she still knows where it is."

"That would be easily resolved, though," Mr Sharif said. "From what I understand, she smashed it. All she'd have to do would be take them back to the spot. The bits are probably still there. Look, I'd better go and comfort my wife. Good *God,* I knew having her back home again was just too good to be true!"

His face contorted like he was about to lose control, then he took in a shovelful of air and strode off after Mrs Sharif. The two MI7 agents looked at each other. They went to their separate rooms, and Alec appeared at Mordred's door five minutes later, with the laptop beneath his arm. He beckoned Mordred onto the landing. "Bring your key, and shut the door," he said.

"What is it? What else has gone wrong?"

"Nothing. We need to find somewhere to videocom. We can't do it in either of our rooms, because they might be bugged. Remember, that's how these people discovered Sebastian Chewton in Great Yarmouth. They've got experience."

He followed Alec downstairs and out of the building.

"Any suggestions?" Alec asked.

"There'll be a bench in the churchyard. About a three minute walk. Pretty secluded."

They set off. The rain had stopped now, but Mordred determined to buy an umbrella in the village on their way. He didn't mind getting wet, but the laptop might not like it. Right now, it was all they had.

Halfway there, he stopped dead. It took Alec a few paces to realise he'd been abandoned, then he did a double-take and turned round.

"What the hell are you doing?" he asked.

"Sorry, I just had a thought." He ran and caught up. "Mr Sharif said, I quote: 'it could be anyone' – he meant, held hostage – 'why her?' Don't you think he may have a point?"

"They think she's still got information about the digital pen, obviously."

"If she was here to find that, she'd do it first, then hit the tourist trail afterwards. The fact that she's at Peak Cavern with her mum and friends strongly suggests she's already taken care of business. Now she's doing pleasure."

"These sorts of people act first and think later, you know that. In any case, they're probably not the brightest sparks in the box."

"Even if they do think later, it's later now. I'm sure they've confirmed the USB pen's smashed. She only needs take them to where she buried it and show them the bits."

"And – what? They'll just let her go?"

"She's no longer any use to them, so yes."

"Why not just kill her?"

"It's not impossible, but they didn't make any particular effort to hide their faces when they were abducting her. Murder's a pretty serious charge. It's not like just abducting someone for a few hours, then releasing them. With murder, you'd make a better effort at concealment."

"Like I say, they're half-wits."

"If the Sebastian Chewton saga taught us one thing, it's that these men are professionals. They don't do *ad hoc*."

Alec clicked his tongue irritably. "Look, John, you've obviously got a theory. Why not just tell me what it is, rather than all this beating about the bush? I've only got a limited lifespan."

"The reason they abducted her has nothing to do with the USB pen. It's revenge."

Alec hooted. "You just told me they were professionals."

"They are. Dimbleton isn't."

"*Dimbleton?* He's in Morocco."

"We don't know that. My guess is he thinks she's outsmarted him and he's out for vengeance."

"Bit petty for a master criminal."

"I've met him, you haven't."

Alec flicked his eyebrows. "There's nothing wrong with adding it to our list of possibilities, I suppose. If you're right, he'll probably want revenge on you as well. I'm sure by now she'll have told him she was staying at The Black Labrador, and who with. She's probably described us. He probably recognised you. You could very well be in a lot of danger."

"I'd already worked that out. The good thing is, if I'm right, he'll keep her alive on the off chance she might be useful in luring me into his trap."

"As usual, it's all about you."

"About me being wiped from the face of the earth, yes. How vain."

"We're probably going to be speaking to Ruby Parker in a moment. I'll mention it to her. We can pass Dimbleton's photo to the police – although I'm pretty certain they've already got it - and have him added to the list of suspects. If he is in the country, that ought to put the frighteners on him. I've read his file. He may be a bully, but he's also a good old fashioned yellow belly."

"Where would a man like Dimbleton hide out?"

"Five star hotel probably, under an assumed name."

"We need a picture, then we can start doing the rounds. There must be lots of five stars round here. We don't have to do all the legwork ourselves. We can probably co-opt a few police officers."

"Sounds as good a plan as any. I haven't the foggiest idea what to do."

They turned right into the churchyard and found a bench in amongst the oldest graves where the grass had been allowed to grow. Alec raised the laptop lid and logged on through four different levels.

"Should we ask her about Gina?" Mordred said.

"Don't be stupid. That would imply we knew something was up, and that would imply we'd been talking about Ian. Besides, it's out of our hands. Just let's concentrate on the matter in hand, shall we?"

Ruby Parker's face appeared. She was sitting behind her desk, looking solemn. It was just like being back in London again. That depressing.

"Where are you both?" she asked.

"In a graveyard," Mordred replied. No point explaining. "Any news on the USB?"

"I hope your laptop battery's fully charged because it's complicated."

"We're good for a few hours," Alec said.

She nodded as if she'd asked the question rhetorically but never mind. "JMCB's looking to get out of private equity and into recruitment. ISIS is looking for people – willing fighters and submissive wives mainly – and it's willing to pay. There's a mass migration right now from various parts of Africa, but particularly the east, with Europe as its goal. Dimbleton's head of a consortium that picks migrants up *en route* at any one of the refugee camps between the Horn and Libya, and offers them safe passage. Once money's exchanged hands, they're loaded into metal containers and driven back to Somali or Eritrea. The containers are transferred to ships and transported through the Persian Gulf to Al Faw in southern Iraq, thence to Mosul and into the hands of the so-called Islamic State. The older and weaker victims are usually dead by this time. The males are then mostly killed, and the women auctioned off as 'wives'. The lorries are then loaded with oil and other sundries for the return journey. You can probably appreciate why it's such an attractive scheme from the perspective of the European far-right."

"It liquidises potential immigrants," Mordred said. "And Islamic State's going to lose anyway. Most of them are going to be killed. Anyone attached to them, even unwillingly, is likely to suffer the same fate. End of problem."

"Where's the oil going?" Alec asked.

"We've a list of recipients."

"Any arrests?" Mordred asked.

"Not yet." She took a deep breath and expelled it slowly. "That's the problem. All the details are on the USB pen, but we haven't been able to find a scrap of evidence on the ground yet. I'm assuming it's only a matter of time."

"I think Dimbleton may be in this country," Mordred said.

"What makes you say that?" she replied in a tone not wholly incredulous.

"I think Aisha's abduction is an act of revenge," he said.

She leaned back in her chair, looking at him through the computer screen. She put her finger on her chin. "It would fit his profile. Why would he have to be in this country, though?"

"He doesn't *have* to be. But you usually want to see your retribution being administered. Make a contribution."

"The best revenge he could take," she said, "would be to load her onto one of his people lorries. To do that, he'd have to get her out of the country, yes. But nothing valuable could be served by having to get himself out as well. He'd be better off just calmly awaiting her arrival in Mogadishu or Asmara or wherever. If he's here to administer retribution in person, it probably means she's already dead."

"John thinks she's not his main target," Alec said. "If that's right, it might be counterproductive to kill her."

"If he can persuade me she's still alive," Mordred added, "and that I've got a chance of rescuing her, he's got me hooked. Or so he probably thinks."

"Yes, I can see that," she replied. "It does make some sense. His men have been following Aisha. They probably saw you together at *Café Stilfuld*. He must have deduced that she has some personal significance for you."

"We're planning on going to look for him tonight," Mordred said. "Alec thinks if he's staying anywhere local, it'll be in the penthouse suite of a five star hotel. It may just be a question of showing his photo around."

"I'll send you our best picture. You can print it off at The Black Labrador. They've got the facilities and they won't stand over you while you work. John, this sounds like a hunch worth pursuing, but not for too long. You've got forty-eight hours then I want you to join the rest of the team."

"What's 'the rest of the team' doing?" Alec asked. "That includes me, I presume."

She ignored the question. "Alec, tomorrow morning, 9am sharp, I want you to report to my office. Bring the laptop back with you. I'm going to introduce you to the two new members of our team, Edna Watson and Ian Leonard. Then you're all going to fly to Djibouti - in between Eritrea and Somalia, so you can cast your investigative net whichever way you like. There, you'll rendezvous with Phyllis and Annabel and await instructions. Morocco was probably a waste of time. John, I want you to go to Manchester airport same time, Thursday morning. Amber will call you tomorrow with further details."

The question Mordred wanted to ask – *what about Gina?* – stuck on his tongue and wouldn't come out. The truth was, it wouldn't come out because it didn't need to. He knew what about Gina. As Alec logged off and shut the computer down, an almost bottomless wave of sadness hit him.

Chapter 25: In Sheffield

"We need to think about how we're going to work this," Alec said, as they walked back to The Black Labrador. "There's too much ground for us to cover alone – we're talking about Manchester, Sheffield, Stoke, Leeds maybe, Stockport."

"Don't forget Huddersfield," Mordred replied, "and Barnsley. Perhaps even Birmingham. Everywhere in between, of course. I notice she didn't mention Gina."

"She didn't promulgate the *never voice her name* decree. That's good news, isn't it? Stop obsessing about Gina, anyway. You've enough on your plate."

They switched to single file to take a short cut along a public footpath between two hedges. The sky was almost completely blue now: only a few little white clouds hurried along like they'd lost their mothers. Birds sang. Tall oat grass, now in the throes of dying back, waved gently in the breeze.

"I wonder what Edna Watson's like," Alec said.

"You mean, intelligent, nice personality?"

"And that. What were the chances of getting another Ian?" He laughed. "Listen to me: trying to make small talk, put you at your ease."

"I am at my ease. Why wouldn't I be?"

"What's the time?"

Mordred looked at his watch. "Two fifty-five."

"We need to get started as soon as we get back to the hotel. Working in the dark increases his advantage. We'll start with the biggest cities and work downwards, yes?"

"Sounds reasonable."

"East-west then north-south. I'll start with Manchester, you start with Sheffield."

"Have we got fake IDs?"

"In my suitcase. You're DI Jonas Eagleton, I believe."

"Him again."

"D.I.J.E. Could be worse. I'm DI Charles Kendrick. Someone in Ops and Docs clearly has something against me. I might take it up with Ruby Parker when I see her."

"How to broach it, that's the problem."

"I wonder how old Edna and Ian are."

They crossed the stile onto the pavement that ran along the main road. Two minutes later they were back in the hotel.

"I'll print off the photos," Alec said. "You go upstairs and fix us a hot drink."

Five minutes later, Alec arrived with his suitcase and two printed head and shoulders photos of Dimbleton. He drank the tea Mordred had made for him in a single draught and flicked the catches and rummaged. "Here's your ID," he said. "Keep your phone switched on at all times. I want you to take this too." He dug down beneath his neatly-folded clothes and pulled out a handgun.

"What's the hell's that?" Mordred said.

"What's it look like?"

"Does Ruby Parker know?"

"I didn't pack this case, John, any more than you packed yours. It's a Beretta 92, the most reliable semi-automatic on the planet, if you believe USCCA."

"What's 'USCCA'?"

"You don't have to know."

"I don't want a gun, thanks. It'll probably go off in my pocket and I'll end up shooting myself in the leg and severing a major artery, like that man in *Band of Brothers*."

"You've seen *Band of Brothers?*"

"Yep."

"Put the safety catch on, that's all. You must know that. Basic firearms training? Look, if Dimbleton *is* out there, and he's trying to lure you into a trap, you'll need something to give you the edge. If he's done his research properly, he'll know you're a complete wuss. He won't be expecting anything like this."

"It's loaded, I take it."

"No, it's just a water pistol. Of course it's bloody loaded, moron. What would be the point of giving you an empty gun?"

"To scare people."

"In my experience, you've usually got to fire at something to do that. Windows are good, so are chandeliers. The sound of clicking just doesn't cut it."

"Okay, okay. Just to please you."

"Gee, thanks. Here: five hundred pounds for taxi rides. We haven't much time so we need to move quickly. Public transport's out of the question, even for long distances. If you need more, get in touch and we'll meet up, but you probably won't until you decide to move to another town or city. Get something to eat too. And coffee, to keep you sharp."

Mordred nodded. Stuff he already knew, but Alec was enjoying himself, so why interrupt? No point bickering. Just keep nodding.

"Call me every hour on the hour?" Alec went on. "Understood?"

"Okay."

"Anything you want to ask?"

"Nope."

Alec picked up the phone on Mordred's bedside. "Hello, room service, could you order two taxis, please? One for Mr Michael Henderson in room five to go to Sheffield, one for Jim Daltroy in room nine for Manchester … Yes, right now, please."

Mordred hadn't been in Sheffield more than half an hour when he got the feeling of being watched. After ten minutes, he still couldn't see anyone who might be responsible. He forced it to the back of his mind so he could concentrate on the task in hand. According to Trivago, there weren't any five star hotels in Sheffield, only four stars. Twelve in total, but they all looked sufficiently classy for the likes of Terence Dimbleton. He located them on Google maps and plotted a route, some of which would undoubtedly involve more taxis.

He began with The Tharamel Sheffield on the city outskirts, then Waternaux Hall a mile further in. By the time he reached the Matlick Arms, a dispiriting pattern was beginning to emerge. As a lone individual armed solely with an ID card and a photo, 'DI Jonas Eagleton' just wasn't that convincing. Ideally, he should have a uniformed police officer or two with him.

5pm. Time to ring Alec. "How's it going?" he asked.

"Not well," Alec replied.

"Do receptionists keep looking at your ID card like it's clearly a fake?"

"I've never had this before. Mind you, last time I did it, I was with Phyllis."

"And that made a difference."

"With the accent and the attitude and the jewellery, I guess she came across as less of a hustler."

"Should we team up?"

"Let's stick with it for the time being. Maybe do another audit in an hour's time. It's my impression that they may be a little suspicious and a lot reluctant, but they are cooperating. After all, the ID speaks for itself, and they don't want to be charged with withholding information if things spin out of control later."

They hung up. At the next hotel, he was more forceful, more don't-you-realise-what's-at-stake-here, and got a much more considered, much quicker negative response. Things were looking up.

Why hadn't he mentioned to Alec that he thought he was being watched? Because he couldn't identify the source of the sensation, that's why. But it was getting stronger.

The Breneman Exner Hotel was next on the list, a modernist style building, mainly glass and white panels, with a decorative tower on the front. He strode into reception and showed his card, then the photo.

The receptionist, a woman in her twenties, looked at it for a moment and shook her head. "I've never seen him before," she said. "I'm really sorry."

"I have," said a woman's voice to his left. "And I can tell you who he is. His name's Terence Dimbleton."

Mordred had already turned to face her. She was about forty, slim and tall, in a trouser suit, a neat beehive, and party make-up. She looked like the kind of person who haunted casinos, not for the direct experience of gambling, but for the abstract curiosity value of seeing others win or lose heavily. There were trace elements of Belarusian in her accent.

"Stella Cassano," she said. "I take it you're with the police." She extended her hand slightly. He shook it.

"Detective Inspector Jonas Eagleton," he said.

"Is Terence in trouble again?" she asked. "Let's sit down for a moment."

They went to a pair of designer chairs opposite a low smoked glass table, out of earshot of the receptionist.

"What's he done this time?" she whispered.

Going by her face alone, she already knew who he really was. *Detective Inspector Jonas Eagleton* had landed like rain on a duck's back. She'd been sent by Dimbleton to reel him in. With serious consequences if she failed, knowing him. Still, no point in letting her know he was on to her.

"We believe he may be able to answer some of our questions regarding the disappearance of a teenage girl in the Peak District this morning," he replied.

"Good God. That would be a new low, even for him."

"We only want to question him. That's not necessarily an indicator of guilt."

"As a matter of fact, I happen to know where he is."

"Right now?"

"I wouldn't normally let on, but with something as important as this, I feel it's probably my duty."

"I'd be very grateful for any information at all, Ms Cassano."

"Stella. And it's 'Miss'."

Like a conversation from the 1930s. "So where is he?"

"My car's outside. I could give you a lift over there."

"I probably need to call for backup."

She looked horribly disappointed. "You've got to understand, Detective Inspector - "

"Eagleton. But please, call me Jonas."

"Thank you ... *Jonas*. I see you're not wearing a wedding ring."

"I'm single." He laughed. "And completely available."

"Sorry, I'm flirting."

"It's fine," Mordred replied. "I know you don't really mean it. It makes a nice change."

"You see, for all his faults, Terence is an old friend of mine. I'm willing to give up his whereabouts if you can avoid causing him any embarrassment. But I'm more reluctant to take a step that might end up permanently breaching our connection. His and mine, I mean, not yours and mine." She giggled. It suddenly struck him she was slightly drunk. "Apart from anything else, we're business associates as well as friends."

He smiled. "Who? You and me, or you and Terence?"

"Oh, you are awful. It's funny that we've only just met. I feel a real connection, like we were together in a previous life."

"In pre-Revolutionary France?"

"Maybe!"

"It's almost clocking-off time for me, actually, Stella. How about a spot of dinner?"

She suppressed a grimace. "How delightful. I'd love to. Where?"

"How about here?"

"H - here? Why here?"

"This *is* where you're staying, isn't it?

"Er, yes."

"I mean, you did appear at reception as if you meant to get your keys."

"Something like that. Of course."

"Obviously, I'd pay. I wouldn't expect you to foot the bill."

She nodded, as if she was re-programming. "Yes, dinner here. That would – we could definitely do that."

"We should begin with a few drinks in the bar. That would be nice."

She looked as if he'd thrown her a life-jacket. "Oh, yes! Drinks! That would be ideal!"

He felt sorry for her now. She was meant to trap him, and he'd turned the tables. She was already close to the limit, both alcohol and discretion-wise. She must have been quite scared beforehand. One or two more and she'd start seeing life from above: a series of choices, and there she went, poor whatever her name really was, making all the wrong ones, and, oh God, she had to do something about it while she could still see the truth. From his point of view, this was usually where it all became pretty sordid.

But he didn't do using people. He'd see she was all right afterwards. Poor Lyudmila. Always on the back foot, always far, far from home. Always tragic.

An hour and four drinks later, they'd exchanged two sentences in Belarusian without her noticing, and she was feeling his biceps. Alec was outside on a bench and he'd booked a room upstairs and sent a few documents to Mordred's phone. Her real name was Tatsiana Krecheuski, and she'd become known to the police first as a sex-worker on April 14 2006, then, a day later, as an illegal. Two weeks after that, she'd been deported and there was no record of her having re-entered the country.

"Would you like to come upstairs to my room?" he asked her.

"I – I don't understand. You're staying here too?"

"I booked it while you weren't looking. I may look like an ordinary DI, but I'm a man of means. I didn't think you'd want to go to yours."

"No, no, of course not," she said, obviously confused. "Lead the way. When are we going to eat, by the way?"

"I'll order food when we get up there. Do you mind if I ask a friend to join us?"

She looked like he'd torn a veil down. Now here she was again, nine years on and still plain Tatsiana K, prostitute. She welled up, then swallowed. "What do you mean?" she asked hoarsely. "'A friend'?"

"From Interpol," he replied. "We simply want to ask you some questions, Ms Krecheuski."

They went up to the second floor, and the room Alec had booked. She sat on the two-person sofa with her back to the window, while he closed the curtains. He made her some coffee and asked her to choose from the menu. He should never have begun this. What the hell was he expecting to get from her? That he'd be able to call the police in, and she'd lead them to Dimbleton? That was probably the very thing Dimbleton was hoping for. After all, no one could pin anything on him. He'd hardly be in the UK if he hadn't already ensured that. His army of lawyers would secure his release, and he'd leave the country. Aisha's body would turn up in a wheelie bin somewhere – Tatsiana's too, probably - and that would be that. Two murders whose sole rationale was the humiliation of John Mordred. A dish best served cold. They'd never see each other again.

He passed her the menu. "Choose anything you like," he said.

"This will probably be my last meal," she said with a tremble in her voice, "once Terence finds out I've talked to the police. So it might as well be a good one. I'll have the pan-fried scampi in freshly milled sour bread crumbs, please. With minted Jersey new potatoes and hand-trimmed Devonshire green beans."

A knock at the door. Alec. "I wasn't followed," he said, as Mordred let him in.

Tatsiana went into the bathroom. They heard her vomiting.

"What's the plan?" Alec asked.

"I haven't got one. Short of using her to get to Dimbleton and then torturing him till he coughs up Aisha's whereabouts. But that's no plan at all."

"He wouldn't necessarily find it unpleasant. He's probably into sadomasochism anyway."

"At the moment, I'm just worried for her." He indicated the bathroom.

"The prostitute."

"Tatsiana, yes." He passed him the menu. "We're having something to eat. Join us."

"I'll have the scampi and spuds," Alec said, after a glance. "So what's going to happen now? Given that neither of us has a plan?"

Mordred picked up the phone. He turned to Alec. "Two plates of scampi. Should that be 'two scampi' or 'two scampis'?"

"Who cares? Bloody hell, get a grip."

"Ah, hello. Room fourteen, yes. I'd like to order some food to eat in. Two scampi with potatoes and beans, and one vegetable lasagne. *Mange tout*, please. Plus a large bottle of mineral water."

He smiled, said "that's fine", and replaced the receiver. "Have *you* got a plan?" he asked Alec.

"Yes, but it's incredibly complex, so stop me if there's anything you don't understand. We get her to tell us where Dimbleton is, then send the police in to arrest him."

"They won't have enough evidence. He'll be out within a day."

"We've got reason to believe he's connected to ISIS. Under the Terrorism Act 2006, he can be held for fourteen days without charge. If we fly to Djibouti tomorrow, you as well, we can get the evidence, I'm sure of it."

"I don't share your optimism."

"Well, that's a subjective fact about you. Or has it any basis in reason or fact?"

"I'm pretty sure from Ruby Parker's tone of voice on the videocom that she doesn't believe it either."

"And ...?"

"I don't believe that what the USB pen says is happening is what's really happening. Women for oil? There must be quite a lot of surplus women in ISIS territory right now, given how heavily they're losing fighters. Fifteen hundred wiped out in Kobani, nine thousand in coalition airstrikes, that's about a fifth of their army. They're falling apart. They don't need more mouths to feed."

"No but they do need slaves. And they've developed a taste for sex slaves."

"Even so."

"Come on, John. They've got lots of oil and hardly anywhere to get rid of it. They'll probably trade it for anything at all right now. And outside-world contacts like Dimbleton can be useful to them. Even if they're giving him more than they're getting back, in the longer term, the whole thing might be worth it. It's about networking. Show the customer a good time – or better still compromise him - and he'll come back. That's what these guys are about: extortion. It's the main way they make their money."

"I can't see how it might work. In detail, I mean."

"You've lost me then."

"You herd these men and women up into a container in, say, northern Sudan. You then drive them three thousand kilometres to the Somalian coast and load that container onto a boat. You then sail them up the Persian Gulf into Iraq – about two thousand nautical miles; ten days or thereabouts - then drive them another thousand kilometres to Mosul. We're looking at nearly *five thousand miles* all in. What do they eat and drink? How do they cope with the heat inside the containers? And the freezing cold at night? Where do they go to the toilet? They'd all be dead on arrival. Every last one of them."

Alec looked at him. He seemed about to say something then didn't. "You're right," he said at last. "It's just not possible."

The bathroom door flew open, and Tatsiana ran out, her hair flying. "I've got to get out of here!" she said in Belarusian. "I've got to get away! He's going to kill me!"

Mordred stood in front of her and spoke to her in her own language. "We can help you. If you run away now, we won't be able to do anything to stop him. He'll probably find you if he's not behind bars. We can protect you."

She put both hands on the dresser and took deep breaths. "What - what can you offer me?"

"We'll hold onto him once we've got him and put you on Match.com. You're beautiful and intelligent. You need a new life. That might get you one."

"I'm not here legally."

"We're secret agents, we're not policemen. We can accommodate that."

"I don't actually know what language you're speaking," Alec said, "But did I just hear you mention *Match.com?*"

"I'm trying to think on my feet. I don't want to promise anything we can't deliver."

A knock at the door. Alec expelled one of his trademark *another of your barmy schemes* sigh, and went to get it. "I'll eat while you talk to her," he said. "I'm bloody starving."

He opened the door. It flew at him with force and knocked him sideways. In what seemed like a single lightning movement, two men entered the room. One overcame Alec's ineffective attempt to compensate for what had happened, crashing through his defences with a truncheon to the head; the other discharged a pistol fitted with a silencer, and hit Tatsiana in the heart.

"Close the door," Dimbleton said calmly.

Farole dragged Alec's prone body to the centre of the room and, in no particular hurry, obeyed.

Chapter 26: Leaving On a Jet Plane

Just in case Tatsiana wasn't dead, Dimbleton crossed the room and fired two more bullets into her chest. He sat down on the sofa. Farole searched Mordred, removed the Beretta from his pocket, then hauled Alec onto the bed. He began to remove Tatsiana's clothes. When she was naked, he put her clothes inside a black waste bag. He checked Alec's pulse and nodded. Still alive.

"This is my own hotel, Mr Mordred," Dimbleton said. "One of several in this part of the world. As soon as your friend booked this room, an hour or so ago, I installed cameras and microphones."

For a few seconds, none of the three said anything. Mordred wasn't interested in the technical details. The cleverness of cameras and microphones eluded him to the point where he'd no sooner heard the sentence than he forgot it.

"I understand you wanting to make an entrance," he said, "but was it really necessary to kill Tatsiana?"

"The prostitute?" He laughed. "Oh, my, you're one of those godforsaken milksops who tries to find out their names with a view to treating them like 'human beings'. *Tat-see-arn-ah, you poor fallen angel, I don't want sex. No, no, I just want us to talk, to make a* connection."

"It's probably not as bad as murder."

"There was nothing lascivious about what I did. Simple business, that's all."

"We're going to find it difficult to communicate if you can't stop talking in clichés."

"I'm serious. I'd like to keep the police busy for as long as possible. Obviously, they'll work out your friend Cunningham didn't do it in the end, but it never hurts to buy a little time. I own exactly seven hotels within a twenty miles radius of Peak Cavern. I was wondering which of them you'd turn up at first. When my contacts told me you were in Sheffield, I rushed over."

"Where's Aisha?"

"You'll find out soon enough." On the far side of the room, Farole took the pistol and placed it in Alec's hand. "In fact, you'll know within the hour if we hurry."

"How did you find out we were in the Peak District?"

"I'm lucky enough to own a helicopter, and I'm qualified to fly both it and any one of my private jets. I go all over the country on business and, being a rich and generous individual, I have plenty of contacts in the aviation world. Once I knew that's how you'd left London, I just did a little ringing around. A helicopter's a big thing, Mr Mordred. It's not as easy to hide as you obviously thought. After I'd got to the bottom of that, all I had to do was enquire of hotels and guest houses. I've many connections there too. And, believe it or not, in the police. It wasn't difficult."

"What happens now?"

"We're going to kill you, obviously. But not right away. That would be too easy."

Mordred smiled. "In books, that usually means I'm going to get away."

"We're not *in* a book, though, Mr Mordred, are we? Just as helicopters turn out not to be as easy to manipulate as you wanted to imagine, so with real life. But keep telling yourself that if you want to. It may come as some comfort when you're burning to death in a metal cage. We're going to put it on Youtube, by the way, so all your friends and family can share the enjoyment."

"Well, that's nice. Thanks."

Farole handed the Beretta to Dimbleton. He took out a pair of handcuffs and gestured for Mordred to present his wrists. Mordred obliged.

"Well done, by the way," Dimbleton went on, "for working out that the little women-for-oil thing was a ruse. It wasn't meant for you to find. It was the story we told our rightist allies. It helps to have friends in politics. Obviously, we'd rather you hadn't found it, but no harm done in the long run. If you'd found it a little earlier, things might have been different."

"So what's the truth?"

"I'd like that to be a surprise. You see, I know you're not going to escape, but clearly, I'd like to stop you trying. Now you're *not* going to try – not properly - until you know what's really happening. So it only makes sense for me to tell you when you're inside the cage and soaked in petrol. Doesn't it?"

"Yeah, I suppose so. What about Aisha? You can let her go now, can't you? That would be the honourable thing to do. I could respect you then. Even while you're burning me to death."

"Your unbridled 'respect', what a moving offer. Unfortunately, she's coming with us. Here's teaser to keep you guessing. Although I'm not selling women to ISIS, I am selling them something. And a few of them know Aisha Sharif – 'Sufi Seven', as she used to call herself - of old. They're looking forward to meeting her – the British contingent especially - as much as, if not more than, they're looking forward to meeting you. Anyway, let's move on. What's going to happen now is that you and Farole are going to accompany me down the corridor, and we're going to leave the hotel via the back entrance. We're going to get into my car, where I'll give you a little something to make you sleep. When you wake up, you'll see 'Sufi Seven'. Don't worry, she's quite unharmed. I promised to deliver her in pristine condition, and I tend to keep my word. Good business."

Farole hauled him to his feet. He didn't resist. Dimbleton cleared the room of cameras and microphones, putting them in the same bag as Tatsiana's clothes. Then they went to Dimbleton's car. Mordred felt something sharp enter his arm and his world dissolved.

When he woke up, he was strapped to a padded seat. It took him a moment to realise he was in the well-lit passenger compartment of a luxury plane, in flight. His original handcuffs had been replaced by rigid bar cuffs. A pair of leg irons bit into his ankles. In front, there were two seats facing away, one occupied by Musa

Farole, apparently asleep. To his left, a window and outside, darkness; to his right, Aisha Sharif, similarly manacled.

"Hello, John," she said in a croak. She cleared her throat. "Hello, John."

He smiled. "Nice to see you again."

"Don't worry, I've got a plan," she whispered.

Keep her positive. Without seeming patronising. "What is it?"

"Remember, how I converted to ISIS before I ran away?" she said loudly, and nudged him. "Well, I'm still convinced they're right and we can set up a new caliphate. And I'm so glad I persuaded you of that too. We can fight the infidels together now."

He nudged her back. "Death to all *kafirs!*"

She nodded. "I'm still frightened," she whispered.

"Don't worry, I can be very persuasive."

"What if they ask me to behead someone, to prove my sincerity?"

"Try not to think of that."

She wiped her eyes with both cuffed hands. "I can't help thinking about my parents as well. They're going to be so sad."

"Try to think about nice things. Where did you go on holiday last year?"

She had to think for a moment. "The Cairngorms."

"I guess you're probably into walking and climbing."

"My mum and dad are. I don't mind it. Going downhill's best."

He laughed. "Did you climb Ben Macdui?"

"The bottom bit, yes. We got bitten to pieces by midges so we gave up. We were going to try again next year, but with special protective gear. Helmets with glass in the front, my dad said."

"I didn't know you could buy anything like that."

"That's what I thought. Then I had an idea: you could make them and present them on *Dragons' Den*."

"My dad was on *Dragons' Den*."

"You're joking."

"No, honestly. Hawking a meditation clock, 'T.M.'"

"I remember that one. That was *your dad?* I don't believe you."

"How much do you want to bet?"

"Really? It was *your dad?*"

"Why would I lie? If I wanted to make something up, I'd say it was Roots Reggae Sauce or The Magic Whiteboard. Make myself look good with a major success story."

"You'd pretend your dad was Levi Roots? Do you think I'd believe that?"

"Maybe not."

"Besides, it's Roots Reggae *Reggae* Sauce, not 'Roots Reggae Sauce'."

"I had no idea I was speaking to an expert."

She didn't say anything. He turned to her. She was facing straight ahead, trembling and gasping. "Oh, God. We're going to die. We're both going to die. Allah, please. What are we doing? Why are we sitting here talking about *Dragons' Den*? We're going to die!"

"Try and think about your plan."

"I can't! It's stupid!"

He moved both hands across and took hers. He'd never seen anything quite like this before. She looked like she was literally going to have a fit. Her eyes bulged. She whimpered then cried. The noise was enough to rouse Musa Farole. He rose languidly, picked something up and came over. He grabbed her face, rapidly thrust whatever it was into her mouth and held her jaws shut till she'd swallowed it. A minute later, she was asleep.

In all the time he was force-feeding her, Musa Farole didn't look across once. Even so, Mordred couldn't help noticing something odd in his expression.

Compassion.

Which raised the question of why he hadn't beaten Mordred up yet. If anyone might feel justified in seeking vengeance, it was him. He'd suffered all the physical injuries: he was still limping, for God's sake.

Then it became obvious. Because he didn't want to upset Aisha. Maybe he imagined he was in love with her, or perhaps he had children of his own.

Either way, it could be useful.

Mordred estimated they were in the air about seven hours. He'd woken up *en route*, so flight-time was anything plus that. The sun rose orange above the clouds. Next to him, Aisha slept with her head forward and a string of dribble coming from her mouth. As the plane circled to descend, it became clear they were somewhere very hot – the design of the buildings and the spread and type of foliage, the distant sea and the direction of the sun suggested the eastern shores of Africa. Given what he already knew, likely Eritrea, Djibouti or Somalia.

He hadn't come close to sleeping and he didn't feel tired now. He was completely responsible for Aisha now. Whatever happened to her next would be *his fault*. That meant he had to think fast – but he couldn't. Just her 'plan', that was all they had, and even she saw it didn't stand a chance. Apart from anything else, Dimbleton had known for a long time exactly whose side she was on, and he'd hardly be bringing her here if anyone was prepared to overlook that. No, their only chance lay in Musa Farole.

There were almost certainly cameras and microphones hidden in here, but it was a risk he had to take. Besides, even if they were switched on, Dimbleton probably wasn't listening – he was probably in the cockpit concentrating on landing. Even if he *was* listening, the devices might not be sensitive enough to pick up a whisper.

"Ustaaz Farole," he called, and went on in Arabic: "please could I speak to you? I need to say something urgently."

Farole stirred and looked at Mordred incredulously, as if he couldn't believe he was hearing his own language from an Englishman. He stood up and sauntered over. "Was that … Arabic?"

"Obviously, I know I'm in no position to bargain, but before I die, I'd just like to apologise for what I did to you in London. I'm sorry."

Farole looked at him with his head on one side as if he'd never seen anything so strange. A talking chimpanzee.

"My fate's sealed now," Mordred went on, "but the girl – Aisha, she's called - still stands a chance. Dimbleton's planning to hand her over to ISIS. You're the only one who can save her. Put her in a burkha or something and help her to safety. *Please*."

"Amazing." He laughed. "Incredible!" He gave Mordred a friendly slap on the shoulder. "Beyond belief."

"Her parents will reward you," Mordred whispered. "Her father's a minister in the British government. You can hold her hostage. They'll pay whatever you ask, believe me. You don't even have to take her to England. It can all be done from over here. Get rid of Dimbleton and you can become rich. Don't you see? She's your ticket to a better life."

Farole slapped him hard across the face. What he'd expected, so he wasn't fazed.

"I can help you get rid of Dimbleton," he went on. "Even with the manacles on. Take Aisha, leave me behind and put a gun within my reach. By the time I get to it, you can be long gone. I'll hold Dimbleton up for you."

Farole laughed. "What is wrong with you? You're supposed to look good for the video, but if you carry on like this, I'm going to end up making you unrecognisable. Don't make me. Shut your face now, and keep it that way."

He turned his attention from Mordred to Aisha. He spat something large onto the palm of his hand, grabbed her face again and put the chewed blob into her mouth. He pushed it to the back of her throat and held her lips closed and pinched her nose. She swallowed.

"What's that?" Mordred asked.

"Khat." He smiled. "It'll wake her up, but she won't be worried any more."

"You're lucky she didn't suffocate."

He laughed. "Wait till you see what Mr Dimbleton's got in store for her before you call that 'lucky'."

He went back to his seat. The plane banked and levelled and came in to land. There was a gentle bump as its tyres hit the ground. Aisha woke up.

"Hello, John," she said. She looked around and seemed to remember. She shuddered and sighed. "We're still here then."

"I need to ask you something. Did you get a chance to talk to Musa Farole before I appeared?"

"Who's 'Musa Farole'?"

"The man over there."

"You mean, begging him for mercy and crying and that sort of thing? A bit. Why?"

He lowered his voice as far he could. "I told him your parents might be prepared to pay a ransom. I need you to confirm that. I think he's weakening."

"What about you?"

"It's going to be very difficult to think of a reason for letting us both go. Apart from anything else, it's going to be much easier to smuggle a fourteen year-old girl out of the country than her plus a six foot tall man."

"I don't want to go if you can't. I'll feel guilty for the rest of my life."

"I'm not saying I won't escape. Obviously, I will. And I'll succeed. We've got to do it separately, that's all."

"You don't understand."

He waited for her to elucidate. He had the feeling no amount of gainsaying was going to get him anywhere right now.

She let out a stream of air. "You probably thought I was in love with you at one time. I guess everyone did. Remember when we were in that café and I nearly cried and then I said something lame like, 'I thought I'd never see you again'. I bet you thought I had a crush on you then, didn't you?"

"If I *had* thought that, I'd have been flattered. Obviously, there's the gargantuan age difference - "

"Do you want to know the reason I like you so much? Truthfully? Because you remind me of Sebastian. You don't *look* like him, but you're like him inside, I think."

"I'm doubly flattered. And I'm not just saying that."

"Do you know what the last thing he said to me was? 'We can't get away together. We have to separate. Then we'll be okay.' And I believed him. The truth was, he sacrificed himself for me."

"I see."

"Have you ever thought of killing yourself? Because I have. I think about it all the time now. Part of me thinks it'll actually be quite good to meet all those crummy ISIS women. At least I can tell them to their faces what losers they are."

"We won't separate then. Your call."

"I really *am* a Sufi, you know. It's not just a name I made up for myself. My mum's an actual Bektashi. We have monthly meetings in our house upstairs. We all get round and chant 'Allah'. Like that: Al-Lah, Al-Lah. Men and women, Shi'a and Sunni, Christian, Jew, Hindu, old, young, it doesn't matter."

"We'll stay together."

"Do you believe in life after death?"

"Yes."

"Really? Or are you just saying that?"

"Obviously I don't know for certain, but I think it's more likely than not."

"I'll introduce you to Sebastian then. Torture's just a bridge we've got to cross. This time next week, we'll all be in *Firdaws*."

The khat was obviously doing its job. But it wasn't just the drug talking. He regretted talking to Farole now. God willing, they'd stay together.

The plane was stationary. Outside, he could see a van approaching, small and squat. The aircraft door opened and a set of metal steps unfolded to the ground.

Farole stood up and leaned over him. "I want you to accompany me outside," he said. "Are you going to come nicely, or do I have to punch you unconscious?"

"The former, please," Mordred replied.

The Somalian undid Mordred's harness and pulled him to his feet. The leg irons were sufficiently restrictive to make walking almost impossible. In the end, Farole picked him up and slung him over his shoulder. At the top of the steps the heat rushed hard against their faces.

On the runway, in the back of the van, Dimbleton was waiting for them on his haunches. "Enjoy the flight?" he asked, as Farole dumped his charge like a bundle of logs.

Not my most uplifting experience or *I was gripped throughout?* No point in making a joke of it, though. Dimbleton had won, and there was no getting past the fact. A moment later, Aisha landed in a rough heap next to him. The rear doors slammed, Farole assumed the driver's seat, and they drove off at speed, the engine roaring infirmly.

"The good thing is," Dimbleton said cheerfully, "it should all be over in a few hours. Nothing lasts for ever, as they say. Sometimes that's a bad thing. In this instance, from both your points of view, it's going to be a positive blessing. Now, first we have to put you somewhere while I go and pick up my money. We've got a small lock-up garage in the town centre. That's where you'll be staying for an hour or so, and sadly, it'll almost certainly be the last time you see me. When the door opens again, you'll be face to face with the people who've paid for your flight over and all the hospitality. Be nice to them, please. For my sake."

He didn't speak again. Twenty minutes later, the car stopped. Farole got out, and a door scraped open, metal on concrete, somewhere nearby. He got back in, reversed and stopped. Dimbleton opened the rear doors of the van from within, and Farole came round to help unload. The two passengers were hauled roughly out and landed on the floor of a corrugated building just bigger on all sides than the car itself. Farole resumed the driver's seat and the car exited.

In no particular hurry, Dimbleton closed the door from outside. Complete stifling darkness. The sound of a padlock being attached.

"Are you okay?" he asked.

"I'm scared again," Aisha replied.

He edged over awkwardly and took her hand. "Don't be," he said. "Listen, Aisha, this may be it, so I want you to do *exactly as I say*. We're both going to make a really big effort to keep what's going to happen next out of our minds. If we can do that, we won't go mad, and there's still hope, because where there's life there's always hope. I'm going to talk to you about school, and I want you to ask me about work. If I ask you a question, you've got to think about the answer and *nothing else*, then you've got to say that answer as calmly as you can. And then you've got to ask me a question, and when I'm answering, you've got to *listen really intently*. Block everything else out. It won't be easy, but it is possible. There are two of us, so we can do it. No one-word answers allowed, understand?"

"O – okay."

"Good. Are you ready?"

"Yes."

"Tell me anything you can remember about your first day at school in Year Seven."

For a moment, he thought she wasn't going to answer, then she said, "We were made to write about what we'd done in the summer holidays. I'd been to Tuscany, to this villa that belonged to a work friend of my dad's. It was painted cream and it had a balcony."

Silence.

"That's good," he said softly. "Now you've got to ask me a question."

"What's – er, what do you usually eat for lunch at work, and why?"

They carried on for about fifteen minutes, but it became clear her concentration was flagging. Maybe it was the unbearable heat. Her voice began to tremble and she kept stopping mid-sentence to swallow. His answers became longer to compensate, and he tried to test her on what he'd just said, but he could see he was fighting a losing battle.

Eventually, they heard the sound of a key in the padlock. Neither of them said anything. She squeezed his hand and puled.

The door didn't open all the way. When the gap was about a foot broad, a man squeezed in and came over to them. After the complete darkness, even this little bit of light was blinding, so whoever he was, he was even less identifiable than a silhouette. He dropped something beside them. Mordred felt a key thrust into his handcuffs, then release.

"Get up, both of you," the man said. "Put these on. There isn't any time to lose."

Musa Farole.

Chapter 27: Hideout

Somewhere between losing Dimbleton and coming here, Farole had undergone a complete change of clothing. He wore a long white *khamis*, a turban and sandals. Once he'd unbound Mordred and Aisha he helped them quickly into the garments he'd brought them: two loose-fit dark-green *jilbabs*, and headscarves. Women's clothes. And two pairs of sunglasses.

"Follow me at three paces when we get outside," he said. "But keep your heads down. Don't speak, and don't look around. It's just round the corner."

What is? didn't seem worth asking. So long as it wasn't ISIS – which seemed somehow very unlikely now - it could happily be anything at all.

They left the garage. Farole replaced the padlock and set off at a brisk pace without looking back to see they were there. Brilliant sunshine, grey and pastel shopfronts, a wide, sandy road with lots of litter, overhead telegraph wires in all directions, the smell of the sea. Lots of young men, a bounce in their stride, some with weapons slung across their backs. An RPG? That couldn't be normal, even here.

Then it hit him anew. Even *where?* Where were they?

After about a hundred yards, Farole ducked into an abandoned side road with tall buildings either side. They followed as fast as possible while trying not to look panicked. A jeep raced round the corner from the opposite end, driven by a thin black man in a khaki peaked cap and combat gear, and stopped abruptly beside them. Farole lifted the passenger seat to let them in then swung it back and got in front. He pulled the door shut, rammed a large pair of mirrored sunglasses on his face and they took off.

Mordred expected them to drive to the town limits then gradually accelerate across the desert, or a wasteland, or through a jungle, until they were somewhere far from Dimbleton. Instead, they drove round several blocks and across three main roads, never exceeding twenty miles per hour, and never looking like leaving wherever it was. When they finally stopped, in a grim-looking side-street, they were in front of a tall grey building that, for all Mordred knew, could be the same one from which the jeep had picked them up.

Farole got out and gestured for them to follow him. They all went inside the building via a badly-fitting metal fire door and climbed three flights of moulded concrete steps.

Whatever was happening, their chances of surviving had increased exponentially. Even though, paradoxically … he had no idea what was going on. Freeing Aisha to get a ransom made sense. But if that was your plan, you'd best leave her would-be protector out of it. Maybe they thought they could get a deal for him too. But then why remove his handcuffs? The leg-irons, yes, he could understand that, because of speed. Bloody hell, as far as he could tell, Farole didn't even have a gun. God, Allah, whatever *is* going on, please let it be good. It looked it. Relatively.

When there were no more stairs to go, Farole turned right onto a broad, grimy looking corridor strewn with rubbish. They walked three doors along and he turned and held up his palm to bid them stop. He knocked. The door opened immediately, and he stood aside to usher them in.

Inside, there were three or four chairs, a pile of guns of different types against a wall, and an old-fashioned dresser that looked French or Italian. On a single bed on the far side of the room lay a fat man of about forty in a plain blue T-shirt, shorts and bare feet. He looked at them and waved listlessly, without smiling. The woman who had apparently let them in looked at Mordred in the same way Farole had on the plane – as if here, at last, was something new under the sun – and went to stand at a table in the centre of the room, where two young men stood anxiously discussing a map and a laptop in low tones. All three wore battle fatigues. Suddenly, everyone stopped talking, and turned to Aisha with portentous expressions whose precise significance Mordred couldn't decipher. Maybe a hostage demand *was* on the cards, after all. Perhaps he was to be the middleman: the only English-Arabic speaker. Of course. That was it.

Farole went to the dresser, took out two cups and filled them with orange juice. He gave them to the newcomers. "Welcome to Eritrea," he said.

Aisha took Mordred's hand. "Have we been rescued?"

"Maybe," he said.

She drank her orange. "Thank you everyone," she said loudly. "Not just for the juice, obviously. For saving our lives, if that's what you've done."

Everyone continued looking opaquely at her. Farole translated her words into Arabic. The three people at the table nodded an acknowledgement without smiling. The one on the bed grinned. "Come and sit on the bed with me, honey," he said in a Miami accent.

"You're American?" she said. She forgot about Mordred and went to sit with him as if there was no risk whatsoever he might be a paedophile.

"Reginald's my name. You must be Aisha."

Mordred came and sat next to her. Might as well be aggressively positive. Shows you can be aggressive. "I'd like to add my thanks for saving our lives. I'm John."

"Hey, loser, we only brought *you* here so we could shoot you dead!" Farole said, in English. "... Which is what's called a 'joke'," he added, when Mordred tensed. He extended his hand. "I work for the *Servizio per le Informazioni e la Sicurezza Militare,* the Italian Secret Service. It took me quite a long time to get close to Dimbleton, and before your little visit to One Canada, he was looking to fire me. Thanks to you, he didn't. I know I picked up a limp, but assuming I survive what's coming, I expect to be promoted, so don't be too hard on yourself."

Mordred shook his hand. "You've no idea how relieved I feel right now."

"I'm Reginald Kondylis, CIA," the fat man said. "Welcome to my lair. The three guys at the table are Saudi secret service officers."

"Excuse me," Aisha said, "I'm really sorry about this, but I need the toilet or I'm going to burst."

"Through there, honey," Reginald said.

"What's going on?" Mordred asked, when she'd gone.

"That's what we're just about to figure out," Farole said. "You're in the southernmost port of Eritrea, almost on the border with Djibouti. From what we've been able to ascertain, lots of armed men have arrived here from the south and the west of the continent over the past two weeks or so. By 'lots': thousands. The town's in lockdown now, so no one's getting in or leaving, with the obvious exception of known quantities like Dimbleton. We've lost all phone and internet connections, so we're completely shut off from the outside world. Something mega's about to happen. But … we've no idea what. Our best guess is an invasion of Djibouti, create a new state of some kind. We've got – we *had* – intelligence that a similar gathering of fighters is happening in northern Somalia."

"We uncovered a truckload of information in Britain," Mordred said. "The world's biggest red herring. It detailed a plot to transport African refugees up the Persian Gulf into Iraq."

"So I heard," Farole said. "I was listening to you on the hotel microphones. What you don't know – and I couldn't get away to tell you - is that there may be more to that information than meets the eye. And we're about to find out what it is." He took a little blue stick from his *khamis* and held it up. "Recognise this?"

Mordred examined it. A portable flash drive. Blue, plastic casing with a little 'S.C.' etched into the side. How the hell - ?

Farole smiled. "I was assigned to watch her while you were in the Peaks. You might recall, the first day there, she went out on a search with her mum and her friends. Well, she found it then, but she didn't tell anyone. She took it away from where it was hidden, and my guess is that when she got back to the hotel, she transferred the information to another one. The next day, she planted the replica then 'found' it. I guess the original had - has - sentimental value. Since the information was the important thing, not the physical artefact, she doesn't think she's hurt anyone. She sewed the genuine article into the lining of her top so she wouldn't lose it."

Reginald smiled. "She's taking quite a long time on the toilet. Maybe realised her lucky rabbit's foot's gone missing."

"What use is it going to be?" Mordred asked. "Either she's wiped it clean, or she's copied it. Either way, we're left at best with a fictitious plot about shipping African refugees into Iraq."

Aisha returned looking pale and animated. She went straight to Mordred. "We – I – um - "

"It's okay," he told her. "I know what you're looking for. Musa Farole just needs to borrow it for a while."

She seemed torn between indignation and embarrassment. "I'll get it back, won't I? Sorry for keeping it, but - "

"Both of you get some sleep now," Farole interrupted. "You're going to need it. And that's not a request."

There were two adjacent cots in the adjoining room, each with a thin mattress that smelt of diesel. The floor, walls and ceiling were the same even shade of pale grey and a pair of boards stood at a single window, blocking the light and some of the heat. In one corner stood a half-filled black rubbish bag. Outside, the sound of vehicles and men calling to each other. Right now, they could have been twelfth century Mongols for all Mordred cared. Farole had been right: he was dead beat.

Aisha went straight to the bed on the far side of the room and lay down. "We're going to be okay now, John. I can feel it."

"I hope so."

"You're definitely going to get us out of this."

She adjusted herself on the bed. She didn't actually bid him good night, but the finality of her cheerful sigh did the same job.

It hit him again: she was his responsibility. She was fourteen, that's all. The death of a child trumped the death of an adult, didn't it? That meant if he had to kill someone to get her out of here, he couldn't hesitate. No qualms, no moral prevarication. Not like the usual him. Just shoot and go. Keep her with him, yes. Shield her in whatever way necessary. Don't flinch.

It was a long time since he'd known for certain he'd have to kill someone. Four years ago, his trainer advised him to prepare himself mentally beforehand, because he obviously wasn't one of those who could do it 'cold'. Later, he'd discovered the *Bhagavad Gita. Bhishma, Drona, Jayadratha, Karna, and many others are already slain. Kill those whom I have killed. Do not hesitate. Fight in this battle and you will conquer your enemies.* He heard Aisha snore. A few minutes later, he fell into a light sleep that would allow him to spring up at a moment's notice.

He awoke because someone entered the room. He had no idea how much time had passed, but he sat up.

Musa Farole. "We've cracked it," he said.

"What do you mean?"

"Come outside and I'll tell you."

"I want to hear," Aisha said from the other side of the room. She raised herself and stood up.

They went together into the room they'd come from. The two men and the woman were still standing at the map. They were talking more excitedly than last time, but with a kind of scarcely concealed dejection. Farole gestured for Aisha and Mordred to sit down on the bed alongside Reginald. He poured them two more cups of orange and pulled up a chair.

"It's like this," he said. "There's an encrypted level below the cock-and-bull story about ferrying women slaves from the Sudan to ISIS. The words of the story itself – exactly as they appear on the flash drive – contain the key to revealing and decoding it."

"And?" Mordred said.

"The guys outside wandering the streets of this town are a mixture of Eritrean military, Al-Shabbab and assorted *jihadis* from the East: including Boko Haram and AQIM."

"I thought Al-Shabbab had been virtually wiped out by the Somali government," Mordred said.

"That's what they want you to think."

"So what are they doing here? Preparing to engulf Djibouti in a pincer?"

"Far from it. Preparing for an invasion of Yemen. They've switched their allegiance from al-Qaeda to ISIS. The aim is to link up with Sunni *jihadis* in south Yemen on the pretext of crushing the Shi'a Houthis in the north, then, once that's done, carry on into Saudi Arabia. Meanwhile ISIS has agreed a temporary ceasefire with Assad in Syria; it's rushing troops down into southern Iraq. The idea is that both factions penetrate the Saudi border together, these guys from the south, the rest from the north."

"They're unlikely to succeed, though, aren't they?" Mordred said. "The Saudis may be relatively few in number, but they're well armed. Britain and America have seen to that."

"Except that not everyone in Saudi Arabia's a patriot in the western sense of the term."

"What do you mean?" Aisha asked.

Farole turned to her. "There's a significant bloc, within Saudi Arabia itself, who believes the House of Saud has departed from the path of Ibn Abd al-Wahhab, the fanatical eighteenth century preacher whose teachings form the foundation of their way of life. 'Departed' by introducing limited rights for women and not doing enough to discourage foreign influence. We've got all their names. Some of them are senior figures within the administration. Together, they're capable of short-circuiting any attempt to repel a two-pronged invasion."

"And once ISIS gets its hands on the Saudi oilfields," Mordred said, "not to mention the Saudi arsenal, it'll consider itself invincible."

"Next stop Damascus," Farole agreed, "so the prophet Isa can descend on Mount Afeeq with his hands resting on the shoulders of two angels and destroy the Al-Masih ad-Dajjal at the Gates of Lud – or whatever it is they keep saying's going to happen. Then Tehran, kill off all the Shi'as. Then Israel, then… well, anywhere you like."

"So how are we going to stop them?" Aisha asked.

"'We' are not going to do anything," Farole replied. "I'm going to shave your head and fix you some different clothes to make you look like a boy, and you're going to stay here and drink the rest of that orange juice."

"On my own? I don't think I can do that. I seriously don't. I'll freak out, big time. I'm sorry, but I will." She grabbed Mordred's arm. "Don't let them."

"I think what Aisha means," he said, "is, how is *anyone* going to stop them? I assume you and I and Reginald and those guys at the table have a role to play?"

"*I* want to play a role," Aisha persisted, bobbing up and down with a pained expression as if she was desperate for the toilet again.

Farole ignored her. He handed Mordred a card. *Julian Etchingham*, JMCB London, and a photograph of someone about Mordred's age. "Something's interfering with the internet and phone access," he said. "If we can take that interference out and resume normal service, we can alert the US forces at Camp Lemonnier in Djibouti. That would give us access to four thousand service personnel and thence Saudi and US airpower."

"Who's 'Julian Etchingham'?"

"He was in charge of JMCB's interest here until Dimbleton arrived. We got hold of his card after he 'dropped' it during a visit to a rent boy."

"Does he know he's lost it?"

"He hasn't lost it. The boy returned it. After we bought it and took a copy."

"So Etchingham's still at large."

"But in such a big town, there can be more than one of him. Remember, he can't ring ahead to let anyone know he's coming."

"What's JMCB's interest in this anyway?"

"Way back in the early last century, King Abdul-Aziz bin Saud reconquered the Arabian peninsula with a fanatical Muslim army called the *Ikhwan*. After a while, he thought better of the association and despatched them. Then he invited the US to share his oil wealth. From terrorism to respectable trade within a generation. Moral of the story? Get in early. ISIS won't last for ever, but its descendant might, and its descendant's friends – JMCB included - probably will."

"Do you know where Etchingham is now?"

"No."

"Presumably, I'm going to pretend to be him. And the real McCoy could turn up at any time when I'm doing the impersonation. To what end?"

"To restore internet and phone access by destroying the thing that's interfering with them."

"Do we know what that is?"

"We're pretty sure it's in the engine room of the Majestic James Cook, one of six 400 metre container ships, currently awaiting sailing orders, a mile out at sea."

"So I'm to travel over there and do what? Plant a bomb?"

Farole shrugged. "Bombs are what we've got lots of and do best. Unless you've a better idea."

"Typical men," Aisha said. "Always blowing things up. *I've* got a better idea. How about we just switch off the disabler? You know, like take the plug out of the socket? I could go with John, we could locate find out where its wires are and I could sneak in, and even cut them if need be. I mean, there must *be* wires. You can't have a wire-less wireless system. It would eat its own tail."

"That's what I've always said," Mordred told her.

"So I can come along?" she said.

"I didn't say that."

"Make your mind up," she replied tetchily.

"I have."

"Well, so have I!"

Reginald put his palms up. "Hey, hey, *hey!* Be nice to each other!"

"Look, John," Farole said, "Aisha may have a point. I'm not saying her plan's any good or anything, but maybe we can use her. You think there are no children in Aden or Sana'a or Riyadh? You think they're all going to come off well if we fail? Thousands of lives may be at stake here. We can't afford to be precious about the so-called 'rights of the child'."

"Hear, hear," Aisha said sullenly. "For your information, though, I'm actually not a child. I'm fourteen."

The three intelligence officers in the centre of the room suddenly started shouting to each other frantically. One of them swivelled the laptop round. They gathered in front of it barking instructions at each other in Arabic. The woman emitted what sounded like a single word over and over again in a gradually rising pitch until she banged one of the keys and the same word turned into an exclamation of elation.

Farole frowned. "Is that what I *think* it is?"

"Internet access," Reginald replied. "Believe it or not, they've just successfully emailed Camp Lemonnier. Ooooh … Just in time. It's died again. What the hell's going on?"

"Does that mean we don't have to do any unplugging or blowing up?" Aisha asked.

"Something's wrong," Mordred said, breaking the thick silence.

Farole put his fingertips to his forehead. His eyes widened. "Oh, no. Oh, God. What the hell have we been thinking?" He strode to the laptop, hit a few keys then picked it up and showed Mordred the screen. Three head-and-shoulders photos, side by side: him, Farole and Aisha. "Probably every mobile phone in this town has this now. With full instructions to find us and bring us in. Plus a big reward. The guys from ISIS are in town and I'm guessing they're pretty livid."

The three Saudi operatives began hurriedly packing their things. They each grabbed a gun from the pile and examined it for utility.

"We've got to get out of here," Reginald said. "Grab yourselves a revolver."

"We can exit by the window," Farole said. "I'll lead the way. John, you take charge of Aisha. Hiba, Salman, Abdullah, flank the girl. Reggie, you bring up the rear. We'll head towards the old market." He picked two pistols from the pile and tossed one to Mordred and one to Aisha.

Mordred put his hands up. "Stop, everyone. Just - just listen to me for a moment."

Farole looked at him as if he was mad. "What the hell - ? Have you gone *insane?* We've got to get *out* of here! *NOW!*"

"I've got a plan," Mordred said calmly.

Chapter 28: Mordred's Brilliant Idea

"You've got exactly ten seconds," Farole said, "and I expect you to talk while we move. And it better be good, because we can't afford dead wood on this team. Dead wood equals dead team, understand?"

"Don't go out of that window," Mordred said, "or dead team is what you'll get. Sooner than you think."

"Get the hell on with your 'plan', dude!" Reginald hissed.

"As we know," Mordred said without moving, "Dimbleton put a message and three pictures out to all mobiles in the area. From his point of view, the problem is, most people aren't going to have their mobiles switched on. Why would they, since they must have worked out, or more likely been told, that there's no possibility of making a phone call, and no internet access? If it was me, I'd have turned it off long ago to save the battery. I'm guessing a lot of them have done, or maybe even been ordered to do, the same. So stop panicking. In all probability, hardly anyone on the ground has accessed Dimbleton's message or even knows it exists.

"Secondly, we know exactly where Dimbleton is."

"How so?" Farole asked. He'd stopped scurrying and looked like he was listening hard.

"He must be on the Majestic James Cook," Mordred said, "assuming that's where the 3G interference system's located. Because he must have delivered the instruction to restore internet access in person. He wouldn't have been able to do it remotely. I'm assuming there are no landlines hereabout, but even if they were, they wouldn't reach one mile out to sea. His ISIS friends are probably with him.

"Now, if Dimbleton has worked out what I just have – although he may not have, just as you didn't: techno-psychologically I think he's still in London – he'll have sent someone from the Majestic to shore, to order everyone in his little mercenary army to switch on their mobiles. That instruction's going to take time to spread, so we've still got lots of breathing space. If the Majestic's one nautical mile out to sea, and Dimbleton despatches a launch – let's say it's a go-fast boat, for the sake of argument – that's about three minutes to port. We've got to intercept that boat as – if - it comes in."

"Lord be praised," Reginald said. "You may actually be right."

"Somehow, we've got to take out the messengers, replace them with ourselves and go straight back to the Majestic, either in that or in another boat. It'll be the last thing Dimbleton's expecting. And, of course, with our email already sent, the cavalry should be on its way, depending on how long it takes Camp Lemonnier to analyse and authenticate the contents."

"We should do it under cover of nightfall, if possible," Farole said.

"There won't be time for that," Reginald told him. "By that time, Dimby'll know his message hasn't got out."

"How?" Aisha said.

"If he's got the foresight to despatch a go-fast boat," Reginald replied, "he'll probably make arrangements for regular updates. When those updates don't arrive, he'll know something's up."

"We could use that to lure him from the ship," she said.

"We can't rule out the possibility that he'll keep randomly restoring wireless for short periods," Farole said. "Keep in touch with his men on the ground that way."

"We can deal with that," Mordred replied. "If we intercept the people in the boat, we can grab their mobiles. To all intents and purposes we can become them. We've still got Etchingham's ID card. That could come in handy too."

"By 'take out' and 'intercept', you mean, 'kill', right?" Farole asked.

"I suppose so," Mordred replied. "Obviously, if - "

"Just wanted to be clear," Farole said. He grinned. "Your reputation's reached Italy, John, but everyone knows you can be a soft boiled egg." He glanced at his leg. "At times."

Mordred held the door open for everyone. "We've got a boat to intercept. We'll discuss the rest of the plan on the way."

Reginald picked up a machine gun. "There's more?"

One of the Saudi guys – Salman, Mordred thought – took the wheel of the first jeep. He and Aisha got in the back, as before, and Farole sat up front with his sunglasses on; the other three followed them in a vintage Mercedes saloon whose chassis almost scraped the road. They drove as quickly as the narrow, short streets, the potholes and the density of armed men in the way allowed. Aisha and Mordred kept their heads down. No one in their path showed the least sign of wanting to investigate them. Dimbleton's message had obviously – almost literally – fallen on deaf ears.

"So what's the rest of your plan?" Farole said.

"It's more of a standby than an addition," Mordred said. "It occurred to me that if Dimbleton's with the guys and gals from ISIS, and I'm brought to him there, they may not want to kill me immediately. The idea's to film me burning alive in a metal cage. They may or may not have brought their camcorder, but I doubt they'll have brought the cage. That'll mean another trip to shore."

"They'll torch you tied to a mast," Farole said, "and film it on their phones. They won't need 3G for that."

"Even so," Mordred replied, "it's going to take time."

Farole hooted. "Not much!"

"It means we've got some wiggle-room," Mordred said.

"They're going to have to be careful," Salman said in an upper-class English accent. "The Majestic's choc-a-block with explosives from what I understand. Lighting any sort of fire aboard it's a massive risk, let alone a petrol-based one. Why not just wait till the US or the Saudi air force arrive?"

"Because we don't know they will," Mordred said. "You must have heard of Mailer-Daemon Failure Notice. We may have sent an email, but we can't allow ourselves the luxury of assuming it's been received. Or even taken seriously."

"Either we go after Dimbleton," Farole said, "or we allow him to come after us. There's no real hiding place in this town, so we can't just lie low and hope he doesn't find us. There's no middle ground."

"When we get to port," Salman said, "Hiba and I will go aboard the speedboat if there is one, and secure it. You wait here until we give you the signal. What's your precise plan once we've gained control of it?"

"Have you got silencers for your guns?" Farole asked, as if that was the more important consideration.

"Standard issue," Salman replied.

"My precise plan," Mordred said, "has changed a little since I first thought of it. I think we should all travel to the Majestic. Salman, I'm assuming Dimbleton doesn't know you or Hiba or Abdullah, so you'll pose as the guys who captured me, and you'll hand me over to him. You'll then salute and leave. Next, you lower a ladder to Musa and Reginald. They bring the bombs aboard, you all plant them, then kapow."

"By which time, you'll have been torched," Farole said.

"If there's an electronic interferer in operation," Mordred said, "you're not going to be able to detonate anything remotely. It'll have to be good old fashioned light-the-fuse-and-retire stuff, or a clockwork mechanism. There's a very good chance we'll *all* end up getting torched. Where are the bombs, incidentally?"

"Boot of the Merc," Salman replied.

Mordred laughed. "So another two or three potholes and we could all be flying into orbit."

"John, I've got to come with you," Aisha said.

He sighed. Not again. "No, you don't. Absolutely not. You're staying on shore. Dressed as a boy."

"You haven't even heard my arguments!" she said.

"I don't want to."

Farole turned round. "I've already told you to ditch any kids' rights bullshit," he told Mordred. "Let her speak."

"If we let her speak," he said, "it'll only reinforce her obstinacy."

"My obstinacy? And another thing: stop saying 'her'. 'If we let *her* speak; '*her* obstinacy'. I *am* in the room, you know!"

"Correction," Mordred said. "It's not a room: it's the back seat of a clapped-out old Eritrean jeep."

"Don't diss the ride," Farole told him as they went over a huge bump. "It's unlucky."

"I'm going to tell you anyway," she said.

"I thought you might."

"If I go with you," she continued, ignoring him, "they'll think everything's sorted. It'll relax them. You know: closure. Salman, you can tell them you shot Mr Farole and you've got his body on shore, and say you can show them later. They'll be so happy they'll cry, and their brains will flood with endorphins, and they'll all be besty-best friends again, and it won't even occur to them that they're closer to their doom now than ever."

"It's a good pitch," Farole said, after a little thought.

"It's the worst idea I've ever heard," Mordred said, although actually it was pretty impressive for a fourteen year-old. Maybe he should go with it. At least he could keep an eye on her.

"I'm coming anyway," she said. "Like it or lump it."

And the truth was, anything might happen to her on shore. She'd be alone unless one of them elected to stay with her. But even then, bad things might happen to her.

"I think she may have a point, John," Farole said.

Besides, who could he trust to stay with her? Reginald seemed like the obvious choice, but he didn't look like he'd be much good in a fight. And could she even pass as a boy? Even with her hair clipped? Where was she going to get a boy's clothes at this short notice?

"Please, John," she said. She was almost crying. "Please don't leave me here."

He tossed a mental coin, unconsciously rocking his head left and right to clear the stress and see the result. "Okay," he sighed. "Okay, you win."

She burst into tears and put her arms round him. "Oh, thank you! *Thank you!"*

He almost welled up himself. Then he laughed out loud at the cruel absurdity of it, of himself. Thank you, John, for leading me to my death.

"Just one thing, though."

He laughed incredulously. "What, you're imposing conditions now?"

"It's important, John. I wouldn't ask you if it wasn't."

"Go on."

"If I get killed – no, *listen!* - If I get killed, and you can get close to me, I want you to whisper in my ear, 'There is no God but Allah, and Mohammad is his prophet'. That's all. Just that one sentence."

"Yep, fine, got it." He saw Musa Farole and Salman the driver exchange significant looks. "Hey, I'll do the same for you guys too, if I can," he said.

They each extended him a friendly palm.

They arrived at the port just in time to see what must be Dimbleton's emissary approaching: a inward-bound, large white speedboat with an enclosed bridge and an easy-planing hull. The coastline here consisted of a long sandy beach and a broad harbour with two long grey stone walls extending about three hundred yards into the ocean in a pincer. Alongside each, men boarded motorised pontoons and RIBs – Mordred counted sixteen, although there were others at sea, and yet still more parallel to the beach.

"We need a way of transferring you to the speedboat that isn't going to draw more general attention," Farole told Mordred. "Get out, both of you. I'm going to tie your hands."

They did as they were told. Hiba and Abdullah got out of the Mercedes and came over for a conference. They grabbed the two prisoners by their elbows, and took them to where the launch was coming in: a set of stone steps descending into the water. Two stray soldiers were seated there, smoking, but they got up in response to Hiba's invective and sauntered off looking browbeaten.

The launch powered its engine down and chugged over to the steps. Hiba and Abdullah stood waiting for it with the two prisoners manifest, looking grim. Reginald and Salman took up the rear. Three crew members came out and tossed a mooring rope. Hiba leapt aboard before any one had chance to come ashore.

"We got your message," she said. "And we've got two of the suspects. I've been in touch with Mr Dimbleton. He wants them brought back as quickly as possible."

"We'll take over from here, soldier," one of the three men said, with a grin. "You go get on a pontoon, honey. Take your friends."

"What about the reward?" she asked.

"We'll see Mr Dimbleton gets to hear about what you've done. You'll get your money, baby, don't worry."

"Could I have a tour of your boat?" she asked. "That would be even better than a reward."

The three men looked at each other. They shrugged in an unconvincing effort to look blasé. "Hallelujah," the one in the rear muttered.

The foremost offered his hand for her to come aboard. She led the way down the central steps and out of view. They followed her like they couldn't believe their luck. The last to descend rubbed his hands together, then turned to Reginald and winked. "Back in about an hour, old fella," he said. "Don't go away."

Exactly sixty seconds later, she re-emerged alone. “All aboard,” she said.

Chapter 29: Aboard the Majestic

The deck of the Majestic James Cook was a good fifteen metres above sea level and crawling with men. Reginald Kondylis, Musa Farole and the three Saudis packed their clothes with plastic explosives and climbed aboard separately by four of the twenty rope-ladders draped from the railings. Reginald Kondylis returned shortly afterwards, abseiling down the hull on a rope. He bound the two prisoners in a rope cocoon around their waists and limbs and attached them to the end of a winch.

"It's madness up there," he told them. "More soldiers than you can possibly count. Hardly room to move. Great thing is, everyone wants the reward. They all want the credit for having captured you. I'm telling you, man, once you're winched up, they'll cast me adrift. Made out like I didn't realise, like I'm a complete dumbass, but it suits me fine. I'll wait for you down here."

"Where are the others?" Mordred asked.

"Side-lined by the resident bounty-hunters, just like yours truly. Better than any of us could have hoped for. Hey, you all right, little girl?"

She nodded. Then retched and vomited over the side. She looked at Mordred and gave an odd laugh-cry. "And I thought going to Rheeming Hall and visiting Mr and Mrs Chewton was scary! Oh, my God!"

"Here," Reginald said. He took two little bundles of leaves from his pocket and put them in both their mouths. "Khat. I don't normally approve, but we ain't doing 'normally' today."

"What's 'khat'?" Aisha asked.

"Like a cure for nerves," he replied.

She didn't have chance to say anything else, because they were both yanked into the air.

"Close your eyes!" Mordred told her. "Don't look down!"

The ocean receded at speed as they sailed upwards. Twenty, thirty, forty feet below, Reginald went through the motions of outrage at being double-crossed. But there wasn't time for vertigo or even for their stomachs to fully turn. It took all of two seconds for them to reach deck-level, where they were met by a hundred outstretched arms and a cacophony of shouts. They were dragged aboard, then clawed and tossed and fought over. Mordred tried to call to Aisha, but the noise of the crowd was deafening. He lost all sense of direction and couldn't even tell whether they moving, or if so, in what direction. Eventually, he heard a familiar voice, trying to restore calm.

"I can see what you've done," he yelled, *"and I thank you! Give your names to Bin Rashid and he'll see you're properly rewarded!"*

Dimbleton. Almost a relief.

That obviously wasn't enough, though, because there were a few gunshots – not that dispatching a little ammunition was ever going to scare these guys – and things began to calm down a little. A space cleared.

"Pick them up!" Dimbleton yelled.

Quiet descended. Obviously, *Eritrea's Got Talent* was about to begin. Mordred found himself – he hardly knew how – standing on what appeared to be a long stretch of deck next to Aisha and with Dimbleton and six young bearded men in turbans and baggy linen in front. Presumably, these were Dimby's ISIS pals.

"So all's well that ends well," Dimbleton said. "Obviously, Mr Mordred, you've caused me a lot of heartache, but I knew you'd never get away. I'm not going to treat you any more harshly, just because you tried to escape. I expected it. No, because I'm such a kind man, I'm not even going to worsen your fate. Burned to death it was, and burned to death it shall be."

"Really appreciate it," Mordred said.

"Aisha, these six men are going to take you below deck and try you out. Whichever one you like best, he'll be your husband. Don't worry, they're all British Muslims. You'll have lots in common."

The six men approached and looked her up and down as if they were so repulsed they could hardly contain themselves.

"You is Sufi Seven?" the first asked, in a Jafaican accent. He turned to the man next to him. "Seriously, this is Sufi Seven? When man first read what she wrote, bruv, man could not *believe* that shit, yeah? And now you're telling me this is she?"

"Is tasty, man," the second one said. He nudged the figure next to him. "Oi, oi, we're gonna have some fun with this one, innit?"

"Big idea, bruv," the third said. "Man is on course to score big time tonight."

Mordred felt his mouth pop open slightly. Of course, he should have known. For some stupid reason, he'd expected them to be sinister, foreign accent types, like stereotypes from an Edwardian boys' magazine. The banality of evil, it never failed to shock … but this was another level.

The first came over to Mordred and patted him on the cheek. "Bruv, we gonna make a major human bonfire out of you, innit."

"And film the show on our tech-nol-o-gee," another said, singing the last word.

"Did any of you used to work in a phone shop, by any chance?" Mordred asked.

"That's enough, boys," Dimbleton said. "What do you want to do first? Burn the man or go downstairs with the girl?"

"You're – you're - " Aisha said. Her teeth chattered. She swallowed. "You're not real Muslims."

They laughed. "Bruvvas, it talks!" one of them said.

"Let's burn the guy," one of them said. "Get the little lady in the mood for love."

"Before you do that," Mordred said, "you might want to check inside my clothes, because I've packed them with plastic explosive. If you burn me to death, probably most of you will die too. As a bonus, the ship might even go down. I'm only telling you because I want to be absolutely fair."

Dimbleton took out a knife and thrust it into Mordred's ribcage. "Not enough to kill you, I'm afraid," he said, with a smile of appreciation at Mordred's wince. "Although I'm sure that's what you were hoping. It's just that, when I withdraw this blade, I'll be able to tell instantly whether you're telling the truth."

He pulled it out. Mordred gasped. Dimbleton put it to his nose and his smile dropped off. "How stupid of you to tell me," he said. "But touching. I guess you were concerned for the girl. Don't worry on that score. She probably won't die, though naturally, I can't guarantee it. I've been involved in several similar cases before and, with the best will in the world, the child sometimes selfishly insists of expiring from shock. Even where her physical injuries are fairly minor." He affected a bored tone. "Help me untie him - but not his hands or feet, obviously. Let's get the explosives out."

They set to work. Within a minute, they'd taken nearly all the rope off and removed the four packets of explosive. They cast it down in front of him to demonstrate its disutility.

"I expect you wish you'd kept schtum now, eh?" Dimbleton said, "Still, never mind. It's an ill wind that blows nobody any good."

Suddenly, three things happened simultaneously. Mordred saw something – a dot - on the horizon. Warplanes. Then there was an almighty explosion somewhere below, in the hull, sufficient to shake the deck and topple everyone, himself, Aisha and Dimbleton included. Thirdly, two of the ISIS fighters developed bullet-holes in their heads.

Almost instantly, there was general panic. Farole lunged from the crowd and cut Mordred's remaining bonds. Then he fired wildly at whoever seemed to be threatening. Another of the ISIS fighters took a direct hit and Mordred experienced a feeling he couldn't quite describe. *Should have stuck with the phone shop, bruv.*

He didn't wait for Farole. Rights of the Child. He scooped Aisha up and jumped over the ship's railings. A second later, they were underwater, going down, down, seemingly for ever. He couldn't fight it, not without loosening his grip on her. All he could do was wait for their natural buoyancy to resume control.

He was still going down when his breath gave out. He sucked seawater, and began to choke, then started to rise.

He broke the surface without even knowing he'd done so. Another yank, harder than the winch at the start of all this. Something hit him on the head, and he scurried to consciousness like the training manual told him he must. He was in a boat, the speedboat. Aisha, yes. Hiba, Abdullah, Reginald at the controls. Fifteen metres above, he saw Farole try to clear the railings but take two or three shots in the back and fall lifeless into the water. What looked like a long way inland, parachutists were dropping in numbers from two large planes.

Suddenly, full throttle. Hiba was cutting Aisha's bonds, not hurriedly, but calmly methodically. The warplanes flew high overhead in formation for a look and separated. Suddenly, all the small-arms fire was directed skywards.

"Salman bought it," Abdullah said, as if it was a Bollywood movie. "He decided to stay put and keep off the enemy."

It didn't look as if Salman and Musa Farole were going to be the only ones. Of course this wasn't the only speedboat in the entire flotilla, and others were on their way. Mordred saw Dimbleton jump off the Majestic into the sea. He guessed he wasn't just saving his skin.

They were making good progress. Aisha was sitting up now, holding onto the fishing-line bars on the deck side. Five or six speedboats were in pursuit, but so distant, they had no chance of catching up unless this one ran out of fuel.

"Where are we headed?" Mordred yelled.

"Djiboutian waters!" Hiba replied. "Get down below," she told Aisha. *"About thirty minutes!"*

Suddenly, there was an almighty explosion in the water, just in front of them, about five metres to portside.

RPGs. And obviously they knew how to use them. This might not be such a walkover, after all. Another explosion, this one closer, then another. The boats themselves were gaining, too.

"Don't worry," Hiba said. She opened a locker, reached into a sack and threw a few spherical objects into the water.

"Contact mines?" Mordred asked.

A moment later, he got his answer. Three of the five boats in pursuit blew holes in their hulls and stopped coming.

"New technology," Hiba replied. "Unfortunately, we've just run out."

Mordred smiled. "They don't need to know that." He reached into the sack and came out with two cans of baked beans and a tin opener. He tossed them theatrically into the water. Aisha rummaged and found an old log-book and threw that in.

The boats obviously saw because they reared like horses. Hiba took out her revolver, aimed carefully and fired.

"Got him," she said, then, turning back to look where they were headed, "Oh no."

Abdullah lay dead. The boat suddenly decelerated, and lost direction. Reginald lay lifeless by the wheel.

"You take over!" Hiba yelled. Aisha was whispering into Abdullah's ear, but Mordred grabbed her. "You can do that later."

He dragged her onto the bridge. "Get Reginald's gun, and keep firing, and keep down. And watch out for Hiba."

"Where – where is she?"

Mordred turned to look. She was in the sea, way, way behind them. Probably dead –the last boat was gaining fast now. At the wheel … Dimbleton? Bloody hell, yes, forever the cliché.

He felt a hard smack his against lower back. For a weird minute, he thought Aisha had hit him with something. But why would she? Then he realised: he'd been shot.

"Forget about firing," he told her. *"Lie down, and stay laid down!"*

Then another bullet, this time through his upper arm. *Lucky*. One more and it'd probably be his heart. He was losing blood too. Had to get them to shore.

He turned the boat ninety degrees and headed directly to land. A gentle sandy acclivity with palm trees and undergrowth just above the shoreline. They could hide in the foliage, assuming he was capable of making it. If not, she could. Those parachutists – they'd have to arrive sooner or later.

"Hold on!" he yelled, as land loomed at thirty knots. They crashed-landed rather than beached. He hurtled forward with the impact and banged his head hard on the glass. He had no idea how Aisha had fared. She might be dead for all he knew. His nose bled. The pain elsewhere was beginning to kick in now.

"Come on," he said, then realised she was standing over him, frantically offering her hand. She pulled him up and they lurched over the side of the boat onto the beach. He could hardly keep up with her.

He heard Dimbleton's boat bang ashore behind them. Another bullet tore through his thigh, and that was it: he stumbled and was out. Energy and blood all on empty.

"Make for the trees," he told her.

She got down next to him and tried to lift him, though he was twice her size. "Come on, John."

"I can't. I think my leg's broken. Get running. I'll try and hold him off."

"How?"

She was right. In his desperation to flee, he hadn't brought a gun, and neither had she.

But Dimbleton had. He got calmly off his boat and came over, swinging his pistol, like he had all the time in the world. He raised it to shoot Aisha.

Then a voice came from farther upshore. "Put down your weapon and *back away!"*

Suddenly, the United States of A emerged from the undergrowth on all fronts. Ten, twelve soldiers. They approached hyper-cautiously with rifles raised, as if there was every chance Dimbleton might turn his revolver on them.

"Last warning!" one of them barked. *"Put down your weapon, sir, and back away!"*

Dimbleton looked furiously at them, and at Aisha. Then he seemed to recover. He dropped the gun on the sand and put his hands in the air.

"Don't think I'm finished," he told her calmly. "I've an entire battalion of very well-trained lawyers in London and, yes, I'll probably serve a few years in prison, but then I'm going to come and get you. Your friend here's dead already, so he won't protect you. You'll spend every single night from now until the end of your life having nightmares about Terence Dimbleton, and when you finally do die, it'll be very, very slowly, at these two hands." He showed her them and grinned. "Do you still think you've won, young lady?"

The soldiers were on their way over, but before they could take charge, Aisha lunged for the pistol and shot Dimbleton in the stomach.

For a minute, he looked shocked and bewildered, as if he didn't know quite what had happened, but something told him it wasn't good. Then she shot him again – Mordred didn't see where, but he heard the yelp of terror – and then a third time. All the while, in the background, someone yelling, *"Put down your weapon, miss, and back off!"*

Dimbleton was still screaming and trying to wriggle away when she shot him in the face. Then a series of clicks.

She threw the pistol on top of him and hurried back to Mordred. She knelt, weeping, and said something quickly in his ear. He was on the verge of blacking out so he didn't hear even roughly what it was. 'John, it's okay, you're going to survive'? 'John, Dimbleton's dead now, he'll never trouble us again'? Neither one of those? Both?

Then he knew. Of course. There is no God but Allah …

Chapter 30: Dear John …

The military hospital at Camp Lemonnier had high, white ceilings, four wards with opposing rows of metal-framed cots, and a large, friendly staff. Mordred's bedside table gradually filled with cards from colleagues at Thames House. Alec had been in on the first day – he'd flown to Djibouti almost as soon as he regained consciousness in Sheffield - but Mordred was still too washed-out to speak. Afterwards, Aisha came to visit him every day at two with either her mum or her dad. Her parents didn't speak much, but they radiated good will, and they always brought him a little gift: chocolates, a magazine, or flowers.

It occurred to him after the third day that Aisha didn't want his company as much as she needed counselling. Their conversations kept returning to Dimbleton. She'd killed someone and, little by little, the darkness of that was encroaching on her. On her fourth visit, they argued.

"No, I don't believe in capital punishment," he told her, "but I do think one person can sometimes be justified in killing another. Not every killing's an execution. Sometimes, soldiers really do deserve medals."

"I don't think I deserve one."

"You've got to get over this, Aisha, or it'll eat you up. It's easy to imagine you could have done things differently, but it's irrelevant. How would you feel if you'd had the chance to kill Dimbleton, but you didn't, then later on he murdered someone close to you? Because he might well have done."

She bobbed her shoulders. "I suppose."

"I know that at school they teach you there's always a clear choice between good and evil. But depending on how unlucky you are, sometimes there are only two or more evils."

"When we get back to England, John, I don't want us ever to lose touch. Only you understand what I've been through. I know you've killed a person too."

He smiled. "And how would you know that?"

"You wouldn't be lecturing me if you hadn't. What was he like? It *was* a 'he', wasn't it?"

"It was a 'they'. And they were bad. If I'd been in your shoes, I'd have killed Dimbleton without thinking. And I certainly wouldn't be obsessing about it now."

"You're probably right. I could have let him live. But that would have been cowardice."

"Wrong again. You'd simply have made a mistake. In the event, you chose correctly, and you acted on your choice. A bad pick doesn't make you, or anyone, a coward."

"Are you coming to the funeral tomorrow?"

"Nobody's mentioned a funeral to me. I've been in and out of consciousness quite a lot."

"Musa Farole. His parents are coming over from Italy."

"What happened to the others? Do you know?"

"They flew Reginald's body back to the USA. Salman and Abdullah and Hiba are going to be buried in Riyadh."

He sank a little inside. "I didn't know about Hiba. I rather hoped she might just have lost her footing and slipped into the water."

They didn't say anything more for a while. She offered her hand and he held it.

"When are you going back to school?" he asked eventually.

"When are you flying back to Britain?"

"Er, I asked first."

She shrugged. "I don't know. I don't know whether I'm fit for Saint Bede's any more."

"That's rubbish. Look, Aisha, remember what I said a moment ago."

"I've got to get over this, yes."

"There's only one way forward for you right now. You need to get back into full-time education, and return to a normal life. I can't really be a part of that. I'm not saying we can't and shouldn't meet up every so often for a chinwag: of course we should. But I can't be a substitute for your peers. And that's what you need. You need Bidisha and Mariam and Fatima and all the other kids and teachers at that school of yours; you need exercise books and PE lessons and *The X Factor* and friends' birthday parties and One Direction and the regularity of school bells and the drudgery of homework. Because once it's gone, none of that will ever come back. And the clock's ticking. If you missed it all because of what you've suffered, I'd feel I'd failed, big time. I'm not joking."

She swallowed. The rims of her eyes became watery. "You could never fail me, John."

"Well, don't make me feel like I have. Listen, we'll make a deal. Your father has a Sufi meditation evening every so often, upstairs in your house, right?"

"Once a month. When did I tell you that?"

"On our plane journey to the holiday of a lifetime, remember?"

She wiped her eyes and laughed at the same time.

"How about this," he continued. "If you go back to school and work hard, I'll come to your father's evenings. If he'll have me."

"Of course he will! All of them?"

"I can't guarantee to attend every month. Sometimes, I'm out of the country. But failing a mission abroad, I'll be there. I promise."

She nodded emotionally. "I know you're right," she said after a long pause. "Everything you've said: I know in my heart of hearts it's true. All of it. Thank you, John."

"What for?"

"Being so honest. And sensible."

"Do we have a deal then?"

She wiped her eyes again and nodded sadly. They shook hands.

About an hour after Aisha left, Alec arrived with Phyllis, both dressed in their Sunday morning best, although it was Tuesday afternoon. They took two seats on the same side of his bed, Phyllis closest. A nurse arrived with a vase of water for the little bouquet they'd brought.

"They told us you weren't up to seeing people much," Phyllis said, as she arranged the flowers.

"I've just finished talking to Aisha," Mordred replied. "I ordered her to go back to school. I told her it's the best thing she could do now. I hope I'm right."

"I'm guessing you didn't let on you were home-schooled," Alec said.

"She didn't ask."

"That yellow one needs to go down a bit," Alec told Phyllis. "It looks like a sodium-vapour lamp up there."

"Like this?" she said

He nodded. "Now pull that blue one up a little. No, not that one; the one on the right, I don't know what it's called."

"A 'flower'?" she asked.

"That's it," Alec replied.

"I take it Gina's still not back," Mordred said. "I was hoping she might come and see me."

Alec and Phyllis exchanged sombre shall-I-tell-him-or-will-you looks.

"Ordinarily," Alec said, "I'd make a joke out of this, but obviously, you've just narrowly survived death, and you're probably not in the mood. So I'm just going to say it straight out."

"What is it?" Mordred asked.

"I'd normally accompany it with 'the curse of Mordred'-type quips. But I realise in the circumstances, that wouldn't be appropriate."

Mordred ground his teeth and sighed irritably. Silence.

"The fact is," Alec said, "Gina's become a nun."

This was obviously too much for Phyllis. She put her knuckles to her mouth and lowered her head to conceal her laughter. "I'm sorry, John," she gasped, as if she was coming up for air, then carried on rocking quietly.

"I'm deadly serious," Alec said. "She entered a convent just outside Athens."

Phyllis wiped her eyes. "I shouldn't crease up. I'm so sorry, John. I know you had a real thing for her. It's just that, as a Guess-What-Gina-Fairburn's-Done it's right up there with, 'She ran away to join a circus' and 'She put a paper bag on her head and she refuses to come out'. If it's any consolation, I don't think she'll stay a nun. Too keen on the home comforts."

"She's a pale ale and *Racing Post* girl at heart," Alec said.

"She wrote you a letter, by the way. A literal 'Dear John'. Ruby Parker's got it."

Mordred closed his eyes, took a deep breath, then blew it out. "Well, at least she's safe. That's the main thing. My worst fear was that she might get a second wind and follow Ian out to Syria."

"Every cloud has a silver lining," Alec said.

"We've got Edna Watson now," Phyllis said. "*The* Edna Watson."

"Olympic and Commonwealth Games gold medallist," Alec added. "Six foot two, but a good figure. Nicely proportioned."

"Six-eight with her shoes on," Phyllis said and laughed. "Try not to mention it when you see her. Even from a distance. Don't, for example, do what Alec did."

"I only mentioned that she might have a bit of difficulty blending in," Alec said. "She wasn't meant to overhear."

"Tell John what happened next. It'll be good for his recovery."

Alec swivelled his eyes and bit the bullet. "The following night, I was coming out of the Albert on Victoria Street with Doug Grusby – you know, from Accounts - when this gang of black lads passed and bumped hard into me. I didn't retaliate. Perfect self-control, quite proud of myself. Five minutes later, in The Speaker, I realised my wallet had gone."

Phyllis nodded. "Luckily, it turned up the next day. Just somehow … there, on the table, during a coffee break in the canteen."

"It didn't have any money in. Instead, it had sixteen head-and-shoulders shots of Ms Watson laughing. She'd actually spent my last twenty in a photo booth."

"Stylish," Mordred said.

"I strongly advise you not to play your 'Station Controller in Budapest' joke on her," Alec said.

"What in *mercy's* name is that?" Phyllis asked.

"It's more of a lame prank," Mordred replied. "Not worth explaining, believe me."

"She's unmarried," Alec said. "When we get back to England, I'll introduce you. You can ask her out and maybe propose to her, and hopefully she'll leave due to unforeseen circumstances."

Phyllis hit him. "Be nice to John. He's not very well."

"What?" Alec said indignantly. "That's how the curse works!"

Three days later, he flew back to Britain. He returned to Thames House the next day with a walking stick. Ruby Parker called him to her office before he had time to request a meeting.

"You were told to take a fortnight off," she said, when he entered. "I hope you're not here to report for duty because the answer's no. I've already told you what I think of macho men, and attempting a return before you're ready falls squarely under that umbrella."

"Nice to see you too," he replied. "I came in because I heard you've been keeping a letter for me. I didn't expect you to roll out the red carpet, but 'how are you' might have been nice."

"That's all you're here for? In that case, I humbly apologise."

"Don't get me wrong. I love working at Thames House. But by the same token, I'm not going to throw away a fortnight's free holiday."

"That's good to hear."

"I don't actually need this walking stick, by the way. I only bought it so everyone here would buy my 'shot several times in various parts of the body' yarn."

"Please sit down. I've already said I apologise, and I meant it. Now stop feeling sorry for yourself." She opened the drawer and handed him a sealed envelope. "Obviously, I don't expect you to read it here. Take it somewhere quiet. I haven't 'opened it for security reasons' or anything like that, before you ask. I've too much respect for Gina – and you – for that."

"Thank you."

"Before you go, I would like to clear up one possible misunderstanding. Once I discovered that Gina was involved with Ian, I didn't call her back here to sack her. I brought her back to tell her it didn't matter. I didn't want her to think she was trapped in a lie. As it was, she'd already made up her mind. There was nothing I could do to dissuade her. I really did try my best."

"I appreciate that." He got up.

"And John?" she said, when his hand was on the doorknob.

"Yes?"

"I'm promoting you. As of the end of this month, you'll be an officer."

"I – well, thank you."

There was nothing more to be said. He left the building and walked to Hyde Park. The sun shone, birds called to each other and, on the grass, a toddler and his parents and their dog played football. Pretty nice for late autumn. Pedestrians ambled along the footpaths looking rushed or pensive, depending on whether they worked here or were visiting. The perfect surroundings to be cynical about a 'Dear John' letter. He sat on a bench and opened the envelope.

Dear John,
By the time you read this, you will know I've gone and, I expect, where. You probably have two questions. As regards the first: it is impossible for me to say whether I am just beginning to fall in love with you, or whether it has already happened. I am not leaving lightly. As one of our best contemporary poets once put it, "you were all the reasons I thought of

staying and you were none of the reasons why I went". You were my best chance for a happy, normal future.

Your second question will be: why. That is much harder to answer, but I realise I must try. Last year, something awful, but irreversible, started happening to me. It was as if I suddenly started seeing all the vileness in the world, and how it clings to everything, almost without exception. I tried to resist it. I even tried medication at one point. Originally, I admit, the feeling was probably ISIS-inspired – 'I Spy Iblis's Stooges': how very true, how profound that sounds now - but later on, I realised, the whole world is awry. Broken, really. Greed, hatred, ignorance, everywhere you look. And finally, I saw: in me too.

You demonstrated beyond doubt that Ian's path is not an option for me. In the words of the cliché, an eye for an eye only makes everyone blind. Besides, the world has now reached such a pass that I honestly think it's too late for guns and mortars. The only hope is that there is a God and we can join Him in fighting the filth on a cosmic scale. Prayer, fasting, helping the poor, tending the sick and the destitute, caring for orphans and widows and the disabled. Forgiveness of sins. Unlimited kindness. The shield of faith, the helmet of salvation, the sword of the spirit.

Anyway, my love, that is why. Please do not be too hard on me. Pray for both of us whenever you can. Because we will meet again.
Gina.

He put the letter back in the envelope. *My love*. He could almost cry. The simplicity of what he thought they had, compared with the unseen complexity. Maybe you never could know another person. *My love*, yes, easy to write. But perhaps love couldn't actually bridge the gap between separate minds.

That would be too miserable to contemplate. Not even love.

Yes, he would pray for her. And maybe for himself too. She was right, they would meet again, but he also knew exactly how she intended that to be understood.

Not in this life.

Three days later, he went to his first Sufi meeting in Richmond. Mrs and Mrs Sharif and Aisha welcomed him like an old friend and served sweets and tea to him and the other guests in the lounge. Bidisha was there, and Fatima. The three girls took charge of Mordred as soon as he entered, and introduced him around. They didn't tell anyone what he did for a living. Most of the devotees were Muslims, but there were two Hindus and a Christian. The conversation was all of work, local affairs and the weather. At eight o'clock, the first snow of the year began to fall, and a few people left, worried about getting home.

At nine o'clock, those who remained – fifteen adults plus the three girls - went upstairs for *dhikr*, meditation. They sat cross-legged on the floor in the Sharifs' games' room, closed their eyes and repeatedly chanted the name of God. Mordred remained focussed for the first ten minutes, then his mood became dark and his mind raced. He thought of Gina in her new vocation, of Annabel on the Thames Embankment that night, of Ian in Syria, of Musa Farole and Reginald and the three Saudis, of all those he'd killed and those he'd saved, of loose ends and broken appointments, of how always, no matter how much joy you tried to import, life was full of loss and error and decay.

Outside, as if in response to the worship within, the snow gradually covered everything in a pristine uniformity. The Sufis' voices filled the room, the house, the suburban streets, the city, the whole world. And though he tried hard to ignore it, behind and beneath the word 'Allah', gentle as a whisper, he kept on hearing an insistent 'My love'.

Books by James Ward

General Fiction

The House of Charles Swinter

The Weird Problem of Good

The Bright Fish

*Hannah and Soraya's Fully Magic Generation-Y *Snowflake* Road Trip across America*

The Original Tales of MI7

Our Woman in Jamaica

The Kramski Case

The Girl from Kandahar

The Vengeance of San Gennaro

The John Mordred Tales of MI7 books

The Eastern Ukraine Question

The Social Magus

Encounter with ISIS

World War O

The New Europeans

Libya Story

Little War in London

The Square Mile Murder

The Ultimate Londoner

Death in a Half Foreign Country

The BBC Hunters

The Seductive Scent of Empire

Humankind 2.0

Ruby Parker's Last Orders

Poetry

The Latest Noel

Metals of the Future

Short Stories

An Evening at the Beach

Philosophy

21st Century Philosophy

A New Theory of Justice and Other Essays

www.ingramcontent.com/pod-product-compliance
Ingram Content Group UK Ltd.
Pitfield, Milton Keynes, MK11 3LW, UK
UKHW041953190726
13854UKWH00005B/1938